PLAGUE WAR: OUTBREAK

ALISTER HODGE

SEVERED PRESS
HOBART TASMANIA

PLAGUE WAR: OUTBREAK

ISBN: 978-1-925711-95-0

CHAPTER ONE

Harry rested his chin on one hand while reading a set of medical notes. The text slipped out of focus before eyes blurred by fatigue. He rubbed at them before checking the time and yawning. 12:30am. He felt like shit. It was his last of seven night-shifts at Randwick Emergency Department, and he was struggling to stay awake. Insomnia had stolen daytime sleep, leaving a soul-destroying exhaustion that blunted his mind and sapped all enjoyment from life.

He stood from the stool and stretched, his lower back cracking. Harry desired wakefulness like a junky lusted for a hit. He pulled out a battered satchel from beneath the bench. Two large cans of energy drink, brimming with unhealthy levels of caffeine and guarana, lay within. He cracked the lid of one, sculling half of the lukewarm contents on the spot. A few drops spilled free onto his chest, soaking into the word "Doctor", sewn into the threadbare scrubs top.

Only another eight or so hours to go, then he'd be leaving for his next contract – a job in Milton on the state's south coast. Harry hadn't completed the exams to qualify as an Emergency Specialist, stalling any chance of career progression. Instead, he'd worked agency contracts between stints abroad with *Medecins Sans Frontieres* (MSF). With MSF, Harry had provided aid in the aftermath of natural disasters, and treated injured civilians during the Afghan war. Most recently, he'd spent three months in Liberia during the Ebola epidemic, working in clinics and occasionally with a "rapid response team", tracking new cases to remote villages. The time there had stretched him physically and mentally. Delivering care in 40-degree temperatures, knowing that any mistake could mean exposure to a virus with an eighty percent mortality rate, was exhausting. He had returned to Australia completely drained, so much so, that he was glad of the enforced twenty-one-day quarantine at home alone.

He'd struggled to adapt back to Sydney, feeling claustrophobic in the city. When the hospital had retrenched his job, he'd been glad for the push, seeing an opportunity for escape to a place where he could breathe more freely. The town of Milton fit the bill perfectly. The village straddled a ridge surrounded by farmland, and had a small Emergency Department that serviced the local population. His application for the role had been approved four weeks ago, and Harry had found himself a rental on the town's northern approach, a house set two hundred meters from the road, and surrounded by green paddocks. On the highway at the front of the property was the landlord's business, a heavy machinery hire service. The previous week, he'd picked up the keys to the property and carted most of his stuff down. All he had to do now, was move in.

With can in hand, he headed to the staff base. It was dim, with most lights in the department turned off to keep a semblance of night. Only essential staff were present, and while Harry took another swig of Red Bull, the ambulance phone started to ring. He cradled the receiver against his shoulder as he grabbed a scrap of paper and pen.

'Randwick Emergency, you have something for us?'

Harry scribbled down the information provided by the dispatch operator, then read it back for confirmation prior to hanging up. Kate, the nurse working in the resuscitation bays with him, was looking over his shoulder at the pad.

'What's coming in?' she asked.

'A retrieval from the airport, sounds like septic shock.'

'No worries, are you going to run the show on this one?'

Harry looked over his shoulder to see what other doctors were around. The roster had been short of late. For senior doctors, there was only himself and another Registrar.

'Yeah, might as well be me.' Harry pushed himself from the chair and followed Kate into the resus area.

By the time the paramedics arrived five minutes later, the resuscitation bay was ready to go. Harry waited at the bedhead while the paramedics hurried towards them. The patient lying on the trolley looked awful. Her breathing was rapid, and skin pale. While one paramedic relayed the clinical history to Harry and Kate, the other ambo slid the patient across on the sheet. Kate cut up the centre of the t-shirt with trauma scissors, then applied an oxygen mask, blood pressure cuff and monitoring equipment for heart rate and oxygen levels.

'This is Beth Hazelwood, a 28-year-old woman with sepsis from the airport,' said the paramedic. 'A call was made by the flight crew requesting an ambulance on arrival. During the flight from Cairns, Beth became unwell, notifying the airhostess of her condition when the plane was thirty minutes out of Sydney. During the remaining descent, she rapidly deteriorated. There's a bite mark on her left forearm that appears grossly infected. Before she became confused, a bat was mentioned – not sure if that's what caused the wound.

'Since picking her up, she's continued to crash pretty quickly. As you can see,' he said, passing across a chart with vital signs on it. 'Her pulse is racing and her blood pressure's bloody low. Her conscious level's also dropped; she's not responding to much now. Any questions?'

Harry shook his head, 'No. Thanks, mate. Make this the last one for the night though, yeah?'

2

The paramedic gave a half smile as he backed the trolley to the ambulance bay. 'You can always hope, I guess.'

Harry started to run through a rapid clinical assessment. The patient's airway was clear for the moment, with reasonable air entry to both lungs. Her heart was beating irregularly, between 130-150 beats per minute, and her blood pressure was so low he couldn't feel a pulse at her wrist.

Harry shoved a cannula into an arm vein, then twisted on a syringe to obtain a blood sample for pathology. The blood he drained was almost black. *Oxygen depleted.* Kate attached a line for the intravenous saline and started pumping it in by hand. The latest blood pressure result flashed up on the monitor; 65/35mmHg. Both Kate and Harry grimaced at the poor reading; things weren't looking good.

Two small puncture wounds, possibly from the incisors of an animal were present on the inner aspect of the patient's left arm. As Harry touched the edges of the wound, rank brown pus oozed to the surface. The surrounding skin was a swollen, virulent shade of red. Trails of crimson tracked up the inside of her arm to the armpit.

Beads of sweat sat upon the patient's exposed skin, running in tiny rivulets to the bed sheets below. Abruptly, it was silent. Harry looked up from the arm wound – the patient had stopped breathing. He placed two fingers below the line of her jaw for a pulse. Nothing. Harry felt a spike in his own heart rate, as adrenaline surged in response to the situation. He turned and pressed the emergency button while yelling out to Kate.

He commenced chest compressions. On the third one, he felt a rib snap under hand. Blood misted from her mouth, falling back in a maze of fine, crimson droplets across the patient's face. Kate appeared at the head of the bed, placing an oxygen mask over the patient's mouth and defibrillator pads to her chest. At the thirtieth compression, Harry paused while Kate delivered two breaths. Another doctor and two more nurses arrived to help. Harry stood back from the compressions, allowing one of the nurses to take over CPR, and filled the team in on the situation as they worked. After two minutes, he called for a pause in compressions to view the cardiac rhythm; a wavering flat line extended across the defibrillator screen – asystole. A non-shockable cardiac rhythm.

'Restart compressions. Suz, give her some adrenaline, please.'

Harry's voice was calm. The team worked quietly, intensely focused on the job at hand. After thirty minutes, it was apparent they weren't making progress. Harry finally recommended to the team that they stop.

'Time of death 0130 AM.'

The other doctor and nurses removed their gloves, and drifted back to their own patient loads. It always sucked to have an unsuccessful resuscitation, significantly more so when the patient was young like this lady. Shortly, it was just Kate and Harry again. Harry grasped the body, one hand on a shoulder, the other on her hips, and rolled it towards him so that Kate could push a body bag underneath. A stream of blood-stained drool slid from the corpse's mouth, soaking into his scrubs while the eyes stared sightlessly ahead. The unnaturally pale skin was still damp, leaving an oily residue on the fingers. Harry paid it scant attention. He was running the events of the arrest through his head, mentally re-checking each step to see if he had made the right calls, while ignoring the blood and saliva oozing through the cotton of his top.

In the next bay, the patient began clawing at his oxygen mask. Harry lowered the body and pulled a sheet up to its neck. Kate and he then moved across to review the patient in distress.

The old man was dry retching. Harry unstrapped the mask and held a vomit bag under his mouth while he heaved up his guts. Kate administered a medication to stop the nausea. Within a few minutes, the patient indicated he was feeling better.

From the corner of Harry's eye, a movement drew his gaze. The arm of his dead patient had fallen from beneath the sheet, to hang down the side of the bed. The fingers flexed into the beginning of a fist, before falling lax once more. 'Surely not...' He rubbed his eyes with a free hand and turned away.

'What the fuck's with that?' blurted Kate. 'The foot just moved, Harry. I'm not joking...' she said, indicating the dead patient. 'I've heard of it, I mean muscles contracting post death, but I've never seen it – have you? Bloody creepy.' She started walking over to get a closer look. 'We didn't call it too early, did we?'

Kate made her way to the patient's shoulder and pulled back the sheet, exposing the chest. She leant forward, placing her cheek over the mouth of the corpse to feel for airflow, while looking out across the chest for movement of breathing.

The head of the corpse jerked upward, bringing an open mouth to the side of Kate's neck. The teeth clenched shut, ripping a mouthful of flesh and carotid artery away. Kate screamed, jerking away from the body. She clamped a hand to her neck, her eyes bulging with agony. An arterial jet of blood spurted between her fingers, crossing three metres between her and Harry. The corpse pushed itself to sitting. The dead woman's eyes were locked upon Kate, unblinking. Blood drenched its chest, bits of tissue hung from an open mouth that emitted an incoherent rasp. It reached towards her and tumbled from the trolley onto the floor. Harry grabbed Kate by an arm, pulling her out of reach of the hellish creature, and pushed her towards the free resus bed, his other hand clamped over the wound.

Staff rushed into the resus bay, drawn by the screams. One of the nurses hit an alarm to bring hospital security. Three nurses confronted the dead patient; when it didn't respond, they moved in as a team to restrain it. The corpse flung one nurse aside, while pulling another towards its mouth, biting through exposed muscle of a forearm. Three security guards ran in, gloves on. With two people on each limb, they wrenched the struggling body back onto the emergency trolley. The mouth of the creature snapped rhythmically, teeth exposed, lips snarled back at any body part within reach. Security manacled each limb to the bed frame, keeping the ankles and wrists pinned to the mattress. It wrenched viciously at the ties, threatening to tip the heavy trolley.

Harry tried to block out the events happening five feet away as he scrambled through the corridors of his brain for a solution to save Kate's life. He had only seconds to stem the haemcrrhage. The gouts of blood pulsing in time with her heartbeat were slowing and getting weaker as she reached a critical volume of blood loss. Harry's front was drenched in scarlet, his scrub top sticking in a congealed mass like a second skin.

With his thumb jammed against her artery to stem the flow, he hooked the procedure trolley over with his foot. In the second drawer, he found a suturing set. He ripped open the packet between one hand and his teeth, pulled free some forceps, and immediately shoved them into the wound to clamp the artery. His thumb moved off the vessel to enable application of the forceps, causing a jet of blood to splatter against his neck. Finding the artery, he clamped it off. Kate's struggles had eased, her features slackening.

As Harry tried next to stop the haemorrhage from her jugular vein, he realized he was already too late. She had stopped breathing, the bleeding had ceased, but only because most of her blood volume drenched the floor and curtains of the resuscitation bay. There was nothing he could do. There was no point commencing CPR, it wasn't a clinical problem that could be solved. He backed away from the bed, only now becoming aware of the blood that covered his front and squelched in his shoes. He rubbed at his eyes with the heel of one hand in frustration and loss.

An inhuman snarl emanating from the middle resuscitation bay brought his attention back. The body was thrashing against its restraints, trying to reach the group of clinicians and security surrounding the bed. The team seemed stuck to the spot, unable to process what was happening. They had seen this woman die. Her heart had stopped for over thirty minutes before they abandoned resuscitation. It was not possible. And yet, she had risen. Had killed a loved member of their staff.

Harry unlocked the controlled drug cabinet and withdrew an anaesthetic used for heavy sedation. He drew up a large dose – enough to knock out a man twice her size – screwed on a needle and jammed it into the thrashing body's thigh.

Nothing.

If anything, its anger and movement increased. An audible snap, like a piece of breaking timber sounded from the left forearm as it wrenched against the restraint. The forearm's shape deformed upwards at the centre. With the next tug, two broken shards of bone ripped through the skin's surface.

The dead woman was oblivious to the trauma, jerking harder at the arm as the wrist slowly tore free. No blood pumped from the wound. It was dry, the flesh a dull brown of old meat ready for the bin. A security guard reached forward to clamp his hands onto the forearm to stop her movement. A spiked end of the bone impaled the security guard's arm in the struggle. He screamed, pulled his arm free and fell backwards clutching the wound against his chest.

They weren't winning. Harry's traumatised mind slowly cogged forward. If they couldn't sedate her with drugs... 'We need to isolate her before that other arm gets free!'

Harry and one of the nurses kicked off the brakes and steered the bed into an empty room at the end of the resuscitation bays. Staff used this space to contain violent patients until they stopped being a threat to themselves or others. It was devoid of furniture, and had a reinforced door that was lockable from the outside. They shoved the bed through the entrance to the back wall and exited, locking the door behind them.

The room did little to muffle the snarling rage from inside. In their haste to leave, both had forgotten to activate the wheel brakes. Now, a repeated thud accompanied the moans, as the bed frame smacked against the wall in time with its occupant's frenzied movements.

Harry walked back to the main area and was approached by the nurse manager with an update. Jill looked like she was barely holding it together. Her face was pale and eyes glassy.

'I've called the police, they'll be here any minute. They've asked you to call Public Health – there's been a similar incident in Cairns this evening after an animal bite.'

Harry grunted an assent, 'Can I get out of these first though?' he said, indicating the gore coated scrubs stuck to his chest. 'How are the staff that were attacked? Is someone treating them?'

'Yeah, one of the new doctor's sorting it out.' Jill glanced down at his uniform. 'Is it ok if you use the patient shower? It'll need a scrub out after you're done. Kind of looks like you stepped out of a horror movie... Sorry,' she stopped herself, her face crumpling as she released a brief sob. 'This is fucked, Harry. It's just shit!' she said. 'I still have to call Kate's family. What the hell am I supposed to tell them? I'm sorry but a patient we thought was dead ripped out your daughter's throat?'

Harry had no reply. Jill held his gaze for a moment longer, tears escaping in a glistening line down both cheeks. She cuffed them away with the back of her hand and walked off.

Harry remained a few seconds more, staring into space. He didn't envy her, nor did he have any advice about how to break the news in a less traumatic way to the parents. Finally, he got going again, fished a few towels and a pair of surgical scrubs off the linen trolley, and left for the shower.

* * *

Harry replaced the receiver. Public Health had listened to his outline of events, only interrupting to clarify certain points, such as the presence of an animal bite wound. The health official had ignored Harry's question when he asked if a similar event had occurred in Queensland. The conversation was closed with a toneless notification that a police/paramedic escort would accompany the patient to a new federal quarantine facility in the city's south.

When he came out of the back office, six police were already gathered outside the locked room. A near continuous moan persisted from within. There was no further thumping of the bed against the wall as the mindless creature had finally overturned the trolley, pinning itself to the ground. Harry introduced himself to the group, and gave a run-down of events. The officers kept quiet during the relay of information, but a few couldn't suppress a smirk. They obviously thought he was full of shit. Harry noted it dispassionately; he still didn't fully believe what he'd seen with his own eyes either.

Two paramedics came through the door of the ambulance bay pulling a trolley. The whole group fell silent as an orderly pushed Kate's body past into a single room. A sheet had been pulled over her body up to the chin, covering the violent means of her death. Her face was the colour of curdled milk, marred only by a fine network of dark red lines emanating from the bite wound across her face. Her eyes stared at the ceiling, as if surprised at her own death. The orderly pulled the door closed behind him, breaking the spell on the group.

As the police organised how they would approach the restraint, the remaining patients that hadn't bolted on their own volition were moved to a different area. Harry hung back; his help wasn't required, and he was quietly glad of it.

The police team opened the door and rushed into the small room. Screams from the dead woman escalated as they pinned the body down, cut the restraints to the trolley and lifted it away. When called for, the paramedics pushed their transport trolley into the room and collapsed it to the ground. The team lifted the flailing body onto the stretcher, and fastened each limb with multiple zip ties to prevent any movement. Harry handed over a copy of the paperwork from the arrest, and the dual police/paramedic team filed out of the department.

* * *

The treatment of the injured nurse and security guard was now complete; wounds washed and dressed. Harry wrote them scripts for antibiotics and analgesia to see them through the next few days. The manager took pity, ushering them out the door with an early mark. Harry joined the remaining clinicians on the staff base where they'd gathered. The police had stretched a blue and white tape cordon across the entrance to the resuscitation area, restricting access to the crime scene. There was still a bunch of junk food lying on one of the desks, but no one was interested in eating. A junior doctor broke the silence by asking the question each was thinking, but reluctant to voice.

'How do we explain what just happened?'

'Maybe the equipment failed, and we got the diagnosis wrong,' offered one of the nurses. 'What did Public Health have to say, Harry?'

'They mostly wanted to know about the wound.' Harry paused as a new thought hit him. 'There's been a murmur on the grapevine about a new disease in the bat population up north that's suspected in some recent human deaths. I wonder if that's why they were so interested in the bite mark. Do you reckon that's what she had?'

The other Registrar cut in. 'We'd have to be unlucky. I think we just stuffed up. She probably had a faint pulse the whole time that was missed.'

'So how do you explain her attack on Kate?' asked a nurse.

'Maybe she was delirious from the infection? Look, I don't know for sure either,' he said, giving up.

'Yeah, you're probably right.' Harry sighed; he knew the hospital executives were going to haul him over the coals about Kate's death. Still, he'd rather deal with that than be staring at the ceiling with a chunk missing from his neck—

A flat smack echoed from the room where Kate lay. Everyone's head turned. On cue, another thump from the inside of the door caused it to shudder in its frame.

'What the *fuck?*' stammered the Registrar.

Harry lurched to his feet, 'It's happening again. Someone call the cops!' He ran towards the door. 'We need to keep her in there – she's fucking dead. She bled out on me...'

He grabbed the handle and placed his weight onto it, his foot braced against the doorframe. One of the nurses joined him and leant their strength. Whatever was left of Kate, heard their efforts. A shriek of anger battered their eardrums as the door bounced from the force of her blows. The minutes dragged on as the unrelenting assault continued.

A police siren escalated in volume as a squad car neared the department, before skidding to a halt in the ambulance bay. Two constables ran in and were directed to the barricaded door. Harry and the nurse were ordered out of the way. One officer stepped forward and turned the handle, pulled open the door and stood back.

Out from the darkness shambled Kate's body. The limbs moved in an uncoordinated lurching motion. Clot-soaked tendrils of hair matted one side of her face, covering the left eye. The right eye snapped its focus to the first police officer. Her lips peeled back into a snarl as she started towards him. The officer moved backwards slowly. 'Stop! Get down on the ground!'

Nothing.

The cop pulled out his Taser, and aimed it at her chest. 'Stop where you are!'

What had once been Kate, lurched forward.

'Taser! Taser! Taser!' shouted the police officer in a last warning to the corpse, then fired the pins into her chest to deliver a debilitating shock. Instead of dropping to the floor in an agony of electric charge, her body was unaffected. Her forward motion continued, now accompanied by a maddening groan.

Shaking hands dropped the Taser in preference of a Glock. The officer's face drained of colour as he provided his last warnings to surrender without effect.

Three shots in rapid succession punched through the corpse's chest, smashing it off its feet. The clot of hair had flung away from the left eye in the fall, freeing both unblinking eyes to bore a hole through the constable's head as it pushed itself back to standing and started forward again.

The constable's hand started to waver as he backed away, firing two more rounds. The first hit her left shoulder; the second entered the right side of her forehead, blowing out a section of her skull to coat the wall behind. The corpse smacked to the ground, lifeless once more. The police officer re-holstered his weapon, took a slow breath and turned around, his eyes searching the people behind until he found his colleague. He maintained a fixed glare at his partner, a *"where the fuck were you during that?"* expression clearly conveyed while he addressed the rest of the room in a rasping voice.

'Start transferring any remaining patients to other departments or hospitals. This entire Emergency Department is now a crime scene.'

* * *

Harry grabbed his backpack and headed for the door. It had taken them another two hours to move the remaining patients elsewhere. He'd never seen patients accepted by inpatient medical teams so willingly before. A further two hours followed of interviews with police and the hospital's General Manager who was desperate to understand what had happened before it was leaked to the media. Harry was beyond tired, scraped to a husk inside after the night's happenings. He needed to find unconsciousness in sleep without any more dissection of events. There was a half full bottle of scotch at home that he hoped could deliver a dreamless sleep.

CHAPTER TWO

Harry jammed the phone back into the receiver in frustration. The bloody police had gained wind of him moving to Milton from hospital management, and had kept him from sleep for a further two hours discussing the night's events on the phone again. They had given him "permission" to leave as planned, stating that he could sign a formal statement via the Milton police. Harry glanced at the bottle of whiskey, untouched on the sideboard. He'd never got the chance to pour himself that drink, the phone had been ringing as he'd walked in the front door. Fatigue now extinguished the desire for anything other than bed.

Harry wandered into the bathroom for a leak and caught his reflection in the mirror. He looked rough. Brown hair curled in rebellious tufts, bloodshot eyes hooded with exhaustion, pale skin and a three-day growth matched how he felt inside. Yawning, he scratched at the stubble on his neck and headed for his bedroom. After moving most of his belongings to Milton, he'd left himself just a camp mat to sleep on for the past week. But with how he felt at the moment, bare floorboards would have done the job. He shrugged off his scrubs, crawled under his sleeping bag and within a few heartbeats, was unconscious.

...Harry walked outside after meeting with the village elders and glanced at the sun. The humidity was oppressive, his whole body felt damp with sweat, turning his clothes to a wet second skin. The village to which they had tracked the latest outbreak was remote, up in the hills with only walking tracks or rough four-wheel drive trails for access. The locals farmed Cassava, a root crop suited to the poor soil quality of the region. Banana trees encircled the living area, immature green fruit hanging in clumps from the upper branches. The lush green of the surrounding foliage somehow acted as a partial antidote to the unrelenting heat of the equatorial sun, you couldn't help but feel alive in such an environment. Alive maybe, but still exhausted.

He looked back towards the hut of concern. Mud brick walls topped by a thatch roof, the stooped low doorway framed a dark interior, appearing black from outside. Inside lay a forty-year-old mother, matriarch to eight live children – an incredible feat considering child-mortality rates in the region. Despite her resilience, she had fallen ill after preparing her uncle's body for funeral the previous week. Her uncle was a village trade representative, responsible for transporting produce to local markets and negotiating sales. He had encountered an infected person on one of these trips, however had not become ill until well on his way home. Unfortunately, he had managed to spread Ebola to three separate villages – including his own – prior to his death.

Harry and two other colleagues from MSF were setting up a clinic in the village to treat locals exposed to the virus. Running a clinic in a remote setting such as this was always a huge challenge. He had to achieve sufficient trust with the locals for them to accept treatment, whilst preventing Ebola transmission to his team during care delivery.

Harry and another MSF volunteer unpacked their equipment from the back of the twin-cab Ute. Methodically, they helped each other apply the protective gear necessary to prevent exposure to the virus. Once dressed, a plastic suit encased their bodies from head to toe, making all movement ungainly and difficult. Respirators and eye shields covered their faces, erasing all features of humanity. Harry felt his pulse escalate, an unwelcome stirring of anxiety at the base of his chest fluttering into existence at the claustrophobic nature of the all-enclosing suit. The heat and humidity under the layers of plastic was immense, and a sheen of sweat soon coated his skin.

Harry and his colleague entered the woman's hut and set up the required equipment for treatment. There was no cure for Ebola. Treatment focused on supporting the body while the immune system fought the virus. Occasionally it worked, with around 20% of infected patients surviving. Looking down at his latest patient through fogged glasses, he didn't think this lady would make that lucky group.

The woman on the bed was slick with sweat, her breathing rapid and shallow. She had soiled herself under the sheet, and as Harry pulled it back, he found red blood mixed with the diarrhea – not a good sign. A small number of Ebola victims displayed haemorrhagic symptoms and began to bleed from their orifices; mouth, nose, anus and sometimes eyes. As Harry inserted an intravenous catheter into her arm, a blood-stained tear rolled down her right cheek. The woman suddenly opened both eyes; the whites were scarlet due to bleeding beneath the conjunctiva.

She looked at Harry in terror and confusion, not understanding why an alien-looking figure was sticking a needle in her arm. She began to fight and grabbed hold of Harry's facemask and hood, ripping it off his head. Harry backed out of the room as quickly as possible, holding his breath and keeping his eyes and mouth shut, praying that none of the woman's blood or saliva had touched his skin or mucous membranes.

Now that he was outside again, Harry opened both eyes, took a deep breath of the fresh air; and froze. Kate stood in the middle of the clearing. Her blue scrubs, clotted with blood, clung to her slim frame. The ragged bite wound in her neck gaped open, glaring evidence of her violent death. Her eyes fixed on Harry, unblinking in accusation.

'You couldn't save her,' she croaked, pointing at the hut from which he had exited. 'And you gave up on me. Some fucking doctor you are.'

Harry sat bolt upright, chest heaving. He leant forward, resting his forehead on his hands as he tried to slow his breathing. The Liberian woman had disturbed his sleep for weeks after returning from his last MSF placement. Now the dream was back, hijacked by Kate in a combined protest at his failure. He walked to the bathroom, twisted on the tap and splashed some water up to his face. There was no point going back to bed, from experience he knew the dream would pursue any further attempts of sleep.

Coping with intimate exposure to death was one of the harder components of working in health. Harry had prevented many deaths, however, it wasn't possible to save every person. In the advent of a patient death, Harry compulsively reviewed his actions to see if he had made the right decisions.

During daylight hours, he could usually shut his mind down on the subject, but occasionally he found an underlying anxiety would persist, keeping him awake for hours at night. His involvement with Kate and her murderer was something entirely different. He *knew* he hadn't misdiagnosed either. They had both died; their hearts had stopped, breathing ceased. There hadn't been any fault with the cardiac monitoring – blaming these items just sought to ignore the possibility that they had both re-animated after death.

As soon as his mind tried to contemplate this, it reeled away, still refusing what he had witnessed with his own eyes. Nevertheless, it had happened, and whatever it was that had come back, was empty of consciousness or compassion, containing only a murderous rage and unassailable hunger.

Harry pulled on a pair of jeans and t-shirt, then stuffed the last few items of clothes scattered on his bedroom floor into a large duffle bag. He rolled up his mat then crammed the sleeping bag into its sack, and slung it over his shoulder.

After a last glance around to ensure all lights were off and windows closed, he left the house key on the kitchen table for the real estate agent to find, shut the front door and walked to his car. It was mid-afternoon, late to be starting a six-hour drive to Milton, but he needed to leave the recent events in Sydney well behind. Putting the car into gear, he pulled out and headed for the Princes Highway and South Coast.

CHAPTER THREE

Steph hooked her toe under the rim of an empty chair and pulled it closer, before crossing her ankles on it and easing into a comfortable slouch. She took another sip from a tall glass of orange juice then set it aside. The air was warm and humid, the slight breeze cooling a prickle of sweat on her brow. Light dappled the ground, filtered between vivid green foliage that cocooned the small, seated area. She felt contented.

The dent in her savings to attend the rainforest retreat had been worth every cent. After months travelling and living out of crowded backpacker dorms, she had decided to splurge on five days at a secluded retreat outside of Cairns. The eco-resort had a focus on "wellness" activities, offering yoga, meditation, diet detoxes and personal trainers along with a lecture series on the local forest environment for those with an academic bent. The only downside to the place that Steph could see was the lack of alcohol, all part of the "detox" she supposed. Although any holiday for her usually involved a few drinks to unwind, she hadn't missed it as much as expected.

This was the first lecture that she had attended so far. It was day four of her stay, and she'd had enough of yoga – there wasn't a muscle that hadn't been stretched to breaking point. Her sleep debt was repaid, she couldn't be bothered doing a gym session, and listening to a tape of whales gossiping long-distance didn't fit her bill as meditation. That left today's lecture provided by a local park ranger as her best option for distraction.

Steph was one of six people that had shown up for the presentation. Hurried footsteps approached along a path towards their clearing, and shortly, a man in an olive-green uniform appeared lugging two covered cages. The ranger introduced himself while placing the cages on a trestle table. He removed the covers gently to reveal a pair of bats hanging upside down.

The ranger presented his charges, two different species of Flying Fox common to tropical Queensland. In the cage to the right hung a "Little Red Flying Fox", named for the russet fur that covered the torso of the breed. Two glistening black eyes blinked in the light from a head covered in grey fur. The bat clasped light brown wings about its body, covering it from toes to shoulder. In the second cage hung a "Black Flying Fox", a much larger creature encased in black fur from head to belly. This creature was a relative giant of the bat world, owning a wingspan of up to one metre.

The ranger displayed a talent for public speaking, his easy stance and evident passion held each person's attention closely. The exuberant expression on his face as he described the local bat colonies and eating habits began to fade as he discussed a new disease responsible for a sharp decline in Queensland bat numbers. During the last six months, civilians had provided multiple reports of dead bats to the forestry service. Flying foxes were renowned, despite their almost canine heads, as gentle giants in the bat world. Their diet comprised fruit and nectar of flowering blossoms, and they rarely came in physical contact with humans, however, three people had recently experienced minor bites and scratches when inadvertently disturbing their feeding on low branches.

The victims had developed a variant of Lyssavirus – a disease closely related to rabies found in some Australian bats. Each person had succumbed despite aggressive treatment at the Princess Alexandra Hospital in Brisbane. At present, Public Health officials hypothesised that a mutation of the Lyssavirus was responsible for decimated bat populations in Northern Queensland, along with greater susceptibility of transfer to humans. The University of Queensland had launched a research project into the virus, and the ranger proudly informed them that the bats on display were part of the study.

He invited those present to come up for a closer view on the proviso they keep their fingers away from the cages. Steph was one of the first to accept the offer, keen to gain some quality photos of the creatures. She pulled a digital SLR from a bag sitting next to her chair, threw the camera's strap over her neck and walked to the front. Both bats had eyes open now, warily watching the humans about them. Steph snapped numerous close-up shots of the smaller bat, fascinated by its liquid black eyes. A vocal older woman elbowed her to the side to gain a better view. Steph stood back, dumbfounded at the brusque rudeness of the woman.

'I want to see how big their wings are. Make the bats stretch them out,' demanded the woman of the ranger.

The ranger looked caught off guard. He gently explained how the bats usually slept through the day, and that he didn't want to disturb them further. At his refusal, the woman decided to act herself, giving the table a sharp kick to rattle the cage.

It was enough to collapse the trestle table legs at her end. Both cages slid to the side, smashing onto the brick pavers. The bats were terrified, frantically clawing at the wire to escape. The ranger quickly grabbed each cage in turn, placing them right way up on the ground, anxious to prevent the bats from harm.

As he grabbed the smaller bat's cage, the fox-headed creature latched onto his index finger, inflicting a vicious bite. He swore under his breath, jerking his fingers back. A small jet of blood squirted from the wound before he clamped pressure onto it with his thumb, the teeth having severed a small artery. A representative from the resort obtained a first aid kit and wrapped a bandage around the wound while the ranger grimaced in discomfort. Steph looked around to see what had happened to the woman who'd caused the whole incident – but the bitch had quietly left without even an apology.

The presentation was evidently over. Both bats had settled down after the ranger placed canvas covers gingerly over their cages.

'Those bats weren't infected, were they?' Steph asked, concerned for the ranger.

'No, they're part of a control group. I'll still be stuck with a course of bloody antibiotics anyway,' he replied, frowning.

During the previous five minutes, the ranger had broken into a sweat and the skin on his hand above the bandaged finger was turning a light shade of red.

'Are you sure you're ok?' asked Steph. 'You're not looking so good.'

'I've had a sore throat the last week, probably just the flu. My head's started to bang though,' he said, massaging his temples.

'Talk to the staff at reception; they should have something for the headache. Maybe they would let you crash in staff quarters for a while until the pain killers kick in?' Steph suggested.

'Yeah, might be a good idea.'

He declined her offer to help move the cages back to his truck, so she left him to it and returned to her room for an afternoon nap.

Steph had been on the road for five months since leaving London. Starting in New Delhi, she had spent four months exploring India, Nepal, Thailand, Vietnam and Laos before landing in Perth. During the past four weeks, Steph had touched base with the main tourist attractions in Western Australia and Northern Territory before taking a small connecting flight to Cairns, beginning a journey down the east coast of Australia.

It had been her first experience of travelling, a trip she'd dreamt of completing since being a teenager, however, there had always been some reason to put it off. First, it was university, and then a career and relationship. At the start of the year, however, her boyfriend had dumped her unexpectedly. Turns out, he had been dating a colleague on the sly for months and she hadn't noticed a thing. Or, more accurately, she'd decided not to read anything into the frequent late nights at work, or the times he supposedly crashed at a mate's place after a boys' night out. It was the wake-up call she needed to take her life back. She had stayed an extra month until her lease expired, then packed her belongings into storage, resigned from work and hit the road. The freedom she had now, to be able to go wherever she wanted with only a backpack for company, was something that she'd find hard to explain to her old self.

Steph pulled her blond hair into a ponytail, kicked her thongs off and lay back on the bed to flip through a dog-eared copy of the Australian Lonely Planet guide. A light breeze caused by the circling ceiling fan played with the hair of her fringe as she read. Within minutes, the book dropped from limp fingers as she fell asleep.

CHAPTER FOUR

Penny's stomach growled. Her lunch had been delayed indefinitely when the job came through. As a police officer stationed at Kogarah, Penny had drawn the mundane duty of preventing unauthorized media access to the Federal Quarantine facility. Overnight, police had chaperoned a patient transfer, and the media had got wind of the story. A series of rumours had circulated amongst police that morning about the events at Randwick Emergency.

The stories ranged from the absurd – new rabies virus turns patient into crazed killer; to the hilarious – dead patient rises again, attacks co-workers and ignores gunshot wounds like mosquito bites.

Her colleagues were obviously bored and trying to outdo each other, but then again, it made for a good laugh compared to the real-life depressing situations they usually dealt with.

Penny and one other officer were standing outside the main gate to the quarantine facility, feeling rather redundant. The security surrounding the place seemed extreme for what was essentially still just a medical facility. A three-metre chain-link fence topped with barbed wire separated the quarantine grounds from the public, each stretch of fence under the surveillance of CCTV cameras. The main entrance was a reinforced metal sliding gate, from which a driveway proceeded thirty metres to terminate in front of the only building on site.

The three-storey structure with a flat roof, was constructed of drab, fawn-coloured brick. Small rectangles of tinted glass dotted the upper-most part of each floor, giving the appearance of cell-block windows. Although they allowed natural light within, they provided a view of nothing but sky to the inhabitants.

The building's foyer was similarly comprised of dark tinted glass, preventing outside sight into even this inconsequential area. With such measures taken, Penny saw little risk that the media would gain access to any information that wasn't first volunteered by quarantine management, or leaked by an employee – neither of which necessitated her kicking her feet at the front gate, bored brainless.

A rumble of an approaching truck engine drew her attention as a camouflage-painted troop carrier rounded the street corner. As the truck drew near, it began to gear down before swinging into the driveway and halting. A detachment of ten soldiers spilled out of the back, each in battle fatigues with webbing and rifle in hand. A soldier with Lieutenant insignia on his shoulder approached her.

'You in charge here?' he asked.

Penny glanced at her partner who just shrugged in reply.

'Yeah, you can talk to me. What's going on?' she asked. The officer ignored her question, instead handing her a sheet of paper from his shirt pocket.

'We've been ordered to take over security at this facility. Police command have been notified.'

Penny gave the paperwork a brief scan, not giving it much credence. She handed the paper back, the officer roughly folded it and replaced it in his pocket.

'Give me a sec, yeah?' Penny indicated to her partner to remain at the gate while she radioed in to verify the information. Interestingly, the Lieutenant's story held true. Kogarah station confirmed receipt of the order only minutes prior. She hooked her radio back onto her vest and walked back to her partner.

'It checks out. We're off.'

The detachment of soldiers continued as if the pair of them had already left. The Lieutenant was at a communication box at the side of the gate speaking to someone inside. As he stepped away, the gate began to move, sliding with a squeal of oil-starved metal. Two soldiers peeled off from the group, remaining outside the gate where Penny and her partner had been standing. The rest of the group walked up the driveway, the truck following slowly behind. As the truck cleared the gateway, it shut once more.

She stood and watched as the truck parked and the soldiers entered the foyer into the building, disappearing from sight. She sighed; at least now she could maybe get some lunch finally. Penny climbed into the front passenger seat, her partner stuck with the driving responsibilities for this shift. In the distance, an intermittent sequence of popping sounds escalated in intensity before stopping abruptly.

Was that a scream?

She looked at her partner. 'Tell me you heard that as well? What the hell are they shooting at? It's a quarantine centre, not a bloody war zone.'

Penny grabbed the door handle to get out again when the radio came alive.

'All units return to base. Multiple occasions of violent assault reported. Riot squad response being formulated, further instructions to follow at station.'

Penny snatched the mike off the dashboard. 'This is car SG 112, we've heard shots fired at the Quarantine Centre, request permission to delay our return to investigate. Over.'

'Car SG 112, that's a negative. Quarantine is the army's responsibility – return to base *immediately.*'

Penny affirmed that they had received the order, jaw clenched in frustration as she signed off. Her partner switched on the lights and siren, wheels squealing as he stamped on the accelerator.

Penny looked over her shoulder at the receding quarantine facility, her stomach clenching slightly. Was there some truth to the rumours about the Randwick ED virus and homicide? If the army was already involved, maybe it was some sort of terrorist attack. She caught her train of thought and shut it down, no point worrying about unlikely scenarios, she'd find out soon enough back at the station.

Penny pulled out her mobile and sent her husband a quick text, asking him to pick up their son from afterschool care and then stay at home until more news came through – it looked like there was going to be some mandatory overtime this evening.

CHAPTER FIVE

Harry exited the airport tunnel and crossed the Cooks River bridge onto General Holmes drive. He was making good time. The roads were more empty than usual, which was fine by him. To his left, the waters of Botany Bay were an angry grey as a southerly whipped the surface into white caps.

He'd been brainstorming a possible cause for the events of the previous night, and the only answer that got past the first base of interrogation was infection. His original patient had been bitten by something before boarding her flight from Queensland. A typical biological response to an overwhelming infection had followed before she had died.

And then re-animated.

But had she come back to life? There had been no bleeding when she ripped her own arm off. Had the virus somehow reprogrammed how the cells were working, making the body a mere vessel to continue virus transmission from host to host? The patient had bitten Kate; however, the injury's severity had prevented the escalation of infection symptoms to the point of death. Kate had bled out instead – a much quicker route to the same end point. But there *had* been a bite, and the virus had been transmitted, leading to the same eventual outcome of reanimation and violence.

If he was somewhere near the truth, then the virus was extremely quick acting, and with each infected person attacking anyone within reach, the rate of spread through the community could outrun a wild fire. In his experience with Ebola, it had been hard enough to treat infected people when they were only scared of dying. How the hell was he to treat an infected person while they were actively trying to kill him?

As his mind leapt forward to the worst-case scenarios, his thoughts leant towards ongoing survival. He'd need to stockpile food before the supermarkets closed – any wide-reaching quarantine would bring general trade to a standstill. What tools were at the farm? He'd need a basic set on the property to make it liveable in isolation for any length of time. Harry flipped his indicator, turning right onto Presidents Avenue. From memory, there was a Bunning's Hardware store and supermarket at Rockdale.

At the supermarket, he filled his trolley with an assorted range of canned goods, both vegetable and meat, and anything that looked non-perishable. He grabbed a few four-litre bottles of water for good measure, unsure whether the farm had a working bore. From the fishing section at Big W next door, he found a sheathed bait knife and machete.

At the hardware store he stocked up on a few essentials: hatchet, axe, pinch bar, spade, hammer, battery packs, torch, wrench and screwdriver set, and two jerry cans for fuel. By the end of it, he'd filled the back of his Pathfinder.

His next stop was the petrol station. He hauled the jerry cans out and filled them to brimming along with the car's tank. Luckily, the Pathfinder had some external attachment points for the jerry cans, so he wouldn't have to get high on the fumes all the way down the coast. At the counter, his eyes were drawn to the cigarettes behind the attendant. Whenever he went on an overseas contract, he inevitably picked up a smoking habit again. Being conscious of his own health was something he only seemed to worry about when he was in his own country.

'The petrol at pump six, thanks.'

'Would you like anything else with that, Mars Bars are two for one with a petrol purchase,' said that greasy-bearded attendant, spouting an obligatory sales pitch.

Ah, fuck it. 'Yeah, give me a twenty-pack of Styvo's and a lighter. Stressful day an all...' Harry tailed off.

He didn't know why he was making excuses to the guy behind the counter; it's not like he'd bloody care what Harry was breathing into his lungs. Harry shoved the smokes and lighter in his pocket and ditched the receipt on the way back to his car.

In the driver's seat once again, he pulled out a smoke and lit up. His car was facing in the direction of the city centre. He waved the smoke towards the window, and then realized the haze wasn't of his own making. At least three different streams of grey smoke rose above the suburbs ahead; there were some major fires ongoing.

He turned on the engine, and caught the end of a news broadcast. People were being urged to stay at home, with multiple riots across the city. The broadcaster was unsure of the cause or origin of the violence, but reports were of multiple deaths and assaults.

Harry pulled out onto the road with the newscast continuing in the background. He'd made the right choice to up and leave this afternoon, Sydney looked like it was in for a rough couple of weeks.

CHAPTER SIX

Penny filed into the station's conference room amidst a crowd of other police officers. The atmosphere was strangely muted, with this many officers in one place, the noise would usually be deafening. Penny had heard multiple stories being swapped in the cafeteria while awaiting the meeting, and if even a tenth of them were true, this was going to be like nothing they'd ever faced. The few quiet conversations still in progress died off to silence as the Superintendent walked to the front.

'I'm sure most of you have heard rumours of atrocities committed in the last few hours, some of you may have even been involved in trying to stop them. We have experienced an unprecedented level of violence on the streets, people attacking each other and, unbelievably,' he paused, a look of revulsion twisting his mouth, 'cannibalism has been observed. I can assure you, that we will succeed in confronting and stopping this threat to public safety. It will be the toughest, and possibly most dangerous job that we've faced in recent times.' He paused and leant to plug a USB key into the computer at the podium, opening a video file.

'The quickest way to illustrate what we are up against is a video of a police engagement that took place in Newtown only an hour ago. Without seeing it for myself, I wouldn't have believed it possible.'

The video was from the squad car camera of two constables from Newtown station. The footage clicked into life as one of the constables exited the vehicle and approached two men huddled over a body on the ground twenty metres away. A muted challenge was heard from the officer as he approached, demanding the two men stand and place their hands behind their heads. At the noise, one of the men slowly stood and turned to face the constable. A crimson slick covered his mouth, chin and neck. Dried, black blood coated one side of his face and shirt, a flap of tissue and skin hung from his right temple in a palm width slab, obscuring the eye and ear on that side. His skin was deathly white where it showed through the gore. The man began to move towards the cop, lurching forward unsteadily, like a 3am drunk.

The policeman drew his Taser, ordering the man to stop and lie on the ground. There was no response from the approaching figure other than an animalistic snarl. The officer fired the Taser pins into the man's chest without effect. The distance between the two rapidly diminished, only four metres now separated them. The cop drew his Glock, again demanding surrender. The killer's hand reached for the officer as he fired three rapid shots into his chest – centre mass.

The impact of the bullets caused the man to stagger one step back; but that was all. He started forward again. The police officer now retreated slowly, continuing to fire, emptying his magazine. Many of the bullets flew wide of their mark as fear overtook his aim.

The policeman's partner could be seen entering the scene from the side of frame as the killer grabbed hold of one hand and wrenched the constable into a savage embrace, locking teeth onto his face and ripping free the cop's upper lip and nose. The policeman screamed, battering with both hands at his assailant, but it had all the effect of a child against a giant.

The killer pulled the police officer to the ground, ripping into his neck while one free hand stabbed forward, up and under his tactical vest, fingers pressing through the skin of the abdomen like a crude knifepoint. The policeman's eyes bulged in agony and the body convulsed as he was eviscerated.

The other police officer could be seen emptying a magazine into the killer's back without effect as it feasted upon his partner. The officer on the ground was no longer moving, now mercifully silent. Whether by blood loss or a stray bullet, at least his suffering had stopped. The partner, realising failure, ran back towards the car. The view of the officer on the ground, with his killer hunched over, rapidly shrunk on the screen as the squad car reversed at speed. The screen went black as the Superintendent stopped the video.

The room was silent for three heartbeats before a wall of noise rose as the audience demanded information, clearly disturbed by what they had witnessed. The Superintendent held up his hands for silence.

'We don't have all the answers to explain what you have just seen. It doesn't fit any pattern of terrorism as we know it, and the instigators are of multiple nationalities and religious backgrounds. We can't pin it on any of the groups currently being watched by our intelligence services. Our best bet is it's some type of infection passed from attacker to victim through body fluid exchange during a bite, as there are witness accounts of victims taking on the behaviour patterns of their assailants.'

'That guy in the video got shot at least five times without going down, how is that possible?' asked one of the constables.

The Superintendent shrugged and sighed. 'The best answer given to us, is that the infection has switched off brain recognition of the body's usual pain response system, so they're just not feeling physical trauma any more. My guess is that the heart was missed, and our video didn't go on long enough to show him collapsing from blood loss. Further studies are being completed at the Federal Quarantine facility on an infected person taken from Randwick Hospital yesterday.' The Superintendent's hands gripped the rostrum tight, white knuckles at odds with an otherwise calm facade. 'They're updating security forces as more information comes to hand about what precautions are needed to prevent infection transmission to our people. We're still left with the immediate need to contain this violence. There have been outbreaks in at least six locations around Sydney within the last few hours, the closest to us is in Newtown, and we'll be sending half of you there to assist.' His gaze roamed the room, briefly making eye contact with many of the officers. 'The rest are to remain in our area, ready to confront any local occurrences. Our focus is on containment and restraint of the infected if possible, however, your safety remains paramount – if required, escalate the level of force appropriately. All officers sent to Newtown will be armed in riot gear.'

As soon as he stopped speaking, at least four people asked questions from the audience. The Superintendent cut them off. 'I'd like to spend more time answering questions, however, time is short and we have to move *now*.' He pointed to the back of the room where A4 sheets of paper were being pinned to a notice board. 'You'll find your deployment details there. Officers allocated to Newtown, you'll be leaving in thirty minutes.'

He gathered a few pieces of paper off the rostrum, and departed for the central command room where overall coordination of the operation would occur.

'Absolute bullshit,' muttered an officer to her left.

Penny glanced to her side at a younger cop, a bloke called Dino who was fond of spouting conspiracy theories. She sighed, not having the energy to put up with his shit.

'What, the deployment strategy?' she asked in a disinterested voice, wanting to avoid the conversation.

'No, the Superintendent's rationale. We just saw a guy get shot five times in the chest, and he says it's because the *heart was missed?* With that many hitting home, even if the heart *was* missed; his lungs, arteries or something would have been taken out – that's why we're taught to aim for centre-of-mass for gods sake!'

'Get to your point, Dino,' said Penny, keen to get moving.

'I'm saying, that the reason that monster didn't go down, was because he didn't get shot in the head.'

Penny groaned, finally losing all patience. 'For fucks sake, this isn't an episode of "The Walking Dead". Those people out there might be diseased or mentally deranged, but that doesn't make them bloody *zombies*.'

Dino smarted at her tone, looking like she'd just slapped him in the face. 'OK, when one of those freaks attack you, keep on shooting centre of mass and see how long you last. But as for me? I'll be aiming for the head. Ain't no freaking zombie having *me* for lunch.'

Penny turned away, cutting off the conversation and joined the crowd closing in on the deployment notices, hoping that she was in the group staying in Kogarah. No such luck. There she was – Penny O'Brien, under the Newtown list.

She squeezed down on the ball of anxiety that wanted to rise and break free of her chest, and instead forced herself to think of what had to be done before leaving. Pulling out her mobile, she dialled her husband, David, and gave him an update, an update that deliberately excluded anything that would worry him unduly – therefore, pretty much everything.

CHAPTER SEVEN

The setting sun cast shards of light through a gap in the curtain, slicing across Mark's face like knives. He was lying on the couch under the front window of his Glebe terrace, asleep. Or, more accurately, passed out after drinking himself into oblivion the previous night.

He'd only returned the day before from a stint in Afghanistan as a sapper with the Australian Army, and instead of being met by his girlfriend for a long-anticipated reunion night of drinking and shagging, he'd been dumped by text message. At least she'd waited until he got back to give him the news, though it didn't make it any easier on reading.

She hadn't given a clear reason, just said she wanted other things – what the fuck was that supposed to mean? Mark had coped with the news in typical army fashion, by getting so drunk that he couldn't remember his own name, let alone hers. He'd bought a slab of Victoria Bitter and bottle of vodka and headed home, parked his arse on the couch in front of Netflix, and began to work his way through the case of beer. He then made a decent effort of the vodka before slumping unconscious.

The first thing that registered was pain; his whole head ached, a vice-like pressure clenched his temples, the pain fluctuating its intensity with each heartbeat. As he opened his eyes, the light on his face lanced a burning poker of agony through to the back of his skull.

Mark groaned and raised his hand to shade his eyes, silently cursing before pushing himself to sitting. He sat there for a few moments, bent forward, breathing deeply and rubbing at his eyes with the heels of his hands as if they could crush the pain out of his head. His mouth was dry, and tasted like some bastard cat had shat in it. He climbed to his feet and stumbled into the kitchen; his stomach churned and spit flooded his mouth as his gorge rose. He made it to the sink in time to empty last night's pizza out of his stomach. The sweet waft of vomit made him gag again, retching until nothing more would come.

He wiped a slick of cold sweat from his forehead, and tried to spit the taste from his mouth before pulling a bottle of coke from the fridge, swilling the carbonated bubbles around his mouth and spitting once more. With the next mouthful, he washed down a couple of Panadol and Nurofen, then waited next to the sink to see if it would come straight back up again. His stomach gurgled angrily, but kept its contents within for the moment.

Mark made himself a black coffee, extra strong, before sitting at the kitchen table, his forehead resting on folded arms while the cup cooled enough to drink. He sat like this for a good while, trying to ignore his headache and self-pity that had prompted the binge, and waited for the tablets to take the edge off his pain.

His terrace was an old two-storey building he had managed to buy with a mix of inheritance and money saved from multiple tours of Afghanistan over the past five years. Unfortunately, the cash had only been enough to secure the building and service the loan, not enough to begin renovation, of which it was desperately in need. Stuck in the orange and browns of the 1970s, it was small, but it was his. The severity of his headache began to recede as the painkillers took effect, the vice grip on his temples lessened and he could open his eyes without wincing. His house was quiet, the TV silent, and there was no sound other than an occasional screaming bird in the distance. It was this absence of sound that drew Mark's attention; usually there was a constant fluctuation of noise and vibration from traffic outside his terrace.

He rotated his head to listen. There it was again. But it didn't sound like a bird now that he was concentrating, it sounded like human screams. *What the fuck?*

Mark got up from the table and padded barefoot to his front door. He stepped outside onto the damp stone of his front step. An involuntary shiver worked through his upper body at the cold breeze swirling about the street, his old jeans and faded singlet providing little protection from the cold. It was early June, and the evening temperatures were steadily dropping as winter took hold.

He craned his neck, looking up his street towards the intersection with Glebe Point Rd. There was a fire somewhere nearby; grey smoke-smeared eddies swirled in the distance, the smell acrid to his nose. A few figures staggered through the smoke, grabbing at other running people that occasionally flitted between them down the main street. *Something's wrong.*

Mark closed the door behind him then turned on the television in the living room, flicking to the ABC News channel. Two news anchors sat behind their desk, strained expressions accompanying a looping discussion of the violence hitting Sydney streets. Mark sat, attention rapt to the screen, incredulous at the situation described by the reporters.

Multiple outbreaks of general disorder throughout the city, civilians turning on each other with mindless violence. The government had declared a state of emergency and citizens were encouraged to stay at home while police and defence personnel brought the situation under control. The violent behaviour of individuals was thought to have resulted from a mutated virus.

An infected Australian woman travelling from North Queensland had attacked staff at a Sydney Emergency Department, killing one and biting others. Although police transferred the infected person to a Federal quarantine facility, the virus escaped into the general community via bitten staff members released home on the night of the attack. The subject under investigation at the quarantine facility had tested positive for a new variant of Lyssavirus – a disease closely related to Rabies, found in Australian bat populations. Security forces theorised that the woman was bitten or scratched by a bat in North Queensland, however, had not ruled out the possibility of biological terrorism, and a deliberate release of the modified virus into the community.

The footage cut to an infectious diseases expert to explain virus transmission. The doctor looked exhausted, his clothes a creased mess of someone who had slept fully dressed.

'The new virus had been named "Lysan Plague" due to its rapid spread through the community to date. Lysan, like its predecessor Lyssavirus, is a vector borne disease, although unlike malaria or dengue fever where the disease is transmitted by the humble mosquito, the vector in this case is our own species.' The doctor paused, listening to questions off screen.

'What's a vector? Ah, ok… I'll try to speak in plain terms. Well, a vector is any creature, whether human, animal or insect, that carries and transmits an infection into another organism. The virus is transmitted from the host during a bite, where saliva is inoculated into the victim's wound. The infection rate is one hundred percent, with the speed of conversion varying dependent on the injury site. Patients with superficial wounds take some hours to deteriorate, displaying symptoms of rampant infection before deteriorating to a point of apparent death. In patients with trauma to larger blood vessels, the process occurs more rapidly, sometimes in as little as thirty minutes. Post "death", observed subjects become active once more; however, normal cognitive processes are absent, replaced with a senseless urge to pass on the virus through biting. Thankfully, we have not observed any airborne transmission of the virus to date. What we don't understand so far, is why carriers of the disease in many cases continue to eat their victims…'

The report cut back to the studio once again, where a police representative reported that two other outbreaks in Cairns and Brisbane were also active. He sought to reassure viewers that police were implementing a strategy across Sydney to contain the areas of violence and infected citizens, and advised people to remain indoors, lock windows and doors, keep lights off and remain quiet as carriers of the infection sought out noise and human activity.

In the advent of an attack upon a friend or family member, the police representative urged viewers to lock the person in a secure room by themselves, and to notify the police and Public Health for retrieval, as

Public Health was still hopeful they could identify a cure for the infection. Lastly, he advised against fleeing Sydney to prevent road blockages and further chances of infection transmission in public.

Mark rocked back in his chair and looked up at the peeling paint on his ceiling. Surely it had to be a large-scale prank, like the ones the BBC did each year on April the 1st? The ongoing screams in the distance, accompanied now by intermittent sirens said otherwise.

He secured the curtains properly, locked the front door, turned the lights off and muted the television. Mark knew he couldn't stay in the house; for one thing, he had no food, and he would likely be recalled to the army base at Randwick.

Shit. His phone had been off since last night. Not wanting anyone to disturb his drinking session, he'd turned off his mobile and left it in his bag upstairs. He took the steps two at a time, grabbed his backpack off the bed and rummaged in the front pocket for the phone. After taking a bloody age to start, his iPhone alerted the presence of a bunch of messages. First was the duty officer at Randwick, demanding an immediate return to service at seven this morning; a variation of this message was present at roughly forty-five minute intervals through the rest of the morning. More alarming however, were the five messages from his now ex-girlfriend, Georgie, who was living on campus at Sydney University. She sounded terrified.

He immediately called her. On the third ring, she picked up.

'Mark, is that you? Are you all right?' she asked rapidly, her voice cracking.

'Yeah, I'm ok. I've just woken up, got your message and seen what's happening on the news – is this for real?'

'I bloody wish it wasn't.'

'What, have you seen something yourself?'

'I was in Newtown for lunch. I saw the start of it. I saw them overrun the cops,' she said, her voice trembling.

'Saw what overrun the cops? You mean virus infected people that the news is talking about?'

'They don't just look sick, Mark. They look like walking corpses; it was too surreal to be happening. Lucy and I were at the cafe there when we saw the police vans scream in and deploy a riot line across King Street. We thought it must have been an exercise or something, so we walked out onto the street to watch. Damn, I wish we'd just run then...' she said, her voice trailing off.

'What happened next?'

'The police were attacked, and before you knew it they were in retreat back down King St. And then they came after us.'

'Georgie?'

'Mark, there was hundreds of them. Most followed the cops, but a lot came our way. We ran a block towards RPA Hospital, that's where most of the people in the cafe went to, thinking we might be safe there. Fucking stupid, I mean what good are a few hospital security guards going to be when a line of armed cops didn't hold them?'

'Did they follow you to the hospital?'

'Yeah, they came right after us. Broke down the doors into the main entrance within minutes. We just kept going, deeper into the hospital, and escaped out one of the rear buildings into the University grounds. It's the patients I feel sorry for, the "Infected" – is that what you called them?'

'That's what the news report named them.'

'Well, they left us well alone when they found easier targets. All those poor bastards stuck in beds, unable to escape. They were eaten alive, I mean that literally, Mark. I don't think I'll ever get their screams out of my head.' Georgie's voice was trembling as she tried to hold it together.

'Where are you now?' Mark asked. 'I'll come and get you, take you to the army base with me at Randwick, it'll probably be the safest place to go.'

'I'm in one of the Science buildings, but we can't stay here. Everyone seems to be heading to the old Quadrangle. People think we'll be able to barricade it and keep them outside. Can you make it there?'

'Ok, I'll be there as soon as I can, at the northern entrance. Keep an eye out for me if you can and phone at hand, yeah?'

He hung up, and started grabbing his stuff together. He'd yet to unpack after returning from overseas, so it made the job easier. A large duffle bag filled with army uniforms and civilian clothes went over his left shoulder, a webbing belt over his right. He got to the front door before pausing. He dumped his stuff on the ground and ran back upstairs to the spare room. He might not need it, but it would make him feel better having a weapon close at hand, even if it just got left in his Ute. Mark entered the digital code to the safe, swung open the door and pulled out his rifle, a Sako .22 bolt action, and four boxes of bullets to service it. With rifle slung over shoulder, he returned downstairs, picked up the duffle bag and webbing and headed outside.

A brief glance up and down the street showed no one nearby, however, a man was at the end of his street, stumbling in his direction. Mark jogged across the road to where his Ute was parked, a twin cab Ford Ranger. He threw his bag and webbing in the back seats, placed the rifle carefully on top then climbed in the driver's side behind the wheel.

The figure thirty metres up the street was coming his way now, angling off the path towards the Ute with an odd shambling gait.

Something about the man made Mark want to avoid any interaction if possible. He slid the key into the ignition, and revved the engine to life. Mark turned the wheel and pulled out, accelerating rapidly to get past the approaching man. He failed.

The man walked straight onto the street, his eyes locked upon Mark in the Ute. Mark tried to swerve away from him, but ran out of space against the parked cars to the left. His side mirror hit one of them and snapped off with a violent crack, then the man lunged into his vehicle's path. The high front of the Ranger knocked him onto his back and the front wheel bounced over the body's hips. Mark hit the brakes and the body became stuck under his back wheel as the Ute skidded to a stop.

Mark was appalled at what had just happened, breathing heavily with his pulse racing. He turned to the back seat, grabbed the rifle and loaded a magazine of five rounds before checking the side mirror to see where the body had come to lie. It was a couple of metres behind the end of the tray. Mark opened the door and walked towards what was left.

The injury was horrific, the skidding wheel carrying the weight of the car, had almost completely torn the bottom half of the body away from the torso. Only a hand's width of flesh at the right side of the abdomen connected the pelvis and legs, however there was no spurting arterial bleed from the major vessels, the tissue was a dry, brown-red. The man was a carrier of the virus. His eyes watched Mark, a hiss exiting its mouth as the teeth snapped together, hands reaching forward. Mark stood and watched in horror for a moment, until the torso and arms started to drag itself towards him, trailing the hideous bottom half of the body in its wake.

The creature wasn't alive in the accepted sense, it wasn't "human" anymore, there was no blood supplying its tissues, it should have bled out within seconds and died from such a catastrophic injury. Mark backed out of reach and jumped into the Ranger, slamming the door shut. He pulled away and headed for Glebe Point Rd at the end of his street, a main thoroughfare that would take him to Sydney University.

At the intersection, he took a left onto his chosen route, and found he was driving into the remnants of a massacre. Wisps of grey-black smoke whipped through the air; there were pools of congealed blood on the ground and in some cases splashed against the windows of shop fronts. The bodies responsible for the spilled blood were gone, converted by the virus to killing automatons. He saw a few shuffling figures further up the street, heading in the direction he needed to go. He drove forward, weaving around an abandoned car in his path and up onto the footpath.

Some of the Infected he passed ignored him; others beat their hands on his windows, pale faces fixed in an animalistic snarl. As he continued his trip forward, he found what the walking Infected had been drawn towards. A man was standing on top of a bus shelter, surrounded by eight of them, reaching upwards to his ankles that were just out of reach. An awful noise issued from their throats as they hammered at the sides of the shelter in rage and hunger. Upon seeing Mark in his Ute, the man yelled desperately to him, waving his hands in agitation. The attention of the Infected mob remained on their quarry, ignoring Mark as he reversed up to a narrow end of the shelter. There was a heavy thud as the man jumped down into the tray.

'Drive, mate, drive!' he cried out. He grasped the roll bar, pressing his body tightly against the cab, trying to get away from the surrounding ghouls that crowded the edge of the Ute tray, reaching for him.

'Hold on!' Mark shouted back over the deafening noise of their attackers. He accelerated as quickly as he thought the guy in the back could handle. Two blocks further on, the street was deserted once more. He pulled over and got out. In the back, the man had slumped to a seated position, evidently relieved at his escape.

'You all right, mate?' he asked.

'Fuck, no. I don't think I'll ever be right again after that shit,' he said. Belatedly, he stuck out his hand towards Mark. 'But thanks, mate, those bastards would have had me soon. My name's Peter.'

Mark accepted the handshake. 'No worries, I'm Mark.' He looked over his shoulder towards the Ute, preoccupied, 'I've got to go; my ex is in trouble. You coming any further, or do you want out here?'

Peter looked over his shoulder back down the street; the pack of Infected from the bus shelter had been following and was now only a hundred metres away. 'They make the decision pretty easy, eh?' he said, suppressing a shudder as he jumped out of the Ute's tray to climb in the front passenger seat.

CHAPTER EIGHT

Steph sat bolt upright in bed. Her heart was racing – something had woken her from a dead sleep, a sound that left her gut squirming like a worm pierced on a hook. There it was again. The hairs stood up on the back of her neck. It was a guttural scream, a scream embodying pure agony, terror and despair. Steph looked at her watch; 6.30pm, she'd been asleep for hours. She slipped out of bed, ditched her shorts and pulled on a pair of jeans and runners instead. As she did up the laces, she found a tremor to her fingers. She had to find out what was happening out there.

There was now the sound of people running, and various other cries of fear interspersed between. Steph opened her room door a crack; there was nothing in the hallway beyond. Taking a deep breath to calm her nerves, she stepped out and closed it behind her. There had to be a rational explanation for the noise and commotion.

Steph headed toward the main dining area behind reception, thinking she'd be able to find one of the staff members to explain away the screaming. As she approached the main building complex, the sound of agitated voices rose. People were running away from the building, seemingly oblivious of their surrounds.

One of the girls that usually ran the resort cafe was hurrying in Steph's direction, glancing fearfully over her shoulder every couple of paces. Steph reached out and grasped her arm as she passed.

'What's happened? Has someone been hurt?'

The girl tried to pull away. 'You need to get out of here, it's not safe!'

'What do you mean?' Steph held onto to the girl's arm to prevent her leaving, but she wrenched her arm from Steph's grip and ran.

Steph looked back towards the main building, and after a moment's hesitation, headed on up.

The main foyer was a scene of manic activity. The two doors within the long series of folding glass wall segments that separated the restaurant from the foyer were being slammed shut by a security guard as he evacuated the last bleeding guest from the dining area. Blood smeared several of the glass panes. The guard fumbled with a set of keys until he found the right one to lock the door.

Two employees dragged the bleeding guest to the far corner, where six other injured people lay on the floor. Three others tried frantically to stem the bleeding on the two worst injured guests without much success. One of them had a hideous injury to his face, the right side of his jaw hung in a bloody ruin, a five-centimetre section of the mandible completely absent. The upper lip was ripped free, exposing crimson-stained molars. His tongue fell loose through the unwanted opening left by the missing segment of jaw. The man was choking on his own blood. As he coughed, globs of clot and scarlet mist spattered against the first aider attempting care. A young woman in yoga pants and tank top whimpered as she wrapped the stumps of two amputated fingers in a shirt to stem the bleeding. A third lady lay unconscious, her right arm missing below the elbow. A growing pool of blood extended away from the poorly bandaged stump. The others had minor areas of tissue loss and wounds that were more easily treated with direct pressure and wads of cloth.

Steph stood confused; she hadn't heard any blasts or gunfire to account for a terrorist incident or gas mains explosion, and some of the wounds had distinctive crescent shapes of a bite. She knelt beside a resort manager providing first aid, passing a bandage from a pile of dressing equipment that had been emptied onto the ground.

'What's happened to them? Was there an explosion in the kitchen or something?' she asked as they bandaged a wad of gauze into a leg wound.

'You weren't here when it happened then? It was Jack, the park ranger.'

'Huh?'

'He went mad, attacking people in the dining room – he's still in there,' she told Steph. 'We need to get everyone away before he tries to come out.'

'I saw him earlier this afternoon, he looked sick, but he didn't strike me as a psycho'.

'Yeah, I don't know what happened to him either. I let him crash in one of the staff dorms. Then he appeared again not long ago at dinner. It was as if he didn't recognize anything – he just attacked any person within reach – biting, tearing at them.'

'What…? You mean he caused these injuries?'

The manager nodded.

'How?' Most of the wounds were horrific, too severe to inflict without a weapon. 'Did he have a knife or something?'

The manager turned a tinge of green as she went on, 'No, worse – it was all done with his teeth and hands.'

'Bullshit…' Steph said under her breath, thinking of the bite sized piece of jawbone missing from the choking man.

Steph stood and walked towards the glass partition. A few other survivors had begun to edge closer as well, drawn by the macabre spectacle unfolding within the dining room. Five metres in from the barricaded doors, the ranger could be seen kneeling on the ground, bent over something. It was the source of the heart-rending screams that had awoken her earlier. A woman's body lay in front of the ranger. Half of the abdominal cavity was gone – eaten. Every few seconds he'd lean forward and rip another chunk off with his teeth, gagging it down without chewing. Steph was struck dumb by the view.

The manager appeared at her elbow. 'Poor woman – when he dragged her to the ground, it allowed the rest of us to escape. He started disembowelling her alive. It took an age for her to die while he just ate and ate, pulling her back whenever she tried to escape. While he was busy with her, we were able to pull out the other people that he'd already attacked.' She paused, her eyes taking on a glassy look. She shook her head before continuing. 'I've talked to the police; they're coming, but are still another half hour away. The bastards are sending cops and paramedics from Cairns, but it'll be too late for some of the people we pulled out.'

Steph looked back at the group of injured in the far corner of the foyer. The two suffering the arm amputation and jaw trauma had ceased breathing. *At least their pain has stopped.*

A noise drew her gaze once again to the dining room. The ranger, Jack, had risen unsteadily to his feet. He was standing side on to Steph. His head hung forward, the olive-green shirt, now more black than green from the congealed mass soaking it, hung open with the buttons torn away. His abdomen was grossly distended, pregnant with the flesh of the woman at his feet. From the back of the foyer, one of the First Aid providers cried out in alarm. Jack's head flicked around, drawn to the noise and his gaze found Steph and the hotel manager. He lurched up to the clear wall, hunger plain on his face, and started to hammer on the glass.

Steph and the manager immediately backed away. A second scream from behind notified them of a nearer threat. A lady was pinned to the ground underneath the weight of the dead man missing half his jaw. She desperately struggled, pushing up against the corpse's shoulders to hold the monster's face away from hers. Dark red sludge dripped from his mangled face as he snapped ineffectually, the tongue lolling sideways from the gap. Next to them, the legs of the dead amputee were starting to twitch.

Steph felt like she was stuck in a nightmare from which she couldn't awake, her legs leaden beneath her. Her brain finally started firing – she had to escape. She spun on her heel and ran for the door. The sound of shattering glass in tandem with screams accompanied her exit as the ranger broke through the paned glass barrier.

Within minutes she was back at her room. Steph stuffed her belongings into her backpack then swung it up onto one shoulder. Keys in hand, she headed for the car park, her room door left swinging open behind. A brisk wind had picked up, shivering the leaves overhead as she jogged with her ungainly sixty litre backpack lunging from side to side. The concrete path turned to gravel underfoot as she entered the resort's car park. She made a beeline for her white Toyota Corolla rental car at the back left corner of the lot. The car's orange indicator lights flashed with a loud double beep as Steph unlocked the doors on approach. She threw her backpack carelessly onto the passenger seat, then sprinted back to the driver's side and slid the key into the ignition. The engine fired instantly, and Steph switched on the headlights to drench the surrounds in a harsh white light. She stamped on the accelerator, causing the wheels to spin for a revolution before gripping to lurch the car into motion. Steph exited the resort at speed, blocking any thoughts of what she had witnessed by concentrating on the road.

Once she'd put a few kilometres between herself and the resort, she eased off the accelerator. What she'd witnessed couldn't have been possible; it didn't fit within the laws of nature. She'd seen a man drown in his own blood, then a short time later re-animate and attack like an animal. And the ranger – Jack... there was nothing left of the kindly man she'd met only hours earlier. What was happening?

A light rain had begun falling, making the bitumen road greasily treacherous. Red and blue lights flashed against the foliage at the next corner, alerting her to an approaching emergency services vehicle. She slowed further and pulled to the side of the road to allow passage on the single lane width as four police cars screamed past. She wished them the best of luck, they were going to need it.

As Steph pulled back onto the road, a light bulb blinked on in her mind. Australian rabies, no, it was... Lyssavirus. Jack had talked of a mutating strain of Lyssavirus responsible for human deaths, and bats involved in its research had bitten him. The people the ranger had bitten had also exhibited the same behaviour on reanimation, meaning that he must have been able to transmit the virus through his bite. If her new theory was anywhere close to the truth, Cairns could turn into a dangerous place until the cops got it under control.

Steph reached across to the top of her pack on the passenger seat and unzipped the top compartment. She fished into the pocket blindly, her eyes still on the road. Her fingers caught hold of what she was after, pulling it free, she saw with relief the purple cover of her British passport. She'd had a sudden fear that it had been left in the resort's safe at reception. She typed the Cairns Airport into the car's GPS. Maybe it was time to head to New Zealand for an explore, she could come back to the Australian East Coast sometime in the future once this all settled down.

Steph resolved to get a flight to Sydney and from there to Auckland. She also had a second cousin, Harry, in Sydney that she could probably call if there was any problem getting a flight to New Zealand.

CHAPTER NINE

Penny sat knee to knee with ten other police in the back of a transport van. They were all in full riot gear, clear shields held in front, helmets with shatter proof Perspex visor on heads and stab-proof vests in place. The van was travelling at speed with siren blaring, jostling its occupants against each other with each bump on the road. They were travelling in convoy; one other van with another ten police officers was ahead of theirs.

Penny lurched to the left against the next cop's shoulder as the driver hit the brakes, bringing the van to a sudden stop. A sergeant wrenched open the door, the late afternoon sun shining into their eyes over his shoulder. They were on Missenden Road in Newtown, fifty metres from the intersection with King Street. They had pulled up in front of a string of cafes, whose occupants now stared at the disembarking police officers with open-mouthed curiosity. Penny marvelled at their innocent response, for the public to not run at the first sight of a riot squad spoke volumes about the overall safety of Australian cities.

The squad was directed to form up at the King Street corner, the twenty officers spreading in a loose line facing south. They'd got there with little time to spare. The street was empty of traffic except for a few parked cars.

The air was hazed with smoke from a fire somewhere nearby, while the sounds of a fight carried from farther ahead. A staccato of small-arms fire echoed, then an order to disengage and fall back. The first officers came into sight as they fell back to consolidate with Penny's line at the Missenden Road corner. Every second officer stepped back, allowing space for the retreating cops to pass through, before forming up once more. The sergeant in charge of the first group approached Penny's sergeant, both he and his men were breathing hard, their faces pale, eyes wide.

'Sergeant Novak?' he gasped, trying to catch his breath after the retreat.

Penny's team leader nodded.

'Damn it,' he muttered. 'Command swore they were sending more reinforcements than this.' He glanced back down the road. 'When they get here, don't bother with the usual crowd control measures – just shoot to kill. I've already lost four officers to the bastards.'

'Are you bloody mad? I'm not shooting people without warning,' said Novak, aghast at the suggestion.

'Those things aren't human anymore. They're already fucking dead! I just had a mate killed next to me by a woman dragging her own intestines!'

Novak pushed the other sergeant aside and stepped past him, 'Stay in the back then.'

Penny could now hear the sound of approaching Infected. A multitude of inhuman rasping snarls grew in volume as the first ones came into view. They moved at a walk, lurching forward. They were in various states of undress. The mass of Infected contained bodies that had once been executives, school kids, waitresses and more, of all different ages. Their faces were a pallid grey-white. Many had bloody mouths, fresh crimson staining their white skin. Each showed evidence of an agonizing injury through which they'd been infected. Some were missing hands or limbs; many had parts of the neck, face, and exposed skin bitten away.

The hair on Penny's neck stood on end, her legs heavy, mouth gummed with stringy saliva. The relentless, slow approach of the monsters was sapping the fight out of the waiting police force before they were even attacked. The Infected stared unblinking at the line of officers; the combined volume of their snarling consumed the air. The numbers of Infected became denser further down the road. They had to number in the hundreds.

A police speaker blared from behind.

'This is the New South Wales Police. Stop and lie down or force will be used against you. I repeat, stop and lie down, now!'

There was no response from the Infected. They were now only thirty metres away.

'Cease your movement or you will be fired upon!' roared Sergeant Novak through the speaker. Again, no response. He dropped the microphone, now addressing the police in line. 'Bean bag guns, take aim at front runners.'

Penny raised her beanbag gun knowing that it would prove futile, and took aim at a woman twenty metres away. She had dirty blond hair, raggedly strewn about her shoulders, a soiled white business shirt above a knee length black skirt, her feet bloodied and bare. A chef's knife stood proud from her neck, buried to the last few inches of the wide blade, probably the last act of defiance by the donor of the blood slicked across her mouth. A chunk of flesh was missing from one of her calves.

'Fire!'

Penny pulled her trigger. The gun made a hollow popping noise as the wide round escaped the barrel. It hit the infected woman in her left shoulder, knocking her off balance briefly, before she continued forward again. Down the line, the officers had the same experience, with only two carriers of infection momentarily thrown off their feet by the non-lethal rounds.

'Draw batons!' ordered Novak.

Long nightsticks appeared in the officers' hands, held at the ready beside their shields.

The Infected were now on them, hands groping forward, teeth bared and gnashing.

Penny rammed her Perspex shield into a corpse knocking it off its feet. Another took its place immediately, grabbing the upper rim of the shield, ripping it aside to reach her. She brought the baton down in a savage arc onto the extended forearm, and was rewarded with an audible snapping of bone. Oblivious to the injury, it came onwards. Penny's foot stumbled, her right knee gave way and she was falling backwards, the ghoul following her to the ground. Her shield was lost in the fall. Penny swapped her nightstick to her left hand and reached for her Glock with her right. She managed to jam the baton into the open jaws of the Infected as it fell onto her. She felt its teeth shatter as it clenched down on the weapon, while one of its hands sought the gap between her shoulder and mask into her neck. Jamming the pistol into its chest, Penny fired twice, the torso above her only twitched with the bullet's passing. It raised itself onto its knees to better get at her upper body, and Penny fired twice more in desperation. The first round went through its neck, the second higher, entering its face between upper lip and nose, blowing a large hole out the back of the skull. The creature slumped off her, dead once more.

Penny dragged herself out from underneath the corpse and back to her feet, sobs of terror exiting her mouth. Her training had led her to shoot centre-mass without effect, and yet the accidental headshot had worked. *Jesus; Dino was right, they're fucking zombies.*

The whole line was being overwhelmed. She saw a Newtown officer pulled into the Infected mob and disappear under a tide of reaching hands and mouths. His screams of agony brought bile to Penny's mouth. Another of her colleagues from the Kogarah station was down, his helmet ripped from his face. Penny took two strides closer, pushed the muzzle against the skull of the Infected monster leaning over him, and fired. Brain matter splattered onto the road as it fell motionless to the ground.

She leant a hand to pull him to his feet. They had to fall back, and thankfully, her sergeant had come to the same conclusion.

'Fall back! Disengage and retreat northwards,' Novak yelled, indicating up King Street towards the university.

Half of the group were able to pull backwards and create space, the rest were either dead or being pulled back into the flesh machine and out of reach. The survivors turned and ran as a group. Many of the Infected remained, feasting on the fallen, while others continued their steady, slow pursuit of the riot squad.

The police officers re-grouped at the entrance to the university. They had put a few blocks between themselves and the mob. Penny pulled off her helmet to wipe condensation from the inside of the Perspex face shield, taking a knee on the ground. They had lost half their numbers, an unprecedented failure and loss of police life. The group was clearly shaken; the first sergeant that had recommended use of maximum force had not made it through the second confrontation.

Sergeant Novak radioed to base, requesting pickup for his staff. He was refused. There were no available police units to spare; all were in engaged and unable to be extricated. They were on their own.

'We need somewhere that's easier to defend, Sarge,' Penny said.

Novak nodded. 'Agreed. We'll fall back into the university, find a building with windows and doors raised off the ground.'

'Those things weren't human anymore,' said one of the cops, stating what most of them had been thinking since the confrontation began.

'I shot one three times in the chest and neck, and it barely flinched,' Penny said.

The sergeant closed his eyes briefly, grimacing, then opened them to meet his officers' gaze steadily. 'I fucked up. I should have taken that other sergeant's advice, but I couldn't shoot to kill without finding out if anything else would stop them first. Would you have really wanted that order?'

There were a few heads that shook in a no; most people dropped their eyes, glad to have not been carrying the weight of leadership earlier.

'I won't make the mistake twice,' he said. 'They were human once, but that ended when they died the first time around. Whatever it is that comes back – that's an abomination.'

The surrounding officers nodded in agreement.

'They got a number of our men and women, and I'll never forget that,' he said. 'Did any of you manage to kill one of them? None of the ones I shot stayed down.'

'I killed two of them with rounds to the head,' Penny said. 'I also shot one in the chest and neck, but those spots didn't make any difference, it was only a head shot that worked.'

'Ok, from here on in, we put them down as needed. If there are any legal ramifications – it was a direct order from me. I'll wear the consequences, ok?' said the sergeant.

'Guys, they're coming again, maybe we should clear out,' said one of the cops, pointing in the direction from which they'd come.

Penny looked around, and sure enough, they had more company than she cared for. Not only was the swarm now only a hundred metres away, but the adjacent student union building had just spewed twenty of the Infected onto the street to join the fun.

'Keep close, let's go,' said the sergeant, moving into the University precinct.

The cops took off in a tight group, the last three of them walking backwards to keep an eye on their followers.

As they passed a road between buildings, a snarling issued from the side. They'd walked right into a pack of them. Gunfire buffeted her eardrums as the officers on that side of the group fired at near point-blank range. At such proximity, most shots hit home, blasting heads apart, splattering the concrete with brain matter and splintered bone. The new strategy worked, not one remained standing – they'd found a way to stop them.

The Infected were closing in. Penny took aim and fired at the closest one – a boy of about eighteen with a grossly broken neck. The round punctured dead centre of face, obliterating his nose and flicking the head backwards.

The group was now firing upon attackers on three sides as they kept a steady pace. Making a stand would be certain death; they had to keep moving. Between the gunfire, voices called out to them. They were approaching some of the oldest buildings in the university, the cloisters and main hall. At the top of a flight of steps, two men held a heavy wooden door ajar, yelling for them to come inside.

Novak saw them and led the group in that direction. At the base of the steps, the Sergeant stood his ground, sending the remaining officers up while he held off the approaching Infected. He fired at a metronomic pace, one shot every second. Each shot hit home. He climbed the steps backwards, continuing his fire until the magazine ran empty. Penny stepped forward and covered him, firing as he made his way inside. Penny slammed the door shut and slid the deadbolt home.

They were safe again for the moment; however, the length of that time depended upon how easily they could defend the building. They jogged down a short corridor and found themselves in an open quadrangle. A huge Jacaranda tree had pride of place in the bottom right corner; the rest of the area was an expanse of luxuriant grass. They weren't the only ones taking cover here; at least seventy people were present, a mix of students and staff.

Penny ducked back inside, found a set of stairs that led her to an upper-floor window on the King Street side of the building complex. She looked out over Newtown and Erskineville. Smoke rose from at least three locations. The noise of the infected mass was loud, even from her new elevation.

The university streets were jammed full of a writhing mass of walking dead. They had drawn the swarm from Newtown after them with the sound of gunfire. Penny looked in the direction of her house in Kogarah, and prayed that her family was still safe. She gnawed at her bottom lip as she wiped a lone, frustrated tear from her eye. How the hell was she supposed to get back to them now?

CHAPTER TEN

Mark pulled into the university precinct from the northern entrance on Parramatta Road, then drove slowly up a small street towards the Quadrangle. So far, he hadn't seen any carriers of infection. He pulled into a parking space fifty metres from the building's end, cut the engine and texted Georgie to say he would be at the northern gate in two minutes. The Quadrangle was one of the oldest and most beautiful building complexes in the university, with gothic features reminiscent of Cambridge. Built with golden coloured sandstone in the mid-1800s, it made the adjacent modern buildings seem out of place and depressingly plain.

At the north end of the Quadrangle lay the Great Hall, and behind it a concealed entrance way; it was to this gate that Mark and Peter approached. Mark held his rifle loosely as they jogged through the fading light of evening. Georgie stood in the shadows of the arch, waiting for him. She unlocked the gate, letting them both in and dived into Mark, burying her head into his shoulder. Mark hugged her close with his free hand, then moved backwards slightly so he could see her face.

'My car's not far away, is there anything you need to get before we leave?'

Georgie frowned. 'Mark, we can't go yet. There's a crowd of Infected on the other side of the Quad. If we run into part of that mob, we'd be slaughtered. There's police here as well now, part of the riot squad I saw earlier. Won't we be safer as part of a larger group?'

Mark paused; she could have a point, especially if some of them were armed and trained. 'Ok,' he sighed. Georgie leant forward and kissed him, making his grimace soften. 'Let me get my gear before any of those creeps work their way around to this side.'

Mark jogged back to the Ute in the gathering dark. His vehicle was the last in a line of university cars behind a white minibus. The lights down the street began to pop on intermittently as daylight faded, while the first of the night's bats flitted amongst shadows between the trees. He kept the rifle in hand while reaching in the back door for his duffle bag.

A scraping sound on the concrete made him turn. Mark pulled the rifle to his shoulder as he spun to see who was there. He found himself looking over his sights at a startled Peter, frozen to the spot.

'You might want to give me some notice next time, mate, if you don't want to end up shot,' Mark said, dropping the rifle from his shoulder and picking up the bag again.

'Fuck, but you're quick with that thing,' breathed Peter, now that the end of the barrel wasn't looking dead at him. 'Sorry, I was trying to avoid calling any of those dead bastards to us by yelling out, that's all.' Peter looked past him into the Ute and noticed the webbing belt. 'Are you in the army?'

'Yeah, something like that,' mumbled Mark, as he transferred the boxes of ammunition into the duffle bag.

'My dad was a Vietnam veteran. Refused to talk about it much, just told me that he'd cut me off if I ever joined the forces.'

'Must be a smart guy. I'd think twice before joining up if I had my time again.'

'Did you get deployed?'

'Afghanistan more than a few times. Iraq once.' Mark shoved the door closed, and paused, cocking one ear up. 'Do you hear that?'

They both turned in the direction of the noise. Further down the street, three figures were approaching up the slope. The front person was dragging a damaged leg; another missed an arm below the elbow. Faces were indistinguishable in the shadows cast by the street lighting, but their sound carried, that unmistakable moaning-snarl of the Infected.

'Time to get back, eh?' Mark said.

The two of them jogged back to the Quadrangle entrance. Two tall iron gates topped with wicked spikes blocked the thoroughfare, beyond which lay a wide passage beneath the building above. The passage was pitch black, with the exit into the heart of the Quadrangle a lighter shade of grey thirty metres distant. Walking under the immense weight of stone in the passage felt like entering the confines of a castle, and Mark could now understand the visceral pull the structure must have had on students and teachers as a place of refuge. Unfortunately, although the grandiosity of the buildings gave an impression of permanence and invulnerability, they hadn't been designed to withstand a siege. There were countless entrances through rear buildings, many of which had windows at head height. If the numbers of Infected swelled outside, they'd find themselves trapped.

The three of them exited the tunnel into the interior of the Quadrangle. Brick paths bisected an open square filled with soft grass. The edges of the lawn met covered walkways with vaulted ceilings. The sandstone buildings surrounding the square rose three storeys into the air. On the eastern side, a large square clock tower soared like a castle citadel, commanding an impressive view across the parklands that descended away from the university towards the city.

An old Jacaranda tree dominated the far left-hand corner of the grassed area. The branches had lost their leaves for the winter, stretching outwards like fine silver bones in the moonlight. People were gathering at its base for a meeting called by a police sergeant. Members of the riot squad could be seen gathering people from the covered walkways to take part in the discussion. Without need for encouragement, they headed over to hear what he had to say.

'My name's Sergeant Novak of the Newtown police. As you already know, we have found ourselves in a dangerous situation,' he said as introduction.

'That's the understatement of the year,' someone said in the crowd.

'True. Therefore, you understand the need for us to work as a group to stop the situation from getting any worse,' Novak replied. 'We need to make this Quadrangle as secure as possible, starting with sealing all entrances. The iron gates at each arch are now locked, however, I want them barricaded. The Infected seem to be drawn in by sight and sound primarily, therefore I want fields of vision blocked, and noise kept to a minimum. You can see ten of my officers to the right; divide yourselves between them to make teams. Let's get this done quickly,' he said.

The people on the lawn milled around for a few seconds, looking uncertain.

'If you want us to keep you alive, we need your help, so get moving. Now!' ordered Novak.

The added verbal force to the order got the correct response, as those present quickly lined up behind the respective officers. Once all were accounted for, the groups separated to different areas of the Quadrangle. Bench seats and tables were carried from the surrounding lecture halls and rooms to block each of the entrances to the courtyard. Doorways to adjoining buildings at the back of the complex were locked and covered. Despite the efforts to stifle noise, the movement of heavy items had invariably drawn some of the Infected from the southern end around to the eastern gates; their presence announced by snarls echoing down the blocked stone entrance tunnels.

Penny walked up to Novak who was standing in the open, overseeing the different groups. 'I think we're almost finished, Sarge,' she said.

'Good. I just got an update from the station. They still want us to stay put, reckon they're working on getting us out tomorrow. But the fucking city's falling apart around us, so personally, I doubt it's going to happen,' Novak said.

'I take it that won't be the version you tell the rest of the people here, Sarge?' Penny said, one eyebrow raised in concern.

Mark, who had walked quietly up to the pair, interrupted the two officers. 'We need a better plan than just blocking the entrances and hoping they don't hassle us.'

'And you are?' asked the sergeant.

'Mark. Australian Army, engineers. I've just spent the last three years building defensive bases for the American and Australian troops in Afghanistan. I might be able to help if you let me.'

'OK, what do you suggest?'

'I agree with what you've done so far, but I don't think much can be done with the external rooms and windows. They're head height above the ground in most places, which may be enough of a deterrent anyway. From what I've seen of those walking corpses, they don't seem that smart – just bloody persistent. If they come here en mass though, they'll probably end up climbing over each other to smash through the glass.'

'Personally, I'm hoping we're out of here before it gets to that stage,' Penny said.

'Me too, but let's prepare for it anyway. Keep all people out of ground floor rooms with external windows. And we need a fall-back area that's defendable. I think the Great Hall would do the job well enough,' Mark said.

The sergeant looked over Mark's shoulder towards the Great Hall in the northeast corner of the Quadrangle. It was a massive structure with sandstone walls. Critically, it had only two access points. One massive set of thick wooden doors opened to the park, another smaller set to the courtyard, and all windows were at least six metres above the ground.

'If I was running the show, which I'm not,' continued Mark, 'I'd move all people into the Great Hall where I could keep them under observation, and away from where they'll attract unwanted notice of the Infected. Post sentries around the courtyard perimeters to listen for any breaches in the external windows, then we can direct any response needed, and hopefully stop a break-in before it escalates out of control.'

Mark paused to see if they were taking him seriously. He'd worked under many different leadership styles before, and knew he'd taken a risk in being direct with an unsought opinion. If the sergeant felt insecure in his ability to command, then he might ignore Mark, fearful that he represented a challenge to his authority. Unfortunately, there wasn't time to spare. His primary responsibility was to keep Georgie safe until they could leave, and that meant he had to ensure the whole complex was as secure as possible in the meantime. Mark waited as the sergeant considered his words.

'OK, that sounds reasonable. Penny, can you notify the others to withdraw their groups to the Great Hall once the entrances are secure, and get volunteers for the sentry duty,' Novak said.

Penny nodded, and moved off to convey the new orders.

'Thanks for sticking your hand up, Mark. If you see anything else, let me know,' he said before moving off to his next task.

Mark breathed a small sigh of relief at his unexpected success. Maybe they'd have a chance.

CHAPTER ELEVEN

Harry rubbed at his neck, massaging aching muscles as he drove into the outskirts of Milton-Ulladulla and his new home. He'd pulled over the night before in a truck stop, unable to keep his eyes open any longer. Planning for a short nap before continuing, his body had demanded otherwise, and he'd gained a fitful night's sleep in the reclined driver's seat, waking to every sound.

Somewhat revived, he'd started off again at dawn under a pale blue sky. The road had been busy, traffic all heading south at speed, with many people paying scant regard to the speed limit in their haste to achieve greater distance between themselves and Sydney.

Harry geared down and pulled off onto a long dirt driveway leading to his farmhouse. A large gravelled area, fenced with high cyclone wire, enclosed various types of earth moving equipment his landlord had for hire. The rear section of the yard housed a multitude of long shipping containers. Some were stacked on top of each other, awaiting hire and transport off site; others stood in carefully spaced rows for onsite storage.

Harry drove past the business, throwing a cloud of dust up behind. The farmhouse lay about two hundred metres back from the highway – an old weatherboard, roofed with corrugated iron. The agent had told him the house was over a hundred years old, however, it had been well maintained. The corrugated iron roof had been replaced five years earlier after hail damage, and a recent coat of light grey paint to the outside of the property made it look a fraction of its real age. There was no garage next to the house, the driveway terminating at the side.

Harry cut the engine, climbed out of the car and stretched his back, before fishing the key for the front door from his jeans pocket. The entire house perched six feet off the ground on high footings. A wide, covered veranda circled the entire building, and a set of ten steps led Harry from the driveway up to the entrance. A light, musty smell pervaded the house as he opened the front door. He opened blinds and windows to air the place out and let some light in. The interior of the property was clean but old, with many of the fittings original or at least from an era when a 'life-time guarantee' meant what it said. The kitchen still had the original wood fire oven in one corner, although a cheap gas stove had also been installed. The living room had a wide fireplace at one end that was in good working order. There wasn't any other source of heating so Harry envisioned both the kitchen wood stove and the living room fire getting a good work out during the winter to keep the place warm.

Harry fetched his remaining bag from the car, and unpacked the food and stores he'd bought. The cans and non-perishable food barely made a dent in the cupboards mounted around the perimeter of the kitchen. Food unpacked, Harry took his new tools to the large shed off the rear of the house.

He hadn't seen inside, and was unsure what lay within. A thick padlock held the door closed; after trying four keys unsuccessfully, the fifth caused the lock to spring open with a satisfying click. The door hinge screamed its lack of oil as it swung outwards, exposing a veritable treasure trove of miscellaneous items from half a century's worth of farm maintenance. Fencing material consumed a third of the shed, rolls of barbed wire hung from one wall, star pickets leaned in the back corner. Various tools were arranged above a long wooden workbench on the left. He needn't have bothered with the hardware store, as the farm was well stocked. A quick glance took in wood splitters, axe, hatchet, next to rakes, spades and a pick. A few key power tools were even stacked under the bench. Harry unhinged the first box, finding a huge angle grinder complete with a series of cutting and grinding discs. The second case held a Makita hammer drill. Harry stacked the tools on the bench then headed back into the sunshine to keep exploring. A large, circular rainwater tank collected run-off from the roof of the house to water the gardens. Near to this was a pump to bring drinking water to the surface from a deep-sunk bore.

Harry glanced at his watch, it was already 11am and his stomach was growling. The amount of traffic leaving Sydney had increased his concern this morning. After seeing how much room he still had to spare in the kitchen, he figured he should do another shopping trip while the supermarkets were still open.

In less than fifteen minutes, Harry was driving into the small coastal town of Ulladulla. On the left of the road lay an enclosed harbour, protected by a long rock wall jutting from north and south sides, leaving a narrow passage in the middle for boats to pass. The marina lay on the right side of the harbour, housing numerous small yachts, their masts slowly rolling in the minor swell. The area was a hive of activity as numerous boat owners loaded key possessions and food aboard in preparation to abandon land for the relative safety of open water.

Harry found many of the stores on the main street were already closed, some with hand written signs indicating contact details or apologies to their patrons, others simply had their security screens drawn at the front, quiet darkness behind the windows telling people all they needed to know. Harry pulled into a car park in front of the main supermarket and walked inside. He quickly filled a trolley to brimming with non-perishable items, and then topped it off with fresh food. He didn't bother buying any more water containers; the bore water had set his mind at ease.

His shopping finished, Harry paid the anxious looking clerk at the register, and returned to his car. Now that the necessities were completed, he was keen to get his TV hooked up at the house to access news updates from Sydney. The radio had ceased being any help by the time he had woken this morning. Each of the stations he flipped to on the FM band only played randomized song lists without any DJ interaction or news broadcast. He rummaged through one of the shopping bags, pulled out a packet of muesli bars, tore one free and began to eat while driving back one-handed to the farm.

CHAPTER TWELVE

Steph was sitting on the lower bunk bed with her back against the wall, knees drawn to her chest. She was the only one left in the twelve-bed backpacker dormitory in Mascot; all the others had bolted earlier this morning, heading south. She'd stayed, despite the offer of a ride in one group's minivan, planning on meeting up with her cousin, Harry. That plan had fallen through. Harry wasn't answering his home phone number, an automatic voice message reporting disconnection.

Steph had flown herself to a destination that was rapidly becoming more dangerous than what she'd left in Cairns. Although the news recommended people stay at home and wait for the security forces to intervene, she wasn't keen to place her faith in everyday cops to deal with Infected murderers. Not when the number of police on the streets was finite, whereas their opponents recruited every person they injured or killed to their own numbers. It was a war that risked hitting a turning point where it would avalanche out of control, and in a crowded city of millions like Sydney, that could happen in a matter of days.

Steph screwed her eyes shut, trying to block out fear to concentrate on finding a plan of escape. The infection was likely to spread throughout Australia's cities; plane, rail and car transport would see to that. She had to escape before other countries recognized the danger presented by the virus, and formally closed their borders. Air travel would be the best bet, hopefully the easiest to access.

With a plan of action, Steph breathed a little easier, she found any type of movement better than doing nothing at all. She double-checked her passport and cash, then heaved her pack onto a shoulder and set off.

Steph walked a city block to Mascot Station, and jumped on the next available train to the airport. The carriage she stepped into was standing room only; it appeared she hadn't been the only one to think of escape from Sydney via the air. People of all ages were stuffed in, pressed up against each other to fit. Luckily it was only a few stops to the International Airport. People flooded through the doors as they opened at the terminal, pushing past each other to climb the escalator towards the ticketing area. The scene in Departures made Steph's heart drop as she reached the top of the escalator. The hall was crammed full, the crowd agitated, and anxiety palpable like static in the air. Kids clung wide-eyed to their parents, too frightened to cry at what they didn't understand.

Steph scanned the departure lists on the TV screens hanging from the ceiling, and her stomach clenched. All flights from Sydney

International were listed as delayed without an estimated departure time. Long lines stretched back from each of the airline ticketing desks, most of which were unattended. In the queue next to her, a heavy-set man in his twenties with tracksuit pants and a black mullet cut into the front of the line, much to the anger of those around. A middle-aged, short guy with greying hair pushed him back out of the way.

'Go to the back of the line and wait your turn,' he said.

'Yeah, are you going to make me, bro?' the younger man replied with a vicious smile as he stepped back to his previous position, looking down at him.

The older man grimaced but didn't say a word as he slid his glasses off, passing them to his wife behind his back. Without further warning, he launched a savage underhand punch into the younger man's groin, bending him double, his mouth silently open and eyes wide in agony. An economical knee thrust spread the younger man's nose sideways, knocking him to the ground. His head hit the tiles with a hollow thud. He didn't get up.

Nobody said a word, however the occasional half smile indicated the crowd thought he'd got what he deserved. The only security guard within sight looked the other way, pretending he hadn't witnessed the whole thing. The older man put his glasses back on, then calmly picked up one of the queue jumpers' feet, and dragged him to the side of the room before re-joining the line once more.

The next line across was formed at the counter of Qantas Airlines. A harried-looking young lady in impeccable uniform was trying to keep her cool in the presence of a verbally aggressive father.

'As I have tried to explain, sir, there aren't any seats on today's flights at this stage. We can't sell any tickets as we have no confirmation when or if the plane will be able to leave.'

'What do you mean, "might not leave"? We have to get out of here – don't you know what's happening in the city?' He pointed at his toddler in his wife's arms, 'You think I'm going to let one of those bloody cannibals get my little girl?'

The Qantas stewardess bit her lip, not knowing what to say. Her eyes became glassy with unshed tears at the stress of the situation. 'Please sir, if you could just be patient for a—'

'I want to speak to your manager,' the father cut her off, his voice now raised to yelling.

'I would.... but they've all gone,' she said, backing away frightened, before slipping through the one-way mirrored door and out of sight.

The father let out a cry of pure frustration, picked up the metal bin next to him, and threw it over the counter into the reinforced glass door, causing it to crack and deform inwards. H_s daughter's wail of terror redoubled at seeing her dad lose control.

As the counter staff disappeared one by one without answers, the agitation in the crowd doubled. People hammered on the desks, calling for attention. In the midst of the clamour, a woman's shrill voice cut through.

'She's bitten! I saw it; she's trying to cover it up! Somebody get security! There's an infected person!'

The crowd surrounding pulled away like a tide from the woman identified. She looked scared; skin pale, pulling at her sleeve to cover a bandage on her forearm. A young boy, no more than six years of age clung to her waist. The accuser continued to scream for attention.

For the first time Steph had seen, security took notice. A team of people issued from behind a one-way glass door, pushing a trolley. One security guard forcibly pulled up the sleeve, exposing the bite wound. The woman was torn away from her son and lifted onto the trolley, wrist and ankles shackled to the bed frame. She screamed for her son, raising her head off the bed to try and see him. The boy stood quietly in the same spot he'd been wrenched from his mother, silent tears streaming down his face. The team kicked off the trolley brakes and pushed her back through the same side door, letting it slam behind them, cutting off the woman's distressed cry.

The address system blared into life, the warning chime to indicate an upcoming announcement. The volume cf the crowd immediately dipped, as heads turned upwards, a look of hope or weak desperation printed upon many faces.

A voice boomed out, strained in an effort to sound controlled and calm. 'Sydney Airport regrets to inform patrons that all departing flights have been cancelled due to newly enforced international quarantine restrictions upon Australia. I repeat all departing flights from Sydney are cancelled for the foreseeable future.' A ragged indrawn breath was heard over the speaker as the announcer paused.

'You are encouraged to leave and return to your homes. If the airport precinct comes under attack, the police have advised us that we may not be supported due to pre-existing emergencies in the city. I repeat: please leave and return to your homes for your own safety.'

The announcement went dead. No further information was volunteered.

For a moment there was silence, then pandemonium. As a mass, the crowd rushed the doors to the street, or fled down the escalator to the train station below. Steph looked for the abandoned boy, but he'd already disappeared in the press. *God I hope he wasn't trampled underfoot.* She moved as well, there was no point remaining if the planes were stuck on the ground, but where to go? She couldn't return to the hostel; she might not be even able to get back in if the landlord had locked up and fled. She didn't have a car, so her last option to leave Sydney was via train.

Steph waded against the flow of people, angling for the escalator to the underground airport station. She'd head south, the other confirmed outbreaks were to Sydney's north, and as the airport lay in Sydney's south, it was also the quickest direction out of the city.

She only had to wait ten minutes for the next train, and managed to wedge herself on board amongst the crowd that had reached the same conclusion as her. Interestingly, the carriages rapidly emptied at the first few stops – maybe people were taking the police advice to remain at home, or using cars to continue their exodus. Either way, soon she was able to claim a seat for herself as she watched Sydney, now her least favourite Australian city, slide into chaos.

CHAPTER THIRTEEN

Mark was relieved of sentry duty by one of the police officers. It was mid-afternoon, and he'd been sitting next to the entrance below the clock tower for the past two hours, listening to the ongoing noise of the Infected on the other side of the barricade. None had made a concerted effort to get through the gate, and from the fluctuating noise intensity, he thought it was likely they wandered aimlessly without a target for their hunger.

He rose to standing, stretched the stiffness from his arms and walked to the Great Hall. Someone had rigged a television at one end, and the ABC News channel was airing an update to the outbreak. Mark noted Peter standing at the back of the crowd and headed over. 'What's new?' he asked quietly, looking past Peter at the TV.

'Nothing good, that's for sure,' he replied. 'Quarantine's updated their advice regarding the infection.'

'And?'

'They're saying the infected are, by all normal means of assessment – dead. No heartbeat, they don't need oxygen, they're not even breathing.' He paused, then pointed at the screen. 'Might as well hear it from them, the reports been running on a loop, it's just starting off again.'

'Cheers,' Mark said, already easing his way through the crowd to hear better.

Testing at the Federal Quarantine facility had failed to identify a cure, or evidence of recovery in any test subjects – and the reason for this was in effect quite simple, they were already dead. Humans infected with the virus, now simply referred to by the authorities as "Carriers", did not fulfil criteria for life. There was no heartbeat, circulating blood or self-generated heat, with their body tissue matching ambient room temperature. Most peculiarly, they did not breathe if alone; only in proximity of non-infected animals was air forced past their vocal cords to create a moan or characteristic snarl.

Once the government reclassified Carriers as dead, all rights normally accorded to Australian citizens were withdrawn. The Prime Minister personally confirmed on camera that Australians would be immune to charges for causing physical trauma to a Carrier.

Testing had commenced to determine the quickest method for returning infected civilians to an inert condition, or as the reporter put it, to "kill them properly". Through systematic trial of various traumatic wounds, security forces had found brain destruction was necessary. Other injuries only served to incapacitate depending on the site of trauma, but left function above the site of injury intact. Infected subjects that had been decapitated were found to have functioning jaws, eye movements, and disturbingly – an ongoing desire to bite.

A police representative confirmed that security forces had ceased trying to restrain and contain Carriers, altering their strategy to elimination. He skirted around the fact that rates of infection had soared, and was elusive regarding infection containment success in Sydney. The representative reiterated a need for civilians to remain at home and avoid contact with those infected, alluding to an imminent release of a state-wide plan of management within the next twelve hours.

As the report began to loop once more, Mark turned away, his mind processing the information. He knew it was true. After all, he'd seen it with his own eyes. Yet his mind continued to fight acceptance, as though holding out for confirmation of an elaborate joke of exceptionally black humour.

* * *

'You've got be fucking kidding,' Novak snarled into his radio set. 'So to confirm, I am now charged with protection and evacuation of the university. With no expected support.' He rubbed at closed eyes, taking a deep breath to get himself back under control. 'And where exactly am I evacuating to? Fine,' he sighed. 'I accept. I'll be awaiting further information if and when it comes to hand. Out.'

Novak clipped the radio set to his vest once more. A few officers were standing close by, eyebrows raised expectantly. Novak scratched at three-day-old stubble on his chin, collecting his thoughts. 'Let's call a general meeting; we need a group consensus on how to move forward. We're on our own.'

Novak stood at the front of the room. Excluding a skeleton crew of sentries guarding the courtyard, everyone was present. The air was tense; rumour of their abandonment had rapidly circulated.

He held up his hand for silence. 'The authorities have finally confirmed our suspicions. The Infected are no longer like us, they've lost everything that once made them human. They're dead. But unfortunately for us, they don't seem to know that.'

Murmuring broke out amongst the crowd, someone could be heard crying softly. Novak acknowledged the reaction to the bad news with a nod before continuing.

'Help won't come anytime soon, but we've done well on our own anyway. The next kernel of joy I get to share with you all, is that we're now responsible for our own evacuation. Although I'm still waiting on a destination for extraction, when it comes through, I want our group ready to leave ASAP. We will, however, need a greater capability to defend ourselves once we're in the open. Give me a show of hands – who has defence force experience, police, or general firearms training?'

Mark and one other man raised a hand. Novak swore under his breath. *Is that it?* That gave him only ten police officers, limited ammunition, and possibly two other men he could depend on for help during the evacuation.

Novak waved them over. He grunted an acknowledgement to Mark before glaring at the new guy. 'What's your background?'

'Army. I'm a captain, attached to the Sydney University Regiment. My name's Will.'

'There's an army base on university grounds?' Novak was clearly surprised.

'Has been since before the First World War, but the Regiment only supports officer training for the Army Reserve now,' Will said.

'What weapons are kept on base?' asked Novak. Maybe there was a small piece of good news amongst the shit.

'There's twenty Austeyr rifles in locked storage,' he said reluctantly.

'Ideally, I want more firepower to take on those bastards out there. If we make it to the Regiment buildings, can you access them?'

'Only if they go into responsible hands. Those rifles can do more damage than any foot-dragging dead shit, and a hell of lot more quickly.'

Novak let a wolfish smile escape. Now they had a bloody chance. 'You've got my word. Any fuck up that happens is on my head.' He looked around the group. 'I need people to accompany Will and me tonight. Who's up for it?'

'I'll go. You're going to need something to transport that number of rifles back, and I've got a Ute nearby we can use for the job,' Mark said.

Novak nodded, 'Who else?'

Penny raised her hand.

'Right, that's sorted. We'll wait until after dark, that gives us a few hours to prepare.'

Penny cleared her throat. 'If we make much noise, we're going to risk drawing another mass of Carriers towards us. What do you guys think about trying to leave guns out of the picture where possible? We've got nightsticks, but they're not going to be all that good for puncturing a skull. Have any of you seen anything else we could use?'

Most of the group in the hall had dispersed, leaving the core group to plan their mission. A few however, had stayed to listen. One of these men interjected.

'There's construction work underway in the Nicholson Museum at the south end of the Quad. The tradesmen have stored their tools on site – some of those might serve the purpose.'

Novak thanked him, and then turned to Mark. 'Can you go and check it out, see what's useable?'

Mark nodded and headed off with the man who introduced himself as they walked. Leon had worked as a curator in the small ancient history museum for the past five years. The museum was to the left of the entrance used by the police to first access the Quad. Subsequently, the pursuing Carriers had battered the doors in mindless rage. The bottom right hinge had burst free of the timber, while the top one showed signs of strain. Mark feared the door wouldn't stand up to much more trauma. It would need reinforcement as soon as possible.

Passing through a glass door, the men entered the museum. Various items were displayed in the moon's half-light, gifted through the windows on the external wall. Pieces of pottery, mosaics and statues made up the lion's share of the museum artefacts. The curator led Mark to a screened-off section where a new display room was in mid construction. Sure enough, a large wheeled toolbox stood in the corner of the room.

'What sort of tradie leaves their tools behind? Probably insured for more than their worth I guess,' Mark said as he pulled the three crates of tools apart to see what was on offer.

'Yeah, I thought they were pretty trusting as well. See anything that'll work?'

Mark was looking for any tool that had a long handle and something sharp on the end. He smiled to himself as he found a few items that fit the bill. There were two long-handled mason's hammers that were perfect. One end of the hammer was a small square shape, the other, a long sharp chisel that looked more suited as a medieval weapon as opposed to a modern-day tool. A half-metre pinch bar rounded out the haul, sufficient as a thrusting weapon or club at need.

'These will do,' Mark said, standing with his finds in hand.

On the way back out, something caught his eye. A full suit of Roman infantry armour hung on display, however, that wasn't what pulled his attention. At the armour's side stood a reinforced glass cabinet displaying the weaponry used by a typical legionnaire. A short sword with dual cutting edges and tapered, triangular tip was presented next to a simple leather scabbard. The Roman Gladius had been the primary killing tool of the empire's soldiers for centuries. Designed as a thrusting weapon, the length of the sword was relatively short, only extending sixty-five centimetres from the tip to base of the grip. Two shallow grooves ran the length of the unadorned blade, and a simple wooden handle was fixed below.

Mark pointed it out. 'I'll be wanting that as well.'

'Really?' asked Leon, wincing. 'That's a specially commissioned item from an Italian sword smith. It's the real deal and took me months to convince the board to pay for it. You sure the tools won't be enough?'

Mark gave him a serious look. 'The hammers are make-shift weapons, but that thing,' he said, emphasizing his point, 'was made for killing. If you want us to get you out of here, how about helping us do it.'

Leon grumbled to himself in annoyance, but left to find the cabinet's key. A few minutes later, he returned and opened the door. Mark reached in and picked up the sword. It was perfectly balanced and lighter than expected. He strapped the leather scabbard onto his belt and threaded the blade home. Due to the simple leather exterior of the scabbard and wooden grip, most people would probably dismiss the weapon as a modern machete.

Hammers and pinch bar in hand, Mark returned to the Great Hall. He found the others hovering over a smart phone with a map of the university and surrounding suburbs displayed.

Novak waved him in closer to look at the screen. 'This is where we need to go,' he said, pointing out the Regiment buildings, located on City Road to the south of them. 'Where's your Ute?'

'Not far away, only fifty-odd metres from the Quad's north entrance.'

'Ok, we should circle around the outside of the university campus, avoid any noise that might draw more Carriers to this place. Will's suggesting we make a noise diversion while we're out there,' Novak said. 'Set some speakers up and leave them blaring – hopefully draw most of the Infected to it and away from here, thereby freeing up the area for when we need to break out with the whole group. What do you think?'

'Sounds good to me. Here's what I found,' Mark said as he laid his finds on the table. Penny and Novak claimed a hammer each while Will took the pinch bar.

Time was moving on, the group agreed to break for some shut-eye prior to the evening mission. They'd leave at 8pm.

Georgie was waiting for Mark when he broke away from the group, a worried look on her face. 'You're not heading out with them tonight, are you?'

'Yep, should be all right though. They know what they're doing,' he said to reassure her.

'Isn't there anyone else that can go?'

Mark felt a twinge of annoyance. 'Georgie, you called me, and after your text the other night, I'm sure that was more to do with my ability to keep you safe than anything else. Well now I'm here, and these people also need my skills to give us all the best possible chance of escaping this prison.'

She flinched at the hard edge to his tone. 'Ok, sorry. Just be safe, I'll be waiting for you.'

He instantly regretted his lapse in control, and gave her an awkward hug. 'It won't take long if all goes well, I'll be back before you know it.'

Penny was standing a short distance away, talking to her husband on her mobile phone. They were still at home and safe. She let her husband know that they were awaiting a formal plan regarding evacuation. On receiving this, they could formulate their own plan to meet up as a family again. She made no comment on what she would be doing in the meantime.

CHAPTER FOURTEEN

Since getting the TV to work, the images displayed had gripped Harry's attention. The scenes captured in Sydney defied belief. He'd caught the updated news from the Federal Quarantine Facility and seen the Prime Minister's address. The nation's leader had looked rattled; fingers that gripped the podium for support and an occasional vocal tremor betrayed his nerves and threatened confidence in his leadership. But none of that equalled the horror of live footage shot from the air above Sydney's streets.

Walking dead crowded George Street, transforming the city centre into a third-world abattoir. Images shot by the news helicopter had been distressing enough, but disgustingly, the rival broadcaster sought to trump the level of horror, deploying a drone camera above an active scene of devastation in the suburb of Leichhardt. The drone had hovered nearby as a crowd of the Infected smashed through a glass restaurant front to attack a woman and child. As the lady was ripped through the window, a piece at a time, the broadcaster belatedly realised it had overstepped the mark and cut back to the news desk.

Harry switched off the television. He had already personally witnessed a Carrier in action, so didn't need to be convinced of the horror. Pulling a cigarette from the crushed pack in his shirt pocket, he walked out to the front porch and lit up. His imagined worst-case scenario didn't even come close to matching the reality. It was only dumb luck he left Sydney at the right time. One more day and... Well, it wasn't worth considering.

So far, he hadn't given thought to what his family would be thinking. His parents lived in Hobart, so there had been no need for concern at their safety. On the other hand, they were probably worried about him. Harry stubbed out the smoke on the deck with the toe of his boot then went inside to retrieve his phone from his bag. Sure enough, there was a list of missed calls from his parents.

He dialled his mum and on the second ring she picked up. Harry had to hold the phone away from his ear, as she gave him a mouthful of abuse for not calling earlier. Once she had settled down a little, Harry apologised. His lack of communication was a running sore point with his family. He rarely left his phone on, and when he did, it was usually switched to silent. During overseas contracts with MSF, he rarely checked email and was unreliable in reply. Harry knew it was poor form and only served to stress his mother, but for some reason, he let it happen.

His parents were safe at present. There hadn't been any reported outbreaks in Tasmania, being the only state free of the mainland. The Tasmanian Premier had announced a self-imposed quarantine, barring any contact with the other Australian states. The Federal Government had supported the move by deploying the navy to enforce a blockade of Bass Strait, while the airports were also closed.

English cousins had contacted his mum, worried about their daughter who was travelling down the east coast of Australia. They had struggled to make contact, with her last known location being Sydney. Harry's mum had volunteered him to help. He agreed, not really having another option. His mum said she'd hunt down a mobile phone number for her and then be back in contact.

She hung up after a last request to 'Leave your bloody phone on this time!'

CHAPTER FIFTEEN

Mark eased the window up, then leaned out to check the surroundings. All appeared quiet. He sat on the frame, put his feet over the edge and dropped the four feet to the ground. The group had worked their way through the buildings attached to the back of the Quadrangle until they were as close as possible to Mark's car. He stood to the side, leaning back into the shadow of the building and waited for the rest to join him. Mark adjusted the scabbard at his side, trying to find a less annoying position. He was in two minds now about the sword, but then again, the hammers hadn't seemed any less cumbersome stuck through the waistbands of his team mates.

Once all had arrived, they moved to the car. Mark unlocked the doors, then propped his rifle on the dash within reach. Engaging the clutch, he shifted gear to neutral and gave a thumbs up to Will and Novak who were at the front of the Ute. They pushed the vehicle out of the parking space and onto the road. Once everyone had boarded, Mark released the brake. The road sloped downwards, allowing the Ute to coast silently away from the Quadrangle. As the bitumen levelled out, Mark turned the key, brought the engine to life and pulled left onto Parramatta Road.

A group of Carriers milled about the intersection leading to the hospital. The engine noise immediately attracted their attention, forcing Mark to swing wide around their approach before turning left. The quickest route to the Regiment buildings led straight past the hospital's entrance. The team had gambled that any Carriers should have wandered away from the area during the past twenty-four hours.

Half a block in, Mark hit the brakes. The street was impassable. Hundreds of Carriers blocked the way, lurching across the paths and road. Patients stumbled amongst them, some with IV lines dragging behind. Bloodied gowns flapped open, wet with gore. Nurses and doctors walked between former charges, vacant eyes and blood-smeared mouths attesting to their separation from humanity. The degree of violence meted during the invasion of the hospital was hideous. Most of the walking corpses missed large amounts of flesh, abdomens torn open, and faces gnawed away. Some crawled on the ground, trauma to their lower bodies so extreme as to prevent standing.

Mark's brakes squealed as the Ute shuddered to a halt. The Infected stopped moving, heads snapped around to fixate on Mark and his crew.

Mouths opened, lips curled back and suddenly the swarm screamed their mindless hatred, momentarily stunning the vehicle's occupants.

En mass, the dead attacked. They came from all sides, pressed against the windows. A boy crawled up the bonnet to the windscreen, a victim from the paediatric ward. It fixed a predatory stare upon Will as it bared its teeth and grabbed at the wiper, tearing it away with one hand. No sound escaped its mouth, the upper throat torn out, cartilage rings of the trachea flopping sideways. Countless fists beat against the windows. Bloodied faces pressed against glass on all sides. Penny recoiled from her window where a ghoul clad in bloodied scrubs repeatedly punched the glass.

'Mark!' Penny cried. 'We need to get out of here, they're going to break in!'

'No fucking shit,' he muttered, tearing his eyes away from the dead child on his bonnet.

A large crack spread across Penny's window adding urgency to her warning. Mark glanced over his shoulder, finding the street blocked from behind as well. The closest exit was to their right, a small side street heading west. Mark jammed the gear stick into first and pushed forward into the crowd. Some of the standing corpses were pushed to the side, most couldn't move in the press and disappeared under the front wheels as the Ute bucked and rolled over the fleshy obstacle course.

Forward momentum stalled, the rear wheels spinning. Mark looked in his side mirrors, the back wheels were stuck in exposed flesh on both sides, spinning in a mess of entrails.

The Infected closed in once more. The cracked glass of Penny's window shattered, showering her lap with sharp fragments. She screamed as a hand reached to grab her shoulder, jerking her towards the exposed teeth of her attacker. Penny jammed the chisel end of her hammer into its eye, jelly from the punctured orb squirting onto her chest; a second lunge shoved the spike deep into the brain. Novak leaned over Penny and shoved the body out of the window and off the end of Penny's hammer. Other hands reached forward eagerly to take its place as Mark engaged the four-wheel drive and stamped on the accelerator. With the two front wheels in road contact, the Ute finally launched into action. Heavy thuds jolted the Ute as it collided with bodies, mowed them down and kept going. Bodies bounced from the sides leaving bloody smears behind.

Abruptly they were free of the press. Cold air blasted through the smashed window as Penny and Novak brushed glass fragments away, faces grim. They had to find a different route.

Mark drove another two blocks before cutting south again. This time the group had more luck, avoiding any swarm of Carriers. Will directed Mark to a small car park behind the Regiment building. An empty security box and gate barred their entrance. Will activated the gate with a swipe card, and two CCTV cameras tracked their movement through the raised barrier. Mark parked under a huge evergreen tree, its branches blocking the meagre light of the moon from reaching the ground. Climbing out, Mark surveyed the damage to his Ute. The white paintwork was a mess of smeared blood and tissue fragments, and the panels were rippled with defects that would keep a panel beater occupied for a week.

Penny had to put her shoulder into the door and shove hard to free the damaged structure. Gravel crunched underfoot as the group headed for the covered rear door. Will took the lead, typing an access number into the security system. A red glow and discordant beep indicated rejection.

'Shit, the codes must have been updated this week,' he said, trying the code once more without success.

Mark swore under his breath.

'Would they have updated the code on the weapons locker too?' asked Novak, tension clear in his voice.

'Possibly. I bloody hope not, but we'll need to break in to find out.'

There was a window at waist height leading into the adjacent room. Novak took off his jacket, bundled it up and pressed it against the glass to muffle the sound as he rammed the centre with his nightstick. Penny cleared the left over shards from the frame with her hammer. Novak's jacket was then thrown over the bottom edge to protect their hands as they climbed through.

Mark heard a crunch of a footstep to their right and was met by the security guard, still present after all. His skin was deathly pale, marred by a spider web of broken capillaries across his face, eyes bloodshot and unblinking in the glare of the sensor light above.

They needed to keep this quiet, the car had likely already attracted more attention than they wanted. Mark, suspecting the guard was infected, unsheathed the sword, stepped forward and rammed the short blade, point first beneath the chin and up into the base of the brain. The body went limp and dropped to the ground, dragging Mark's arm with it. He placed a foot on its face and pulled the weapon free, before wiping the blade clean on the guard's uniform. A brief inspection of the body identified a bite wound to the hand; few had escaped the flood of Infected the previous day.

After sheathing his blade, he followed the others through the window. A sweep of the ground floor rooms confirmed the site was abandoned. Will led them to a room, half of which was obstructed by a metal cage. A row of Austeyr rifles hung neatly on the far wall;

ammunition was held separate, in crates on the floor. The metal of the cage was thick, if the Captain's code didn't work, they'd be forced to abandon the weapons and return empty handed.

Will typed a code into the security pad. A green light flashed above the gate as it buzzed, and the electronic lock clanged backwards. Will made no attempt to contain a triumphant grin as he pushed open the gate and led them into the weapons store. Each person loaded themselves up with five rifles. Mark and Novak took an end each of an ammunition crate with a bundle of M9 bayonets thrown on top. Job almost done, they headed back down the hallway. A cursory inspection outside showed they were no longer alone. Six Carriers lurked in the car park, drawn by the earlier noise of the Ute and breaking glass. Novak hooked a finger for retreat and they backed down the hallway.

'We need those bastards away from the car. I reckon two to draw their attention and keep them occupied, while the others load the rifles and ammo. Shall we draw straws?'

Mark glanced up at Will who nodded acceptance. 'Nah, fuck that. This needs to be done quietly, without guns. The hospital's only a block away, we can't afford to draw many more of them in or we'll end up trapped. Will and I have the best training in the group to get it done,' Mark said.

Novak looked pissed. 'Are you trying to say something, army boy? I can take any of those brain-dead fucks,' he said.

'The only thing I'm saying, is that we've had more unarmed combat training,' Mark answered, holding firm.

Novak was about to continue the argument when Penny interrupted.

'If they want to play hero, let them. Number one priority is to get back to the Quad with the rifles. Let's just get this done.' She turned to Mark, holding out her hand. 'Give me the keys to the Ute and we'll load the guns.'

Novak's teeth ground together with restrained anger, but he stayed silent. Mark laid his rifles on the floor then fished in his pocket for the keys.

'Are there any other doors to the car park from this building?' asked Mark.

'Yeah, there's one in the Officers' Mess. Unlocks from the inside,' Will said.

'That'll do then, give us five minutes and we should have them out of your way.'

Mark and Will both did a quick check of their weapons. Once satisfied everything was in order, they left for the Officers' Mess.

'Hey guys?' called out Penny softly. 'You only need to draw them away, no need for anything stupid, ok?'

Mark noted the concern in her eyes, despite her hard words earlier. 'Don't worry, we'll be fine.'

It was always much easier to make light of a situation; better that than acknowledging the real danger to yourself and others. That only risked the mind freezing, and as far as Mark was concerned, inaction was the only guaranteed route to failure and death.

* * *

Penny was waiting in the shadows near the main entrance. She couldn't see or hear anything from Mark and Will. They'd been gone ten minutes; surely they should have been through the door by now? As if prompted by her thoughts, a window further down the building exploded into a shower of glass shards. She looked back at the Carriers to find the focus of their attention successfully transferred. The ghouls moved away from the Ute and lurched toward the breaking window to investigate. She eased open the door and another quick scan confirmed free passage to the Ute. Penny wedged the door open, hooked five rifle slings over her shoulder and grabbed the handle at one end of the ammunition box. With Novak on the other end, the two of them ran for the Ute. Penny's muscles trembled with effort as she helped Novak lift the heavy ammo box into the Ute's tray, followed quickly by the rifles.

The sound of a fight was loud from the opposite end of the car park. Penny frowned to herself, it meant Mark and Will had either chosen to attack, or been trapped and forced to defend themselves. There was nothing she could do about it for the moment, they still had the rest of the rifles to load. Penny sprinted back for the next load, chest burning as the cold air ripped in and out with each breath. She skidded to a halt, gravel flying against the metal work of the Ute, and deposited the last rifles on board. Novak was close on her heels.

The two separated, Penny to the driver's door, Novak to the passenger side. Penny yanked the key from her pocket, and shoved it into the door lock. A blinding pain speared up her right leg as her foot was pulled under the Ute, causing her shin to smash into the base of the doorframe. Penny landed flat on her back, winded as she momentarily struggled to draw breath. Her right foot was tugged further under the frame of the car as her fingers scrabbled for purchase in the sharp gravel about her. A demonic snarl issued from the shadows beyond her foot.

The security light caught the eyes of a Carrier, reflecting dull red. The hairs on Penny's neck stood on end, a sob of horror lodging in her throat. She stamped hard with her left foot into its face. Once, twice – but still it held on. She could now feel a savage clamp on the side of her foot; the creature was trying to bite through the leather of her boot.

Penny changed tactic, bracing her free foot against the base of the Ute and shoving her whole body backwards and away. It worked. Her attacker was drawn out from under the car into the open. Releasing her foot, it pushed upwards to hands and knees. Tangled hair hung down obscuring much of its face in shadow. The Carrier had been a young woman, probably from the university across the road. She wore the remnants of a pink singlet top above a short denim skirt. The right side of the shirt was torn from chest to lower abdomen, exposing mangled breast tissue and shattered ribs. Her legs below the knee were missing, only the bloody stumps of her tibia and fibula remained. A rumbling growl issued between smeared remains of lipstick and fractured teeth, like bubbling phlegm from a Rottweiler's throat.

Penny scooted further back, drawing her legs away before the dead beast could latch onto her once again. She yanked the mason's hammer from her belt. Taking the handle firmly in her right hand, Penny swung it overhead, driving the spiked end through bone at the temple, deep into the skull. The growl died on its lips, the eyes lost focus once more and it dropped with a crunch to the gravel at her feet. Penny braced a foot against the skull and wrenched the hammer free. Novak helped her to stand, then grabbed an arm of the corpse and dragged it free of the Ute.

'Are you ok?' he asked.

'Yeah, I'm all right. How are the guys holding up?'

Penny looked towards Mark and Will; they needed help quickly. Their fight was continuing at the other end of the car park, but Penny had no idea if they were winning or losing.

'Novak, get in the Ute,' she said urgently.

Behind the wheel again, she revved the engine into life and sent gravel flying as she reversed and spun the wheel. The high-beam lights drowned the scene ahead in harsh definition. The men were trapped against the building, surrounded by at least five Carriers, multiple more lay on the ground immobile. Penny ground her teeth and stamped on the accelerator, aiming straight for the melee.

* * *

Mark looked out the window into the car park; four or five slowly-moving figures could be seen in the gloom outside. He tried the handle of the door – locked.

'I thought you said this door opened from the inside?' Mark whispered.

Will stepped past him for a closer look. The door was one large sheet of glass framed by a narrow wooden border. A new deadlock had been installed.

'Cash must have been stolen from the bar one too many times afterhours, I reckon. There're no other doors at this end of the building, we'll be stuck going through the window at this rate.'

'For fucks sake, you got to be kidding,' Mark said. 'Did you bring the pinch bar? Maybe we can lever the bastard thing off.'

Will raised it in his right hand. 'Yep. It was the only piece of shit weapon left as I recall.'

He jammed the chisel shaped end behind the lock. The soft wood gave easily and the deep screws holding it to the frame began to pull free as he levered. The wood at the edge of the door started to bow inwards. There was a large crack as a split in the frame appeared, followed by an explosion of shattering glass as the entire pane disintegrated.

'That got their bloody attention,' Mark said as he looked past Will into the car park. 'Maybe we should have volunteered to load the Ute after all.'

Each Carrier outside had turned to the noise and now approached, mouths open and teeth bared. Mark loosened the blade in the scabbard and drew it out, the blade giving a metallic hiss as it slid past the rim.

Resigned to the inevitable, Mark stepped through the shattered doorframe, closely followed by Will. They walked a few paces forward and paused. Both men stood prepared, knees slightly flexed, up on the balls of their feet. The sword hung comfortably loose in Mark's grip, like it had always been a part of him. Will held the pinch bar raised in both hands, point forward. The first of the walking corpses were only metres away.

In his peripheral vision, Mark saw Penny and Novak sprint for the Ute. Time to begin. Mark lunged at the closest ghoul, stabbing the sword into its face. The blade deflected off the cheekbone, ripping free a slab of brown tissue. He regained his footing and followed up with a chop deep into the side of the skull. The Carrier dropped heavily to the ground, pulling Mark's sword with it. He kicked the head free of the blade then looked around wildly for the next target.

Will had more luck with his first opponent, spearing the sharp point of the pinch bar through an eye, deep into the brain. It crumpled, sliding off the weapon to leave it free for the next attack. Two ghouls closed on Will from the right. One was a rat-faced man in the overalls of a mechanic, the other was just plain huge. A long beard matted with clotted blood hung over a distended gut. Will swung the angled end of the pinch bar at the closer of the two, burying the curved metal point into the bone above the rat-faced man's ear. The bar lodged, jammed in the skull as the body fell to the ground. Will struggled to rip it free, he squatted and desperately worked the bar up and down.

A large hand gripped his forearm, ripping it away from the weapon with crushing strength. He tried to pull his hand away, but it was drawn inexorably toward the gore-rimmed mouth. The teeth clamped down on his middle and ring finger, biting clean through. Will screamed, small arterial spurts jetted from the severed ends of his fingers as he was wrenched closer into a bear hug. The clotted beard slimed over his face and into his mouth, making him gag. He kicked hard, trying to free himself without effect. The Carrier leant down into the angle between neck and shoulder and ripped free a mouthful of flesh.

Mark swung his blade into the neck of a mangled teenager, severing the spine. It dropped to the ground, unable to move its legs and arms, however the mouth still rhythmically snapped in rage. He thrust upwards with the point of the sword through the open mouth of a snarling woman, severing the brain stem. He heard Will scream to his right, and turned to find him deep in the embrace of the massive Carrier who was choking down a mouthful of bloody tissue. He stabbed his sword deep into the eye socket, the metal point grating against the back of the skull. The hulking mass fell backwards off the blade, releasing its grip on Will.

The two men turned and stood back to back. Will had regained the pinch bar in his left hand, the injured right clutched the bite wound at his neck to stem the pulsing of blood. Five more of the Infected had entered the car park from the street, attracted by the brawl. Mark and Will retreated to the edge of the building; the fight had moved them sideways from the doorway, cutting off their retreat.

The Infected mob snarled, lurching forward to continue the attack, their hunger insatiable.

The roar of an engine drowned out all other noise. Mark glanced to the side to find his Ute accelerating towards them. He placed his hand onto Will's chest, pushing him back up against the wall as he also flattened himself against it. The front of the car smashed into the group of walking dead, throwing them forward like spare pins, and swept past within a foot of the two men pressed against the brickwork. As the Ute skidded to a halt, Novak and Penny spilled outwards, long handled mason hammers at the ready. Mark and Will joined them, moving between the corpses to cave-in skulls before they could regain their feet. Within seconds there was nothing but their own heavy breathing to be heard in the cold air.

Mark turned to Will, moving his hand gently away from his neck to inspect the injury. 'Fuck, that looks bad. Sorry mate, I should have got to him sooner.'

Will grimaced at the pain. There wasn't much to say, he knew as well as any in the group that he was living on borrowed time. The bite would kill him; it was only a matter of time until he became a clone of the mindless killers they had just fought.

Mark went back to the Ute and returned with a roll of duct tape and a rag to bind into the wound. There was no large vessel injury, however he was still losing a steady amount of blood. The wound had torn a large segment from the trapezius muscle at the junction of neck and shoulder. He bundled the rag into a ball and pushed it tightly into the wound as Will ground his teeth together to suppress an agonized moan. Mark then wrapped the duct tape over the rag, and diagonally beneath the opposite armpit, across the back and over again, creating a tight ring of tape to hold the dressing in place.

'Sorry, the dressing's pretty shit, but it's the best I can think of at the moment,' Mark apologised.

'Somehow, I don't think it'll be the dirty rag that'll kill me,' Will offered with a weak smile. 'You guys need to leave before any more turn up.'

'Get in the car, Will, we can't leave you like this while you're still alive. Once you're dead, I promise I'll put a hole in your head before you turn – you won't place anyone at risk,' said Novak.

'We still need that sound diversion to draw the crowd of Infected away from the Quad; I might as well do that. There's no point you guys staying, leave me a rifle and a couple of mags of ammo and I'll get it done.'

The others looked at him warily, not wanting to accept.

'Don't worry, I don't plan on getting eaten alive – I'll save a bullet for myself when it's all sorted.'

Penny reached into the Ute tray and withdrew a rifle, passing it across while Mark loaded two magazines of bullets.

'Sixty rounds enough for you?' Mark asked.

'Plenty.'

The group stood awkwardly for a few moments more, then Mark reached forward and shook Will's hand. 'Good luck, mate. Make them fucking earn it, yeah?' he said before turning away and climbing into the driver's seat.

The others followed suit, giving his uninjured hand a quick shake before joining Mark in the Ute. He turned the engine over, and then left Will standing quietly as they drove away.

* * *

Will put the rifle sling over his shoulder and walked back into the building. He soon found what he was looking for. The sound system in the officers' mess had broken a couple of weeks earlier. Instead of getting it fixed, one of the men had bought an old school 'boom-box' stereo from a pawn shop down the road. When not plugged into the wall, the unit could be run on a handful of D sized batteries. Will eased off the battery compartment cover, and to his surprise found it fully loaded. Releasing the catch, he sprung the CD compartment open, ditched the disc in it and replaced it with something more appropriate. He scooped the stereo under his left arm, hung the rifle sling carefully next to the bite wound, and headed off.

Back on King Street, Will dragged an abandoned restaurant table and chair to the middle of the road. A few of the Infected had already spotted him and were heading his way. He rested the stereo on the table, hit play and cranked the volume to max. The first track of the iconic Gunners album, Appetite for Destruction, buffeted his ears.

A half smile kinked the side of his mouth as the opening guitar riff of "Welcome to the Jungle" blared into the night.

He turned to pick his first target. Will took his time, sighting each shot carefully, waiting until they breached an imagined 30-metre barrier where his accuracy was guaranteed. He turned in a slow circle to ensure he wasn't attacked prematurely from behind. Within minutes the street towards the university became increasingly dense as the Infected spilled out in search of the noise.

Will changed magazines, counting the rounds as he methodically dropped corpse after infected corpse. With five bullets left, he stopped. He didn't want to run dry because of an under filled magazine. He sat on the chair and flipped the rifle around, resting the stock on the ground and muzzle under his chin. He glanced up one last time; they were close now, just metres away with a promise of horror in their feral eyes.

Will clenched his own shut and rammed his thumb down on the trigger. His head flipped backwards, the top of his skull missing as his body slumped from the chair. The Infected came onwards, kneeling at his warm body to feed.

* * *

The drive back was uneventful. Mark didn't try to pass the hospital again, taking a large detour, before cutting back across and up to the university and Quad. A group of the police officers awaited, and helped to ferry the rifles and ammunition inside. Mark headed for the south side of the Quad, climbing the stairs to the top level. He pushed open a window and heard Axl Rose's angry whine in the distance, punctuated by evenly timed gunshots.

Below, he could see the crowd of Infected begin to thin, heading towards the noise on King Street. He'd done it then.

There was a break in gunfire, then a single shot rang out.

Mark sent a silent thank you for the sacrifice, then turned and left to find Georgie. It was now up to them to make the most of Will's offering.

CHAPTER SIXTEEN

The train slowed as it approached Berry Station before shuddering to a stop. Steph peered out the window into the darkness, but failed to identify a platform. Above her, a speaker crackled into life.

'Last stop, Berry. The track ahead is blocked; therefore, this service will not be continuing to Bomaderry. To exit the train, make your way to the front carriage.'

She swallowed on a throat suddenly dry. After what she'd seen outside on her journey south, Steph had no desire to leave the carriage that had been a cocoon of safety compared to the horrors she'd glimpsed at speed. Sydney had worn a shroud of smoke, buildings going up in flames while the Infected turned the streets into a blood bath. The southern suburbs had been in chaos as the train swept through, unable to stop at stations turned to slaughterhouses, platforms slick with gore as Carriers feasted.

Steph buttoned up the front of her denim jacket and shouldered her backpack. She was the sole occupant of her compartment. Most of the travellers had exited at Wollongong, with the rest disembarking in ones and twos at subsequent stations until Steph was left on her own. She stood closer to the window trying again to see the station, but the reflection of the interior lights made it impossible to penetrate the darkness.

Giving up, she made her way forward, passing through the adjoining carriages until she reached the front. Steph tapped the exit button and the sliding doors drew backwards with a pneumatic hiss of air. The exit only just reached the end of the platform, the rest of the carriages were strung out down the line out of reach. She pulled her jacket tightly around her and stepped out. Steam billowed with every breath in the frigid air as she turned in a circle to take in her surroundings and decide on a course of action.

A second train was abandoned ahead, taking up the rest of the platform. A few weak lights illuminated the station. The centre globe stuttered intermittent flashes of brightness against the side of the first train. Two windows in one carriage were smashed, the door sliding back and forth, prevented from closing by an obstruction on the ground. Steph hesitantly sought a closer view. An amputated forearm lay on the floor in a puddle of blood, the doors to the carriage clamping every few seconds about the wrist before opening once more.

Steph recoiled, her heart racing. The infection had beaten her here. She darted to hide in the shadows of the building for a moment, listening carefully for the presence of anyone else. Silence. Taking a deep breath to steady her nerves, Steph made for the exit. The street in front of the station was dimly lit, with light posts infrequently spaced down the road. A sign pointed her towards the town centre. She knew that at least one of the Infected was roaming the small country town, so finding a secure place behind a locked door was her priority. Steph drew her pocket knife from a pouch on her belt, a Leatherman 'Super Tool' that had been gifted by her father on leaving home. She flicked open the serrated blade, and with handle gripped tightly, began to walk along the edge of the road to town. Her eyes glanced furtively about the street as she moved, searching each shadow for movement and danger.

To the left sprawled open parks and a large sports oval. Along the right of the street stood a row of huge trees, whose thick canopy blocked any moonlight from penetrating the inky depths about their trunks. A figure stumbled onto the road in the distance, silhouetted against the light of the main street. Steph flattened herself against a tree and froze, watching intently, hoping that she would be lost in the surrounding gloom.

A scream tore through the night.

The figure ahead stopped, head cocked to the side briefly before turning and heading in the direction of the cry.

Steph fought to contain a rising wave of panic. If Carriers roamed the main street, that prevented her from seeking accommodation within any of the hotels. It was only 10pm and she still had to make it through the rest of the night. Carriers were only part of her concern. The temperature was plummeting – her face was numb from the wind already, she needed some sort of shelter before she became hypothermic.

An idea sprouted a tiny kernel of hope, causing Steph to turn back and head towards the oval once more. Sure enough, at one end lay a children's playground. A raised fort was suspended six feet above the ground, accessible only via a cargo net ladder or monkey bars. From what she'd seen of the Infected so far, they weren't capable of coordinated movement or thought, and the simple obstacle of the cargo netting could possibly be enough to keep them away. Also, the fort had a roof to provide shelter from rain if the weather turned nasty through the night.

Steph pushed her pack up and through one entrance, then climbed the cargo net herself. From her pack she pulled out a thick, feather down sleeping bag and climbed inside – fully clothed, boots and all. If she needed to escape in a hurry, she wanted to be able to run immediately. She found the corner most sheltered from the wind, and sat on the floor, back against the wooden panels. Steph knuckled silent tears from her eyes then pulled the hood of the sleeping bag over her head feeling cold, frightened, and most of all, alone.

The mobile phone in her pocket began to vibrate. Her nerves were strung like razor wire and it startled her badly. Steph fumbled the phone out, finding the displayed number unfamiliar.

'Hello?' she whispered into the receiver.

CHAPTER SEVENTEEN

Harry scanned the street margins ahead as he entered the small town in the early hours of the morning. His parents had come through with Steph's mobile phone number a few hours prior. He'd called straight through and found out her location. The conversation had been short as she had little battery left on her phone. Harry had driven as fast as he'd dared on the pitch-black highway, his headlights on high beam, eyes desperately scanning for yet another stalled car to avoid. He'd narrowly avoided joining a pile-up of cars abandoned on the approach to Nowra while exiting a blind corner at speed. He had stamped on his brake pedal, ramming it to the floor in a vain attempt to stop faster. The ABS braking system had taken over, bringing the car to a shuddering halt mere centimetres from the mangled wreck in front.

After his nerves had recovered, he'd driven around the accident site. It was made up of five cars; the front two appeared to have had a head-on crash, the others had likely slammed into the rear on exiting the corner as Harry had so nearly done. Behind the wheel of the first car, the driver thrashed against the smashed window frame, a wordless howl of rage screamed at Harry as he drove around. Whether he had been infected prior to the crash or attacked afterwards while trapped would remain a mystery. But it confirmed that cases of infection were steadily progressing away from Sydney.

Harry slowed his speed as he entered Berry. The town centre clustered either side of the highway, made of quaint shops to service holidaymakers. Cafes, antique shops and the occasional restaurant lined the street, however the scene was no longer peaceful. Harry passed a slumped figure in front of a smashed show window, a pool a dark blood oozing into the shadows. As he passed, the legs began to twitch, then the body pushed itself to standing, another recruit of the Infected.

The Great Southern Hotel was on fire, flames licking the wall behind the bar, grey smoke sifting out from beneath the eaves to join the clouds above. Harry weaved in amongst a number of abandoned cars on the main road, picking up speed again. The number of Carriers had increased, and he now had four figures lurching in his wake.

Following the voice prompt of his car navigator, he turned down Alexandra Street to the train station. He slowed as he came to an oval, searching for the children's playground. Harry pulled off the road, allowing his headlights to play across the park as he turned the car in a circle. Finally, he spotted the kids' fort ahead, fifty or so metres off the road with a head peering over the edge of its window at him. Harry cut the engine, left the lights on and jogged over.

'Steph?' he whispered, 'Are you here?'

A backpack thumped to the ground, followed immediately by its owner, who landed with a feline economy of movement beside it.

'Harry? Is that you?'

Neither cousin had met before.

'Yeah, let's get out of here, this town is starting to crawl with Infected,' he said, grabbing an arm strap of the pack, he headed for the car with Steph close behind. Harry avoided the main street this time, taking a back route and headed for home.

CHAPTER EIGHTEEN

Penny ended the call and slipped the phone into her pocket. She was standing outside on the grass of the Quad, her hands balled into fists to stop them shaking. She took five deep breaths, her eyes blinking rapidly in an attempt to stop any tears from breaking free. Penny had taken a gamble, she'd asked her husband to leave Sydney, to head south and not wait for her. Sydney was only getting worse, the numbers of Infected rising exponentially. She was worried that if they didn't leave now, they might not make it out of the suburbs, or run an ever-greater risk of their home being broken into and attacked.

Her husband, David, had been angry, refusing at first, but she'd laid the unfair guilt of their son's life in his hands, saying that if he stayed and waited he might just be guaranteeing their son's death. The plan had been for Penny to wait for the evacuation, then join them at some point further south. David wasn't aware that a strategy for their evacuation hadn't been confirmed, but she needed them as far away from the risk as possible.

Feeling under control once more, Penny forced her family worries to the side. When confronted with dangerous matters in her line of work, she had always used visualisation to separate competing tasks for her attention. When thoughts of her family threatened her concentration, she pictured placing them in a box that was then gently pushed to a recess of her mind, freeing her attention for the immediate threat. She had found the technique effective, however, she walked away with unease that she was becoming more adept at compartmentalising her life. There were so many things about her now that her husband didn't know or truly understand.

Penny checked her watch – the news update was due in a few minutes. She jogged back to the Great Hall to join the group. Survivors were huddled to the front of the stage, standing shoulder to shoulder. A biting cold chilled the air, as the gas supply had failed overnight. Electricity was still working, but it was unclear for how long that would survive. On the TV, a reporter announced a cross to a press conference chaired by the NSW State Premier.

The Premier looked as though he'd aged a decade. Grey rings hung under his eyes and his suit looked like he hadn't taken it off in days. Penny took satisfaction in his appearance, that it looked as though he actually felt some weight of responsibility. She hoped he felt like a failure, because at the moment, it seemed like the whole state had been abandoned.

The Premier gripped the podium tightly with both hands and raised his eyes to the camera. 'It is with a heavy heart that I bring the following news to the people of Sydney. A decision has been reached, under advice from the state police, military and Federal Government, that our city has been lost to the advancing infection.'

There was dead silence in the Great Hall.

'All non-infected citizens are now advised to make plans to evacuate Sydney. People on the city's fringes are encouraged to head either south, or inland. Inhabitants of the inner suburbs are likely presented with greater risk on leaving their homes. Evacuation points will be available from major sports grounds where the Air Force will be conducting airlifts. Other evacuation points will be via ferry terminals and ports. The responsibility to access these evacuation sites will fall to the individual, however, please note that once accessed, these will be safe locations, defended by the Australian Army. A list of evacuation points will be displayed at the completion of this address, and I advise you to make your way promptly to your nearest site.

'Although this marks the darkest day in our State's history, mark my words,' said the Premier; his gaze was unwavering, expression furious, 'Our city will be retaken. We will come home.'

His eyes drilled into the camera for a few moments longer, then he stepped away and disappeared from sight. A list of evacuation locations began to slowly roll down the screen. As the options began to cycle through once more, Novak took the stage next to the TV.

'I think our best option is the Sydney Cricket Ground.' When a voice from the crowd tried to interrupt, he held up a hand for silence. 'Not only is the SCG the closest option, it's a straight route along Cleveland Street. Once we get there, it should be an easily defendable site. Our challenge will be traversing the four kilometres that separates us, intact.'

Novak's gaze travelled the survivors. 'I want our group ready to leave within the hour. We have twenty rifles, each with two magazines of ammunition. I want volunteers to carry one – however, you must realise that you will be expected to use it in defence of the larger group. Mark and I will be running dry fire training in the Quad courtyard in ten minutes. Everyone else, find something you can use as a hand weapon to take with you.'

Novak jumped off the stage and walked outside to prepare for the training session. The spell was broken; the small crowd in the hall broke up, some following Novak outside, others going for their belongings to prepare. Penny found her mouth was dry as her adrenaline surged. It was finally happening, they would be facing the Infected once more, but this time to reach safety.

Penny's phone began ringing. It was a video call from her son, she walked to the side of the hall to take it.

'Hey Mum, we're on our way. Dad had the car packed already, we were just waiting for you to get home. Where are you going to meet us?' Ben looked worried. At only twelve years of age, he looked very young, his face was pale and eyes wide with concern.

'We're getting evacuated to the SCG, so once I know where we get taken from there, we can make some concrete plans, ok?'

Her son nodded, she could see he was sitting in the front passenger seat of their car. The screen shot started to shake, as David began driving.

'Just make sure you guys don't stop for anything ok? Just keep going and drive around any Carrier that you come across,' Penny said.

'Don't worry, Mum. Dad's got the axe and your big chef's knife, we can take on anything,' her son boasted. Penny's brow wrinkled in concern. Her husband's voice came in from outside the edge of the screen.

'Pen, it's ok – I'm not planning on using them, I just felt more comfortable having something like that with us,' he said.

'Hey Dad, maybe we should go back and try a different way?' Her son's voice was shaking.

'Ah, fuck,' she heard her husband mutter.

'What's going on, David? Is the road blocked or something?' Penny asked.

'Yeah, there's about ten of them on the street ahead. Should be ok, there's a gap to the side.'

Penny heard the engine rev over the phone as her husband accelerated for the gap. Suddenly her son screamed, pointing to the right. She heard David swear, followed by a large bang. The phone was thrown from her son's hand, and fell to the floor in the passenger foot well. She could see past her son's knee to her husband in the driver's seat. He was bleeding heavily from a laceration to his scalp after his head hit the steering wheel.

'David? Dave! What happened? Are you ok?' Penny cried anxiously into the phone.

She could hear her son breathing heavily.

'One of the bastards stepped in front of the car. I tried to swerve, but hit the gutter. Fucking tyre blew and sent us into the light pole – shit.' Her husband was looking over his shoulder at something outside the car.

'Ben, you take the knife. Keep the window up!' David yelled.

Penny could hear him trying to start the car, but the engine refused to launch. Suddenly the glass exploded next to David's head, and she saw bloody arms reach through for her husband. The snarls of the

Infected could be heard over the phone. Her son leaned over her husband, vainly stabbing at the creatures through the window to try and save his dad who was being wrenched out of screen. Penny could hear him screaming in agony as he fought back, punching wildly.

'Ben, get out of here. Run, just run!' he yelled.

Penny saw her boy lean for the door handle and pull it open, then his foot came down on the phone's screen as he launched himself outside. The image went black, her son's phone was destroyed. Penny was screaming at her phone, tears running down her cheeks as she told him to keep running.

Her baby boy was alone, and she was helpless to save him.

CHAPTER NINETEEN

Harry stood in his kitchen, looking blankly out the window to the green paddocks beyond. He had a steaming mug of coffee in hand to dispel the lingering fog of sleep. The trip back from Berry had been largely uneventful; his main battle had been keeping his eyes open.

The relief of finding Steph alive and uninjured had left him feeling exhausted as the adrenaline abated. He'd kept Steph talking, mainly just to keep himself awake, and had heard her experiences of the past week along with a brief outline of her preceding travels. They had finally arrived at the farmhouse after 3am. Once safe inside with doors locked, Steph had taken to the couch in her sleeping bag, Harry had crashed in his room fully clothed.

Of all things, a bloody magpie warbling its joy of the new day had awoken him after only a few hours of sleep. His chest still felt heavy with tiredness, but his eyes had refused to close again. He'd finally given in, and climbed out of bed to make some coffee. Soft padding footsteps roused him, and he looked over his shoulder to find Steph in the kitchen doorway.

'Morning,' Harry said, holding out a hot mug of coffee to her.

Steph gratefully accepted, cradling the cup between both hands to warm them. She blew on the top before taking a sip.

'What's your plan from here?' he asked.

'I'm not sure yet, all I know is that I don't want to get stuck in a city again.'

'Fair enough, me neither. I'm toying with the idea of staying here, weather the storm until the government gets the outbreak under control. You're welcome to stay, if you want,' Harry offered.

Steph looked uncertain.

'No stress, have a think on it. I could do with help to make the place more secure. I've got to go into town, I still haven't touched base with the Emergency Department. I'm supposed to be starting work there in a couple of days, but with the way things are, I don't reckon that'll be happening. Are you all right to hang out here by yourself for a while?'

'Yeah, I'll be fine. Take your time,' she said.

Harry drained the last of his coffee, then dumped the mug in the sink.

'All right, I'll see you in an hour or two.'

After a quick shower and change of clothes, Harry left Steph to catch a few more hours sleep and drove to the Milton-Ulladulla Emergency Department. He parked on the street, and after doing a quick survey of his surrounds for any danger, walked inside. In the forefront of his mind was the spread of infection to Berry where he'd rescued Steph the previous night – it was only 80km towards Sydney, and the prospect of encountering an infected person was now a very real possibility.

The Emergency was tiny compared to the large department he'd left in Sydney. It consisted of a few monitored beds, a resuscitation bay and a handful of consult rooms. The reception was empty with no clerk at the front desk. Harry knocked on the door leading to the clinical area. Eventually a nurse called Tina arrived and opened it, allowing him in after he'd introduced himself.

The nurse led him to the main clinical area to meet the only other doctor on duty. There were usually more staff present, however, since the deterioration of the outbreak in Sydney, the workforce had thinned somewhat. The remaining doctor, a bloke called Ian, welcomed him.

'We're all that's left. From what I've heard, most of the health staff in town have already bolted, heading for the Victorian border. The others have just stopped showing up to work, but then again, so have the patients. I don't know if you've noticed, but the town's become pretty empty in the last 48 hours,' said Ian.

'What's the plan if a suspected infection arrives?' asked Harry.

'So far, the recommendation has been just to isolate them and ensure no contact with body fluids. It's supposedly not airborne, but how they could possibly be sure of that at this early stage, I have no friggin' idea. The government's due to release new management guidelines today; I've been checking my email constantly for them,' he said.

Harry explained his contact with the infection so far, and described what had happened at Randwick Emergency. The colour drained from the faces of his new colleagues as they listened.

A message from the NSW Health Department popped into Ian's inbox, and he clicked on it immediately. A link was provided to a new policy directive for the "Clinical Management of Suspected Lyssavirus". The three workers crowded the screen, reading the short document together. Once finished, they sat back, collectively stunned at the strategy mandated by the government.

'They can't be serious,' said Tina.

'That's not euthanasia, it's fucking murder,' spat Ian. 'It goes against everything our professions stand for. There is no bloody way I'm doing that!'

Harry was sitting thoughtfully, reading through the paper once more. The policy recommended all suspected cases of Lyssavirus infection to be isolated from family and public. Once in a private setting, the patient was to be rendered unconscious via intravenous sedation, and then euthanised. Due to the requirement of brain destruction to prevent reanimation, health staff were advised to use a bur hole electric drill to penetrate the thin temporal bone into the underlying cerebral tissue. Post procedure, the family were to be advised that "due to treatment complications, the patient had died".

The ramifications of such a policy were breathtaking. Doctors were being asked to lie to their patients and family, and then commit state-sanctioned murder. It would irreparably destroy the trust between the medical profession and public, not to mention break the souls of many clinicians who entered their professions to help, not harm. Requiring them to murder the patients they were there to save, was simply heinous.

Harry pushed back from the computer and stood. 'I can't do it. Not this way. Self-defence is one thing, but that…' he trailed off into silence. 'Sorry guys, but I resign. I didn't sign up for this shit.'

'I agree, but the town still needs medical care,' said Ian. 'How do we ensure people can access help if it's needed? We still owe the public that, don't we?'

'If the infection continues to spread down the coast, we're probably better off supplying medical consults from our own homes once they're secure,' said Harry. 'We can leave contact information on the front door, offer treatment for trauma or medical illness that is strictly non-lyssavirus related. What do you think?'

The others agreed, seeing no other viable option. The three then raided the drug room, compiling a stock of medication each to treat the most common ailments presenting to the Emergency, then supplemented it with equipment to manage minor trauma. Harry reversed his SUV to the front doors then loaded four crates of supplies into the back. The nurse attached a list of their contact details to the inside of the glass front door, and next to it, a notice declaring the department was closed.

Tina stood back from the doors looking at the "closed" sign, shaking her head. 'This is the first time the department's been shut since it was built. Doesn't seem quite natural, does it? I mean, Emergency Departments just don't close, do they?' she said.

'Hopefully we get to return all this stuff within a few weeks once this is brought under control,' offered Harry as he prepared to leave.

'I hope you're right. I just bloody hope you're right,' said Tina.

CHAPTER TWENTY

Mark was standing to one side, supervising the dry fire drills and it had him worried. He'd spent the last twenty minutes running through simple weapons handling information, the basics of firing the rifle and changing a magazine. He left out any of the "failure to fire" drills. Trouble-shooting a defective rifle was too much to ask in this setting. If a rifle malfunctioned, it would have to be ditched, or relegated to use as a club. Most of the volunteers had never held a gun before, let alone a high-powered assault weapon such as the Austeyr. In the right hands, it was lethal against the enemy. In the hands of a novice, however, there was just too much that could go wrong. But what choice did they have? If it came to close-quarters fighting, they would almost certainly be overwhelmed. They needed to keep distance between themselves and any attacking Carriers, and firearms were the only way.

A hand gripped his shoulder, pulling him away from his thoughts. Penny took him to one of the covered paths at the side of the grass. Something was definitely wrong – she looked agitated, barely holding it together. Georgie was there also, looking concerned.

'What's wrong? If those guys aren't going to shoot each other by accident the first time they use live ammo, we need to keep going with the drills.'

'Fuck the drills, Mark. I've got to leave and I need your help if my boy's going to have any chance,' she said, her speech rapid.

'Slow down a second,' he said, raising his hands. 'What's happened? I thought your kid and husband were driving south this morning?'

'They did, but David crashed and they were attacked. I was on the phone to them when it happened – I saw those bastards kill my husband in front of me,' she said, her voice cracking.

'Is your boy ok?' Mark asked.

'I don't know; he ran from the car leaving the phone behind. I can't go to the SCG not knowing if he's dead. Will you help me?' Penny pleaded. 'If you can't come, I'll be leaving by myself anyway.'

Mark was torn. He had serious misgivings about Novak's plan to get to the SCG, but he still had to get Georgie out. On the other hand, he owed Penny for the previous night. Without her, he would have died at the Regiment quarters.

Georgie took the decision out of his hands. 'Penny, we can help,' she said, looking up at Mark to see if he agreed.

He sighed, took a breath and nodded.

Georgie gave him a small smile. 'But we'll need to continue south afterwards. Mark what do you think? I'm worried about going to the SCG anyway – that many people on the move in the middle of the city? Surely they'll attract thousands of Carriers in to feed.'

'You're probably right. If we can take a couple of the rifles with us, we'd be safer on our own. It's still going to be dangerous, we've got half a city to make it through to escape south.' He glanced at those struggling through the dry fire drills, sighed again, then turned back to Georgie and Penny. 'And even if we make it out, the news said our next major town, Wollongong, is already crawling with the Infected.'

'Maybe we could skip all that,' Georgie suggested.

'What do you mean?'

'My parents have a yacht at anchor in Kogarah Bay – I've been nagging you to come sailing with me for months, remember? If we go there after finding Penny's boy, we can leave out of Botany Bay and just stay on the water until we go far enough south to skip the badly infected towns. My folks have a farm outside of Milton; it's got a small marina nearby at Ulladulla where we can dock.'

Mark smiled slowly. 'That sounds bloody awesome. Geez, you're full of good surprises sometimes, babe.'

'They wouldn't be surprises if you listened more than half the time, Mark,' she said, deflecting the compliment Georgie turned back to Penny. 'What do you think Penny? Will you come south with us if we take you to Kogarah? Three people would make the boat safer to handle, especially out on the open water.'

Penny looked up at the mention of her name. Eyes glazed, Mark was sure she hadn't heard much of the discussion, that the images of her husband being pulled out the car and her son fleeing occupied her mind.

'Sorry, what did you ask?'

'Will you come south with us on the boat after we look for your son?' Georgie asked again.

'Sure.'

'Ok,' Mark said. 'I'll deal with Novak and get a couple of rifles. You two collect whatever you want to bring. The main group's due to leave in thirty minutes, we should probably aim to go at the same time.'

Georgie and Penny nodded, and parted to get their jobs completed.

Mark found Novak supervising a last fire drill. 'Ok guys, that'll have to do,' Novak called out. 'Go grab your stuff and meet at the north gate in ten minutes.'

Novak slung his rifle over his shoulder, and turned toward the Great Hall. Mark called out to him, the man turning then frowning as Mark jogged over.

'Hey Mark, we need to get going. Can you pass on to anyone that you see that we're meeting at the north gate in ten minutes? I want to pile as many of us as possible into the university cars out there. One of the staffers accessed the keys for them. If we can go in convoy, we might not even need the rifles.'

Mark's expression was tight; he wasn't looking forward to breaking his news.

'I've got a problem, Novak.' Mark motioned to Georgie and Penny. 'We won't be part of the convoy. Penny's family have been attacked – we need to try and find her son, he might still be alive.'

Novak's face was furious, his cheeks flushed. Mark interjected before he could talk. 'It's her kid, mate. If it was yours, you'd do the same.'

The anger began to visibly dissipate, Novak's features relaxed until he just looked worried and tired. 'That's fair enough, but it leaves my job all the harder. Now it's just me and a couple of cops to get this group through four kilometres of infected suburbs.'

'Sorry mate, I don't have much choice – Penny saved my life last night, I kind of owe her.' He paused, then continued. 'One last thing, I need to take two of the rifles and some ammunition.'

Novak's face tensed for a moment. 'Ok,' he conceded. 'I can't really refuse after last night, can I?' He put his hand out and Mark accepted the handshake, 'Good luck.'

Two Carriers were outside the gate leading to the university cars and Mark's Ute. Novak and Mark took one each, dispatching them quickly with efficient head wounds. Novak waved the inhabitants of the Quad out to the waiting vehicles. There were five cars and a small bus. Seven people were crammed into each car, the front passenger of each armed with a rifle. The rest squeezed into the small bus. The seats had been ripped out earlier, allowing the refugees to be packed shoulder to shoulder like cattle. Each held pathetic, makeshift weapons. Most had opted for lengths of timber pulled from tall-backed chairs in the Great Hall. The bus suspension was low once loaded, but it would be safer than attempting to walk the whole distance.

Peter elected to join Mark, Penny and Georgie in the Ute. They waited for the convoy to leave, then with barely a glance behind, headed out in the opposite direction.

CHAPTER TWENTY-ONE

Novak was in the front passenger seat of the lead vehicle – a white Toyota Corolla. They'd made steady progress after turning onto Cleveland Street, ensuring that all vehicles stayed together as a tight group. The bus couldn't safely exceed 40kmph, its suspension bottomed out constantly due to the weight carried. They'd passed numerous of the Infected, but had been able to drive around and continue without incident. They were now over half way there Nevertheless, Novak kept his hope carefully locked down, not daring to tempt fate.

The convoy topped the rise over the train lines at Redfern, and continued to Surrey Hills. Novak swore under his breath. Up ahead the road was blocked at Elizabeth Street. A public transport bus had overturned in the middle of the intersection, blocking both lanes. There was nothing for it, they'd have to turn around and find an alternate route. The convoy of vehicles was half way down the block, with the bus at the rear.

The bus started to reverse for the beginning of a three-point turn when a loud bang rent the air. The bus' suspension had finally snapped under the excess weight, causing the cabin to drop heavily onto the rear right wheel. The driver continued to finish the turn with the tyre pressed up against the top of the wheel well. Blue smoke drifted lazily as the rubber disintegrated under the friction and pressure. As the bus hit ninety degrees across the road, the wheel blew, echoing between the surrounding buildings like a gunshot. The rim of the wheel bit into the tarmac and ground downwards.

The bus was crippled. It could go no further.

Novak watched it with growing horror. There were too many people to load into the cars, and besides, the bus had now effectively pinned them in. They would have to walk the last few kilometres. He opened his door and ran towards the bus.

'Everyone out. We'll finish on foot. Only two or so kilometres to go,' he said, trying to sound encouraging. He waved at the occupants of the cars to get out and join them.

'I want everyone as a tight group, riflemen on the outside. We're going to do this at a jog, ok? No matter what we come up against, we keep moving forward. The end's in sight guys, let's take it home.' Novak attached a bayonet to the end of his rifle and led the way forward, starting out at medium-paced trot, weapon at the ready.

Rounding the large bus that had blocked the intersection, they came across their first Carriers. Numerous shuffling and lurching figures were spread out down Elizabeth Street growing in density towards the city, however, none were close enough to cause immediate harm. The Infected tracked their movement with unblinking eyes, their faces a rictus of anger as they followed behind.

Novak picked out a target ahead. Three Infected men blocked their path, he raised his rifle to shoulder, paused his movement to lay the sights over the middle figure's face and squeezed the trigger. The recoil wasn't as bad as he'd anticipated, and he rose to find his target on the ground missing a significant portion of its face and head. The two remaining Infected were oblivious to the other's demise, pacing forwards with arms outreached in anticipation.

He felt the group bunching behind him and knew they had to keep moving at all costs. Walking forward he came within a foot before firing a second round at point blank range, snapping the head back in a mist of bloody tissue. A staccato of bullets ripped up the torso of the other Infected, starting at the abdomen, the last round collecting the corpse between the eyes. Novak glared at the uni-student who had fired.

'Get it back on single shot and conserve your rounds,' he growled.

They kept moving, the numbers of Infected steadily growing. Fifteen of the walking dead occupied the Crown Street intersection. The group hit them without pause, rifles coughing bullets to knock the Carriers from their feet. The accuracy was poor, most rounds only hitting the Infected in the torso or abdomen, however it was enough to momentarily prevent their attack as they passed through.

From Novak's peripheral vision as they passed Crown Street, he realised they were in real trouble. Towards the city, the street was packed with a slow-moving swarm of Infected. They had to keep onwards and hope the SCG was defended as promised.

A crowd of the Infected emerged from the next street corner, blocking their path towards the SCG. This group was denser and would be hard to break through. Looking behind, Novak found their retreat sealed, the swarm had emerged from Crown Street, preventing their exit back along Cleveland. The sporting fields surrounding the SCG could be seen in the near distance, and yet they might as well have been a hundred miles away.

They were trapped.

The noise emitted by the Carriers was oppressive, their animalistic rage and blood lust drowned out all other sound. Novak halted the group, pulling them into a tight knot. People were terrified. The smell of shit and piss filled the air as some were incontinent with fear. They had seconds before they were attacked. Novak tried to ignore his own terror, he needed rage to overcome immobility and allow him to fight.

He soon found a kernel of anger to stoke. Anger at being left behind by his own police force, anger at being stuck with the responsibility of saving so many people, and pure bloody rage that he'd come so close to succeeding before having it ripped away. He heard the roaring of blood in his ears, reducing the snarls of the surrounding Infected to a murmur.

'Rifles to the outside!' he shouted above the roar of the Infected. 'We go through, or we're dead. Everybody fights. Send these fuckers back to hell!' he screamed.

He flicked off the auto lock-out behind the rifle's trigger to allow the weapon to automatic fire. Novak aimed at general head height and loosed a burst of fire, sweeping an arc across the front of their attackers. Numerous bodies fell, but far too many were left standing. Suddenly they were amidst the Infected, bloody hands wrenching anything within reach, seeking to draw flesh towards ravenous mouths.

Machine gun bursts thundered all around, echoing back off the buildings either side of the street as the rest of the group engaged the enemy. They were slowly making ground. The riflemen were at the front and sides; some firing methodically, others in panic, letting wild spatterings of bullets whip through the flesh of the undead in front.

One of the younger students gripped the trigger on auto without having proper grip of the stock, the barrel rose ever higher into the air. In fear, he still gripped the trigger and fell backwards, spraying bullets through the middle of the evacuees. Screams of agony mingled with those of fear as maimed people dropped to the ground to curl about their wounds. The Infected were thinning numbers at the outer edge of the group, drawing people forward and down into the press to be ripped apart by mouth and hand.

Novak stabbed his bayonet forward between shots, thrusting the point into faces of his undead opponents. He tasted copper as blood slicked across his face and into his mouth from a gash at his hairline. He used the stock like a club on the withdraw, crushing skulls where possible before opening up an area of reprieve with an automatic burst of fire. They all walked on a carpet of flesh now as they advanced through the intersection, a flooring of bloody torsos, slippery loops of intestine and limbs. Stench filled his nostrils, the mix of shit, blood, piss and terror making his stomach churn.

Many of the corpses under foot were still functioning, hands reached upwards to grasp at legs, teeth fastened on unguarded ankles. The evacuees stamped with each step, trying to crush the skulls of those on the ground, smashing downwards with their makeshift clubs, or stabbing over the shoulders of the remaining rifleman into the press.

Novak was out of ammunition, stuck using his rifle as a club and the bayonet as a spear. A female student from his group screamed in his ear, a high-pitched shriek of agony as a Carrier latched onto her arm and pulled her to the ground, savaging her neck. *Too late to help her*. He drove ahead again, stabbing at anything within reach, a high-pitched whine from his damaged eardrum blending with the tortured screams of the fallen.

A last corpse dropped at his feet, the frontal bone caved in beneath his rifle's stock – and suddenly he was free. Open street lay between him and the parkland surrounding the SCG. The Infected on the outside of the throng ignored him, intent on attacking the greater density of people still stuck within. He now needed to widen the breach so that the rest could escape the writhing mass of killers.

Novak began viciously clubbing the Infected between him and the evacuees following, as more people extricated themselves and turned to help him free the rest.

Finally, the last member was pulled from the clutching grasp of a crawling Carrier. Novak quickly scanned the remaining evacuees, as they jogged onwards. Most of the Infected remained thrashing in the crowd, fighting over the bodies of the fallen, only a handful turned to pursue them. The keening screams of those left behind were gradually cut off as they succumbed beneath the torturous teeth and stabbing fingers of their attackers.

The survivors were pitifully few in number; no more than twenty of them remained. He'd lost more than half escaping the swarm, and now they were incredibly vulnerable. Of the weapons, only four rifles remained, none with ammunition. The handgun at his waist was the only firearm capable of firing. Novak urged them onwards, variously with humour or aggression, whatever kept his charges moving as fast as they could. He noted at least four of them were carrying wounds, bite marks to arms and legs. They would have to be dealt with soon, but not yet.

As they ran through the park, three Chinook helicopters thundered overhead towards the SCG, their dual rotors buffeting the grass flat around Novak and the surviving evacuees. He could now see the processing stations leading into the stadium, and the military cordon. They were no longer on their own, hundreds of other civilians were streaming towards the stadium entrances, queuing in agitated lines, desperate for access to the safety offered within.

All Novak could think of was the swarm less than a kilometre behind them. Surely the noise of the helicopters would draw them? And what of other crowds of undead? Each chain of survivors was likely to trail their own Infected followers. He hoped to god that the Army had an adequate plan for defence of the stadium, because if they failed, it was going to be a blood bath like no other.

CHAPTER TWENTY-TWO

'Take the next street, my house is on the left,' said Penny. She was leaning forward in her seat, hands balled into fists on her lap, the skin over the knuckles blanched. Mark made the turn, checking the house numbers as he went. The street was deserted. A lone car was parked in a driveway, abandoned with the driver's door open. Penny shook her head in dismissal as Mark pointed it out.

Mark saw the number he was looking for, a shiny copper nine reflected the sun from its location on the mail box. He pulled into the driveway and Penny was out of the car before it had stopped, running to the front door. Georgie followed close behind. This had been the best place to start looking, hoping that Penny's son may have returned to hide.

Mark got out of the car and leaned against the front bonnet, his Sako .22 rifle in hand as he scanned the street for movement. It was silent aside from the birds. Short, wiry indigenous trees were planted along the street, attracting Rainbow Lorikeets to feed from the flowers. Their cries were raucous, as if enjoying their new primacy as sole living creatures of the street. He glanced into the back seat of the Ute where Peter remained, feigning sleep, and clenched his teeth in irritation at the man's inaction. Even if he was too scared to leave the vehicle, surely he could at least help keep a lookout for Infected.

The women emerged from the house. Georgie shook her head at Mark's raised eyebrow; they'd had no luck, the place was empty. Penny's face was pale and drawn, there was only one other place to look now – the crash site. She directed Mark out of the street, taking the route her husband usually took to the M5 motorway, and within three blocks, they found the wreck.

The gunmetal grey station wagon had mounted the curb half way down the street, crashing into a telegraph pole. The base had snapped on impact, the pole falling to crush the midline of roof between driver and passenger. Surprisingly the roof had stood up to the weight, only bowing moderately under the tonne of wood. Mark pulled up ten metres back from the vehicle. After turning off the Ute's engine, they all heard it; the growling rasp of a Carrier. Penny emitted an involuntary sob. They knew what they would find behind the driver's wheel.

Mark got out and warily circled the station wagon. The driver's window had been smashed out by the attacking ghouls, and through this opening, what was left of Penny's husband now vented his rage at being entrapped. His right forearm was missing below the elbow, and the meat had been stripped and chewed away from the upper arm leaving carmine-streaked bone open to the air. The near side of his face had not fared much better. It had been reduced to a mess of sinew, muscle and bone almost unrecognisable as human. At the sound of Mark, the head turned. The sole remaining eye fixed a glare of hatred upon him as the head whipped about, teeth snapping in anticipation. The seat belt held the undead creature firmly in place, imprisoned by the simplest of restraints.

A scuffing shoe on the ground caused Mark to turn, and he found Penny at his shoulder. She had approached reluctantly, obviously terrified to confirm with her eyes what her ears had already declared as fact.

'Oh David....,' she whispered, hand over her mouth in horror. Tears silently flowed down her cheeks. Mark put an arm around her shoulders, gently steering her up to the path and away.

'Do you want me to end it for him, Penny?' he gently asked.

Penny took a deep, shuddering breath. 'No. I at least owe him that. If not for me, they could have left earlier. Maybe they would have been safe in Melbourne by now.'

Penny hesitantly walked back to the driver's window. She raised her eyes to stare at her husband as he snapped and bucked at the seatbelt, reaching for her with his one remaining hand.

'I'm sorry, David. Sorry for all of it.'

Tears streamed afresh as she drew her service revolver. Clicking off the safety, she raised it in a trembling hand and fired. David's head jerked to the side with passage of the bullet then fell silent.

Penny lifted her free hand to rub at her eyes as if she could erase what they had seen. After a few moments she called to Mark. 'We still have to find Ben.' Her voice was thick with strain.

He nodded, and joined her to begin a search of the block. Peter and Georgie followed in the Ute, close behind. Suddenly Penny darted forward and picked up an item off the ground. It was a bloodstained skate shoe. Mark ground his teeth together, not looking forward to the next find.

The shoe had been on the ground at the start of a concrete driveway that disappeared behind a high fence, concealing much of the front yard from view. Mark offered to check it out alone, but Penny elbowed him aside. The front yard was dominated by a huge avocado tree, thick green leaves blocking much of the sun from reaching the ground beneath. At the base of the trunk was a figure hidden in shadow. They approached slowly, Mark's eyes searching the margins of the garden for any other presence. As their eyes adjusted to the gloom, more details emerged. The grass around the figure had been mulched into the soil, blood having been spilt in such quantities to turn the dirt into mud. The figure itself was little more than shredded flesh and splintered bone, with no identifying feature remaining.

Penny knelt at its side, cold blood soaking through the knees of her pants to chill the skin beneath. She was looking over the body, checking what was left of the hands. The thumb and index finger remained on the right hand, and as she lifted this closer, Penny began to wail, a sound of pure grief. She clenched the hand to her mouth, kissing the finger and thumb, murmuring an apology again and again under her breath as tears streamed down her cheeks.

Mark put a hand on her shoulder. 'Penny, it might not be him. There's… there's nothing left here to identify .. Maybe he got away.'

Penny held up the hand towards Mark. 'Look at the thumb. There's a high ridge down the middle of the nail. Ben's had this deformity ever since his thumb got slammed in a car door. The doctor missed the nail bed injury and when the nail grew out, it had this ridge in it. It's him Mark,' she said, her voice cracking. 'I wish to god it wasn't, but it's him.'

'I don't know what to say, Penny. This is such a shit situation...' Mark looked at his feet, feeling awful for wanting to escape her grief. 'I know it doesn't cut it, no words will, but I'm sorry for your loss.'

Penny looked up at him, tears cutting pale lines through the grime of her face. 'Will you help me bury them, Mark? One last favour.'

Mark glanced once more around the garden, he was getting nervous being in the one location for such an extended period of time. Surely the Infected that had massacred the boy must be nearby.

'Of course. Come back to the car though, let me and Peter get it sorted,' he said as he led Penny down to the Ute.

The next property had a large well-maintained garden at the front of the house. The soil in a large bed of yellow daffodils had been the best option, the loose dirt yielding to the only tools that Mark had for the job – his hands. He coaxed Peter out of the Ute to help, and between them, they scooped out a body length shallow pit, before gently placing the two sets of remains together, son and father to be forever more by each other's side.

Mark was drumming his fingers on the steering wheel in agitation. He sighed and looked at his watch for the fifth time. Peter had been badgering him to hit the road, and as much as the guy was starting to give him the shits, he was right. They needed to get going. If they stayed any longer, they would all end up on the menu.

'Georgie, I don't know what to say to her, but we need to head off. She's going to have to make a choice to stay or join us soon. Do you reckon you could get her moving?'

'It's not like I have any idea what to say either you know,' she muttered, clearly not looking forward to encroaching on the grieving mother. 'Ok, I'll try,' she said, giving in with a sigh. Georgie swung down from the Ute and walked up to the garden.

She found Penny lying on the grass, lengthways next to the grave of her husband and son. The woman was staring up at the sky blankly, gazing into nothing while the fingers of one hand toyed with a daffodil at the edge of the dirt. For some reason Georgie found it mildly unnerving, she would have been more comfortable to find her crying.

Penny's eyes suddenly flicked towards her. 'I just feel numb, like I've been hollowed out inside. I can't cry anymore; it just doesn't feel real. What the fuck's wrong with me?'

'Nothing feels real at the moment to any of us,' Georgie said. 'The last couple of days should only be in nightmares. It wasn't your fault, Penny. I'm sorry, but we have to leave. Will you still come with us?'

Georgie didn't give her time to respond, grabbing her hands and pulling her to standing. She brought Penny to the Ute, leading her like an invalid. Peter opened the back door and helped seat her inside. As they drove off, Penny stared at the burial site, still looking backwards long after it disappeared from sight.

CHAPTER TWENTY-THREE

There hadn't been time to fortify the sports ground to any major depth. The military had instead built a semicircular series of sandbag redoubts facing onto the park at twenty-five-metre intervals. The cordon blocked the road approaching the SCG from the north and south, then extended along the margin of the adjacent paved areas west of the SCG. This allowed use of the area for processing civilians that sought extraction. The redoubts were topped with FN Minimi machine guns, and accompanied by a detachment of general infantry soldiers that roughly directed approaching civilians.

As Novak herded his group between two redoubts, he was pulled up by one of the soldiers, a corporal by the chevrons on his uniform.

'Hold up there, mate,' said the soldier.

The corporal had his rifle raised, aimed straight at Novak's face. 'I don't even want to know how you came across those weapons, but they stay here. Place them at your feet and move away.'

There was no arguing with the man, the rifles were largely useless anyway without ammunition. Novak calmly placed the Austeyr on the ground, followed by the other evacuees that still retained a rifle. Two privates darted forward and retrieved the weapons. Nobody checked for small arms, leaving Novak's service pistol unnoticed. The corporal waved them onwards once more with the point of his rifle, his focus once more directed elsewhere.

Back from the initial cordon, other soldiers directed the approaching civilians to processing stations. Novak and his followers were forced into a long queue passing between two waist-high temporary fences. At the mid-point, a large German Shepherd and handler were on duty, the dog intently sniffing each person before stepping back. As Novak and his group approached, the demeanour of the animal changed. Its tail tucked up between its hind legs, the ears flattened and lips drew back exposing teeth. A deep growl rumbled from the beast's throat. The handler moved his animal out of reach, the back legs of the dog shaking, a wet patch on the underlying concrete expanding as the dog wet itself in terror.

A different soldier now blocked their path.

'Someone in this group has early stages of infection. We need those that have been bitten to separate, and move over there,' he said, pointing towards a shipping container.

The container had an open door at the back, although shadow obscured vision of the interior. Novak's team looked toward him for an answer, the dependence upon his leadership had become absolute. He shrugged, 'I don't think we really have a choice, guys.'

'Just walk over there, and we'll be able to guarantee you won't become one of those walking corpses. We're in a hurry though, so hands up, who's bitten here?' The soldier was becoming more agitated.

Four of the group separated themselves and walked hesitantly towards the container where two soldiers waited. The soldiers ordered the small group into a line, facing away from Novak.

'Get onto your knees, hands behind your back where I can see them,' barked the older soldier, voice tight. Any choice to comply was removed as the men roughly shoved them to kneel on the concrete.

One of the group, a female student with a bite mark on her calf looked over her shoulder at the sergeant, her face pale and eyes wide. 'Novak, what's going on?' she asked, voice shaking.

He felt his gut lurch. Novak turned to the soldier who'd ordered the separation of his group. 'Hey, I'm responsible for these people! What are you guys doing?' When the man didn't reply, Novak grabbed his shoulder with one hand, forcing him to acknowledge his question. In his peripheral vision, the German Shepherd bared its teeth, issuing a snarl of warning as it strained against its lead.

The soldier finally met his eye. 'You know perfectly well what is going to happen. We have no choice – euthanasia's the only cure.'

Novak let his arm drop, feeling like he'd been punched in the gut as he turned back to the four on their knees. There was nothing he could do now other than pay witness.

Standing behind the kneeling people, the two soldiers drew their handguns, and after a silent glance at each other, they each lined up their first victim and fired. Heads whipped forward, faces exploding outwards with the exit of the bullet. Boneless, their bodies slumped forward into a puddle of their own gore. The two soldiers quickly moved onto their next target, finishing the job before their remaining victims had a chance to react. The soldiers holstered their guns, and then taking hold of a body by hands and feet, began to move them into the waiting shipping container.

Outside in the queue, the dog was amongst them again. Gone was the behavioural expression of fear as it darted in and out of their legs, inspecting each person in turn.

'Right, move on through,' the soldier said, satisfied that the early infections had been weeded out.

Novak looked back at those following him and shook his head quietly at his own failure. Fifteen people left out of seventy, and not one of the police officers under his command remained. What a fucking joke. He knew the army had no other option, had figured he'd be stuck with the ugly job himself once the infection started to take hold. Revulsion cramped his gut as he recognised a degree of relief that the role of executioner had been taken from him. Surely he owed them that much, a trusted person to explain why it was necessary and to end it painlessly?

Novak turned away and headed for the turnstiles at the end of the fenced walkway. When he got his people through, his duty was finished as far as he was concerned. It was the army's responsibility from there. If his superiors saw it differently, they could go and get bitten by a Carrier for all he cared. He waited while each of his evacuees passed by and through the turnstile, then stepped through himself. Novak called his group together on the far side. They gathered around looking expectantly at him. The look of dependence steeled his resolve, he needed this part to finish.

'I'm sorry I couldn't get more of you through. Each one of you earned it. You played as much a part in your own survival through that journey as I did. My job ends here though; the army will evacuate you to wherever they think is safe.' Novak looked down, not wanting to meet their eyes.

When he raised his gaze, a couple had already broken off, making for the grassed oval, however most of the group were still there. Not one of them was looking at him with contempt. One of the women stepped forward, taking his hand in her own.

'Sergeant, you didn't fail us. Thank you,' she gave his hand a squeeze, then departed. The remainder of those present shook his hand, mumbling their thanks before heading for the oval. Part of Novak unclenched as the burden was shed.

The sun cut through a gap in the clouds above, casting shadows in stark contrast on the concrete at his feet. Novak felt his heart stutter in shock at the first spatterings of fire from the machine gun emplacements. He felt bile rise at the back of his throat with the realisation of what it meant. Looking out across the park, past the sandbag redoubts, the first of the attacking Carriers could be seen. There was no order to their approach – the dead knew no strategy. The swarm from Crown Street had finally reached the military cordon, attracted by the density of uninfected people and noise of the retrieval helicopters.

A Minimi machine gun was incapable of single shots. Gunners used short bursts to improve accuracy, however, the weapon was designed for stopping soldiers with hideous trauma to "centre of mass" organs such as lung, heart and abdomen. Such a strategy proved useless against the Infected. Anything other than a direct hit to the brain was ineffective. Novak saw multiples of the walking dead knocked from their feet, flattened as machine gun fire hit their torsos, only to crawl back to standing and continue forward, their desire for carnage unchanged.

Novak thought he'd feel panic at such a sight. Instead he felt grim resignation. He'd done all he could, now it was out of his hands and as it appeared; he was screwed. The weight of numbers would overwhelm the poor bastards at the military perimeter, leaving his only chance a helicopter evacuation before the Infected reached the interior of the SCG. Novak turned and ran for the nearest entrance. Other people around him joined in the rush, panic overcoming reason as a base need for survival trumped all other thoughts. Novak saw a young man trip and disappear beneath the crush, trampled underfoot. He found himself in the general admission stand, and joined other people climbing over the chairs to reach the grassed oval.

The north end of the playing field was roped off as a landing area for the Chinook helicopters. The southern part of the oval was crammed with people, shoulder to shoulder in a heaving mass as each tried to push to the front for evacuation. Novak stood at the rear of the crowd, a simmering rage brewing once more. There was no chance that any more than a handful of the crowd would leave here safely. The Infected were likely only minutes away.

A gut-twisting scream echoed from the stands above. Novak's gaze flicked upwards looking for the owner of the cry, and felt the hairs stand up straight on his neck. Carriers spilled from multiple exits, lurching forward to people yet to descend from the stands. Their appearance was hellish, bodies torn by machine gun fire, hanging sections of flesh and clothes, bloody and burnt. The crowd on the oval surged away, breaking through the containment fence towards the remaining helicopter. The Chinook was filled to capacity already and preparing for take-off, the twin rotor blades spinning faster into a blur as it began to lift from the ground. The forerunners of the crowd clasped at the wheels in desperation as it rose into the air, only to drop from the sky as their strength gave out.

The Infected reached the oval, tearing their way forward, a meat grinder of humanity. Novak checked his magazine. Five bullets remained. He would take four of the undead out, and save the last round for himself. He paced towards the advancing line of horror, calmly selecting his targets. As the fourth corpse dropped to the ground he upended the pistol, pressing the barrel end under his chin.

Novak closed his eyes, willing himself to pull the trigger and bring an end to the nightmare. A scream tore open his eyes, and he found a young woman under attack to his immediate right. A pallid ghoul dragging its own entrails had its teeth buried in her shoulder, whipping its head from side to side to rip out a mouthful of tissue. Instinctively, Novak levelled his gun at the creature, and fired; his last round used to save a girl that would soon be dead regardless. The girl ran without a backwards glance at her saviour.

Novak's eyes widened in horror as he realised the death to which he'd condemned himself. He threw away the handgun, drawing out the mason's hammer as his last defence. He swung the chiselled spike with adrenaline-fuelled strength into the face of an attacking Carrier, puncturing the forehead and brain behind. He had become separated from the main body of the crowd, surrounded by the undead. As he wrenched the hammer out of the skull, he felt burning fire lance through his upper arm, as a chunk of bicep was ripped free. In horror he smashed his hammer through the gore rimmed teeth responsible. Suddenly, he was falling, his right leg pulled from beneath. Novak landed on his back, above him the sky was blocked out by four dead faces, crouching down to feed. He couldn't escape, there was nowhere to run, nothing left to fight with. The fingers of a hand stabbed relentlessly into his abdomen with inhuman strength, bursting through the muscular wall and into the coils of intestine, ripping a handful free.

Novak screamed, his whole world reduced to pure agony.

CHAPTER TWENTY-FOUR

Mark parked and cut the engine. Georgie had directed him to a marina on Kogarah Bay, a fan of piers that sprouted from the shore beneath the St George Motor Boat club. A southerly wind had gradually built through the day, sending white-capped waves to smash into moored boats and pylons. Georgie pointed out her boat, a nine-metre yacht with single mast that bucked against its ties. The craft was in beautiful condition, a brilliant white hull standing in direct contrast to the dirty grey water upon which it floated.

Penny allowed Georgie to lead her to the yacht, hair whipping about her face as they traversed the pier out to the boat and below deck. Since being coaxed into the car after burying her family, Penny hadn't spoken a word. She merely stared into space, refusing interaction with a world that had torn away everything she loved. Mark shouldered his pack, grabbing a rifle in each hand before following them out to the yacht. Once on board, he ducked through the low cabin door and deposited his load. The cabin was bigger than expected, able to sleep six people if required. A V-shaped double bed resided at the bow, on either side of a narrow walkway hung a set of bunks, with the lower bed doubling as a bench seat during the day. At the stern lay a galley kitchen with a gas stove and narrow sink for washing.

Georgie started running through a checklist to ready the boat for open water. A frown creased her forehead as she checked the fuel volume, cursing at the low level. Petrol filled barely half of the tank.

'Mark, how much fuel is in the Ute?' she asked.

'Don't know, probably about thirty litres, do we need it?'

'Yep, I want a back-up so we don't have to rely on the sail to move.'

She retrieved a Jerry Can and siphon hose from a storage cupboard and handed it to him. 'Once we've got that, we can leave. I'll start removing the mooring lines while you do it, ok?'

Mark climbed back up to the pier and found Peter standing with his hands in his pockets, looking towards the Captain Cook Bridge east of the marina. The apparent lack of activity or concern in his body language immediately gave Mark the shits; the guy was dead weight. He handed Peter the can and hose along with his keys.

'Have you used a siphon hose before?'

Peter looked blankly at him.

'I take it that's a no then.' Mark gave him a brief run down on how to do it and left him to trudge back to the Ute.

Peter grumbled to himself as he walked away, annoyed with his allocated task. He stopped at the beginning of the pier, looking around the car park for any danger. The place was deserted. Fifteen metres back from the Ute, a door into the boat club swung free on its hinges in the gusting wind. The interior was hidden from sight, and Peter had no desire to go exploring. Satisfied that he was alone for the moment, he walked to the vehicle, unlocked the driver's door and flicked the latch to unlock the fuel cap. Setting up the siphoning rig took only seconds. 'Who wouldn't know how to use a siphon hose? Condescending bastard,' he muttered.

While petrol filled the can, Peter drew the hood of his jumper overhead for warmth. He turned his back to the boat club and looked over at the yacht. Mark and Georgie were moving around, tying off ropes and generally looking useful. He felt something wet soak through his jeans. Looking downwards, he swore to himself in frustration. The Jerry Can had overflowed and now fuel was pouring onto the ground. He jerked the end of the hose from the car to stop the siphon.

A hand clamped around his neck, and fingers like steel bands crushed his windpipe from behind. His vertebrae creaked painfully and prevented his neck from turning to see his attacker. Rotten breath exhaled past his ear as the Carrier drew close, a low growl issuing before it latched onto his left shoulder. Peter whimpered as he felt the teeth finally penetrate the material of his jumper into the skin below. He battered at the hand around his neck then grabbed hold of a single finger, ripping it backwards. The joint gave way with a crunch to leave the finger standing at an odd angle from the rest.

The Carrier ignored the small trauma, disengaging teeth from his shoulder for a less guarded area. One vicious bite and tug ripped Peter's ear clean from the side of his head. He screamed at the burning pain before the grip on his throat tightened, cutting it off. He couldn't breathe, his trachea was crushed. Another bite tore into the side of his head as his chest burned for air. Vision greyed at the lack of oxygen, and then mercifully he knew no more.

Mark stood abruptly, banging the top of his head into the low roof of the cabin.

'Hey Georgie, did you hear that?' He cocked his head to the side listening, but there was nothing more to hear above the hollow whistle of wind through the rigging. Georgie shrugged, unsure.

'I'm going to check it out, be back in a sec.'

He picked up the Sako rifle and climbed back onto the pier. Wind borne droplets of water spattered across his face as he jogged back to land, the wooden slats bouncing under foot with each step. As he neared the Ute, the acrid smell of spilt petrol irritated his nose. Mark slowed, hackles rising on the back of his neck. He scanned the car park for the presence of anyone else.

A loud crash echoed from the adjacent building as wind slammed an open door against the wall, shattering the glass pane within. Shadows moved within the doorway, someone was heading his way. Mark edged around to the side of the Ute with the fuel tank. He saw Peter's feet first, toes to ground as he lay prone on the bitumen. A Carrier knelt on his back with the fingers of one hand locked about Peter's neck. It was wearing dirty blue overalls, a grimy rats tail hanging down the back of a pallid neck. Peter wasn't moving, his face pale blue, eyes bulging with a look of surprise.

Mark chambered a round and shot the Carrier through the back of its skull. It fell to the side and lay still. Mark leant forward and felt for a pulse at Peter's neck, nothing. Movement caught Mark's attention. Behind him, four stumbling men had emerged from the door into the grey winter's light. It was time to go.

He screwed the Jerry can's lid in place, picked it up and ran for the yacht. As he came within earshot, he called for Georgie to cast off. Her head sprang above the back of the boat at her name and her eyes widened at the approaching threat. She disappeared from view for a moment as she started the boat's motor, then leapt above deck, scrambling for the bow to release the mooring line. The chasing Carriers had now reached the wood of the pier behind Mark as he unhooked the stern line and dropped into the back of the boat, dumping the petrol can to the side. Both Georgie and Mark pushed against the edge of the pier, trying to drive the boat away from the side. It gradually moved, the bow pointing outwards, however the stern was still less than a metre from the dock. The first of the Infected reached the pier next to them and blindly stepped off for the boat, arms reaching forward. Its feet missed, however, momentum carried it far enough that the chest landed across the edge of the boat. Growling, it wrenched itself forward with its hands, trying to drag its legs in. Mark drew the sword from the scabbard at his waist, and with a vicious underhand swing, brought the blade up into its face, the metal biting deep into the cheek and forehead. The force of the blow knocked the body backwards to slide beneath the water, its hands vainly reaching for purchase. The yacht was now two metres off the pier, and the remaining Carriers fell harmlessly into the water.

Mark breathed deeply as he leaned forward on the handle of the sword, its point resting on the wooden side. As his breathing slowed, he hung the blade over the edge to wash the infected tissue away.

They were safe again for the first time in days, and despite the icy wind, relief flooded through his limbs like a warm bath.

CHAPTER TWENTY-FIVE

Harry was sitting behind the wheel of his car, thinking. He'd pulled into the driveway of the farm house at least fifteen minutes prior, and yet hadn't moved to go inside; his mind was stuck working through his options. It came down to stay and defend, or run and hope for something better. The problem with running, he couldn't think of a location that would be safer than the farm. The whole east coast of Australia had escalating outbreaks of infection, and if Melbourne hadn't been overrun, it was only a matter of time. Major cities were potential death traps – Sydney being the perfect example. The only state free of infection was Tasmania, however, its Premier had enforced a strict 'turn back' policy for all boat traffic and closed airports to the mainland.

On the other hand, if he stayed on the farm, he thought he might have a good chance at avoiding trouble. Milton was a small town, and half of its population had already fled south. This meant that any large density of the Infected would have to come from elsewhere. His house was in free pasture, with clear lines of sight for any approaching danger. He had a guaranteed bore water source, and good soil for crops if the situation became prolonged. And with the landlord's heavy machinery available, the potential for greater fortifications around the house was also present.

The hire yard was deserted, a note on the door alluded to an extended holiday and business closure until further notice. In other words, his landlord had fled. As far as Harry was concerned, that placed anything in the hire yard at his disposal. Technically, he wouldn't be actually removing anything off the owner's land, just rearranging position. The shipping containers especially caught his attention, if he could work out how to move them, they could be arranged as a fortification around the perimeter of his house making it virtually impregnable.

Harry sprung the latch to the door and stood from the car, his back creaking as he pushed his hands into the base to stretch. He'd made up his mind; he was going to stay and weather the coming storm. Steph appeared at the top of the steps. She looked somewhat recovered, a decent sleep wiping away the grey smudges beneath her eyes. Her hair was drawn into a neat ponytail at the nape of her neck. She was wearing a t-shirt under a black puffer vest, an old pair of jeans showed her knees through rips in the fabric.

'I was wondering if you were ever going to come in?' She paused, her forehead creasing in concern at the expression she saw on her cousin's face. 'Something happen that I need to know?' she asked.

'I've just been debating with myself about what to do. The Emergency Department's closed and most of the town has fled. I've wracked my brain, but I just can't think of anywhere else that's going to be safer than our present location. I reckon I have a better chance of making this house defendable than gambling on a retreat to the unknown. I've made up my mind – I'm staying, Steph.'

He looked up, meeting her eyes for the first time. 'Do you want to join me? God knows I'll need help making this place the stronghold it'll need to be.'

'I take it you've got some plans on how to make it safer then?' She turned around, pointing at the knee height windows at the front of the house, 'With so much glass, it would take mere seconds for a Carrier to smash through.'

'Yeah, I've got a few. If we do this right, those walking corpses won't even make it to the house. I'll grab a bit of paper; let me draw out some plans, then you can see if you think my ideas are plausible.'

Harry left Steph on the door step looking after him. Her face had softened somewhat, an eyebrow slightly raised in curiosity at Harry's confidence as she turned to follow him inside.

Steph chewed her bottom lip as she studied the roughly-drawn plan on the table. Harry had scribbled a diagram of the property, including lines of defence that could be created from materials at hand. She was finding it hard to poke holes in his logic so far, the only troubling factor she saw was the lack of manpower to make his vision a reality in a short timeframe.

Harry had proposed reinforcing the current paddock fences with barbed wire to catch hold of any lone wandering Carrier. If high numbers arrived, the paddock fences would likely fail under combined weight, requiring a closer line of fortification. The house itself was raised six feet off the ground on high footings, circled by a veranda. Removing the stairs at the front and back and replacing them with a ladder, would automatically create another simple barrier against the mindless dead.

He next proposed laying a defensive square of shipping containers around the perimeter of the house. Harry also suggested digging a series of deep holes inside the fence line. If speakers were rigged in the holes as bait, they could potentially attract many of an attacking swarm away from the house, reducing the overall numbers being fought. Reluctantly, she was impressed.

'I like the idea of the shipping containers, but how are you going to move them up here?' she asked.

'There's a truck in the machinery yard that has a crane system on its back for loading and unloading the containers. We just cart them up on the truck, then unload them around the house. I still need to work out how to use the crane system though – that bit I haven't done before. Surely driving a truck shouldn't be too different from a manual car?' he said. 'Either way, I think we should concentrate first on the simple stuff, like sorting out the existing fence line, and knocking out the steps to the house.'

'Ok. Count me in. Anyway, my parents would disown me if I left you here to die on your own.'

Harry looked up at her to find Steph's face was deadpan.

'Glad to take advantage of your sense of family duty,' he replied with a wry smile at his cousin's dry humour.

A crackle of gunfire came over the speakers in the living room, replacing the monotone drawl of the news report Steph had left running on TV. Harry walked towards the other room to investigate.

'Do you know what's going on?' he asked.

Steph got up and followed. 'They were just covering the evacuation in Sydney. It was all fairly mundane, no more close-ups of people being eaten, thank Christ. Too many complaints I guess....' Steph's voice trailed off as she came to Harry's shoulder and saw the screen.

Both Harry and Steph gazed at the television, dumbfounded. A news helicopter was relaying footage from the SCG evacuation, hovering at the height of the surrounding stands. A reporter provided a barely coherent overview, so distressed was she at the spectacle unfolding below. The camera swung away to film the grounds around the stadium, displaying a writhing sea of the undead. The insatiable Infected had erased any evidence of the military cordon during an orgy of terror. The camera panned back to the oval, finding a swarm of Carriers descending into the packed oval of evacuees. Even from the chopper's elevation, the horrendous violence was clear. People were trapped, hemmed in on all sides by the swarm of hungry, dead flesh.

The camera zoomed in, focusing on a single police officer that stood his ground on the oval. Instead of retreating, he drew his gun and advanced, taking four measured shots at the Infected. The officer then paused, and placed the barrel beneath his chin with eyes closed.

'Poor bastard,' muttered Harry, realising the man was about to commit suicide.

Suddenly, the officer opened his eyes and levelled his gun at a Carrier attacking a girl to his left. A headshot dropped the Carrier and the girl ran on. The officer dropped the empty gun and pulled out a hammer, smashing it into skulls of the Infected like a berserker from ages past. But bravery would not be enough. Within moments, he disappeared from view, pulled beneath a bloody mass of Infected arms and teeth.

'He should have saved that round for himself,' said Steph, shaking her head, eyes sad. 'The girl had been bitten, she was dead anyway.'

The news camera changed focus to a transport helicopter that lifted from the crowd, desperate people dangling from its wheels, dropping one by one back to the heaving mass of insanity below. One tiny figure held on grimly, only to finally plummet as the chopper cleared the stands, hurtling to the concrete far below.

Harry turned off the screen, nauseated. Sydney was lost. He turned to find Steph as pale as he felt.

'Let's get to work,' he said. There wasn't much else to say.

CHAPTER TWENTY-SIX

Georgie was standing at the wheel, gazing forward over the cabin's roof as she steered the small yacht towards the bay's heads and an escape from Sydney. They weren't by any means alone in choosing this escape route, with hundreds of small boats all heading to sea, the huge bay felt mildly claustrophobic. The sails were still furled against the mast and boom. Georgie planned on using the sail once out of the bay, however, presently used the motor to aid manoeuvrability amongst the throng of other boats.

A high-pitched whine caused by the air ripping around the wire lines of the mast had eased as the near gale force wind had died down, replaced by a gentle breeze as they'd passed out of the Georges River into Botany Bay. In absence of the driving wind, the small waves decreased in height and lost their white caps. Georgie breathed a sigh of relief; the conditions on the water had her holding down a knot of anxiety regarding her ability to manage the yacht. It had been months since she'd sailed open water outside the heads, and over a year since skippering a craft blind at night. At least with the wind easing, the boat would be less difficult to control, and there would be more of an opportunity to teach Mark and Penny the basics of sailing.

Mark was perched to her right on the edge of the boat, cleaning his sword with a rag. He'd carefully dried away the water on the blade, belatedly regretting the salt water cleansing after dispatching the undead attacker. Mark now coated the blade in a light slick of oil he'd found in the galley to prevent rust from developing.

Georgie watched him from the corner of her eye as he worked. It had been the first time she'd ever seen him fight. If she was true to herself, there had always been some concern about what lay deep within him as a person, what enabled him to enter conflict zones as a soldier time and again. Mark had always been reticent in discussing his experiences away, preferring to park those memories when at home. Unfortunately, this only prevented Georgie from truly understanding what made him tick. What if he went to experience a warrior's blood lust and adrenaline of battle? She wasn't sure if she could stay with someone who viewed the world in such a way.

However, when Mark had been required to fight earlier, there'd been none of the rage she'd imagined must be implicit to such an act of violence. Rather, he had employed a workman-like economy of movement to dispatch the monster from the side of the boat. She'd seen no excitement on his face afterwards, only relief at its conclusion. This made her feel somewhat guilty that she'd doubted his character, but mostly, it made her feel conflicted over having pushed him away. She'd started detaching herself, becoming more distant than usual before he'd left for his last tour, and during it, she'd barely contacted him. She knew army guys tended to think the worst while they were away, and that her avoidance would have only worried him. Distance didn't make the heart grow fonder in her experience, just more jealous and suspicious.

If she was true to herself, she never believed they would have a long-term future together, their backgrounds were too different. Her family wanted for little, enjoying a wealth created by successive generations on the land. And yet, Georgie was keenly aware of her privilege, and it was this awareness that drove her to make the most of the advantages her birth provided. Her parents had instilled a belief that to waste any opportunity presented or earned, was to spit in the eye of luck. She had never shirked a hard decision, and that carried into her private life as well. If she considered a relationship had run its course, she preferred to rip the Band-Aid off, endure the pain and move on. Neither of them had raised the breakup, and considering the new circumstances, she was happy to let that conversation wait.

Happy again with the condition of his weapon, Mark slid the blade home into its sheath and moved next to Georgie. Resting a hand lightly on her hip in an unconscious caress, he appeared oblivious of the scrutiny he'd been under moments before.

Mark looked off to the left of the bow, across to the deep port on the north-eastern shore of the bay. The container ship terminal had been named as one of the evacuation points from Sydney, and a throng of humanity could be seen lining the dock. As Georgie headed for the bay's exit, she'd been forced within a few hundred metres of the port, where multiple ships could be seen loading passengers. Numerous smaller boats were taking part, brave locals using their own small fishing crafts to ferry people back and forth out to large container ships anchored in the bay. A fight had broken out on one of these smaller boats, as the passengers turned on their rescuer to steal the boat. Georgie and Mark looked helplessly on as the captain was dumped overboard. As he tried to climb back on board, one of the men callously chopped down on his hands with a wide bladed knife, severing the fingers to drop like fat little worms as the man screamed and fell back into the water. The captain had been heavily dressed for the cold weather, and the weight of his sodden clothes took him below the surface within moments.

Eighty metres to starboard towered the *Armonda* cruise liner, requisitioned by the government to aid evacuation efforts. It had been loaded earlier in the morning, crammed full of Sydney's fleeing citizens. Unfortunately, numerous brewing infections had passed security unnoticed. Muted screams fluctuated in volume with the breeze. Smoke trailed from broken windows at one location. At the lowest deck on the stern of the ship, a mass of people gathered as they sought to escape the slaughter within. People started to jump the twenty odd metres to the water below. As the attacking dead hit the crowd, those jumping became a waterfall of flesh, desperate to avoid being torn apart.

'Mark, don't even think it,' said Georgie. 'You saw what happened to that captain, that could be us if we pull them aboard, our boat would be swamped in seconds. And how will we know if they've already been bitten or not?'

'I know. You're right, it doesn't stop it from being fucked up though. Let's just get out of here.'

From that moment until they escaped the heads of the bay, the couple stared resolutely ahead, trying to block the screams and cries for aid around them. They passed more than one boat that had become a floating slaughterhouse, decks splashed with crimson. Sharp, triangular fins started to cut the water with surprising regularity as bull sharks were driven to frenzy by the sheer volume of blood mingling in the waves, adding to the horror for those luckless bastards who had been forced to jump overboard.

The bow of the yacht bucked upward into a one-metre swell as they rounded the Kurnell headland and headed south. Under instruction, Mark cranked the main sail up the mast. With a massive smack, a gust of wind filled the canvas, tipping the boat slightly to port as the yacht sprang forward eagerly. Neither looked backwards, taking no pride in their actions of self-preservation.

Some things were better left in the past.

CHAPTER TWENTY-SEVEN

Georgie had made the most of the remaining hours of light, forcing a crash course in sailing on Mark in the hours after leaving Sydney. She was being pragmatic, there was no way that she would be able to captain the boat through the entire trip, and would need spells away from the wheel. In the end they had both been relieved for the distraction as he learnt first how to manage the sail.

Georgie then taught him how to turn the boat's direction by tacking. When he had this manoeuvre sorted, she showed him how to jibe, a more dangerous method of turning the boat. Although Georgie instructed him to keep down, the speed at which the metal boom holding the base of the sail swung mere inches above his head made him wince.

Cronulla, Sydney's southernmost coastal suburb slipped by in the distance, giving way to the greenery of the Royal National Park as Mark enjoyed his first stint behind the wheel. The southerly continued to blow steadily into the evening, requiring him to make frequent small turns of the bow across the wind to maintain their progress down the coast. Although they had GPS, Georgie elected to keep the coast within sight, a decision Mark was more than happy to support.

As the light faded, Georgie took back control of the wheel. Four hours of sailing brought their yacht within reach of Wollongong; however, the port city was almost unrecognisable at night. The electricity had failed, leaving most suburbs in an impenetrable darkness. A low layer of cloud blocked the moon above, while reflecting a blood-red glow upon the city centre where a massive fire burnt out of control. Thick plumes of dirty grey smoke billowed upwards from the inferno, while smaller fires burnt holes in the pitch black across the city.

Wollongong had descended into the chaos seen so shortly before in its northern neighbour. Mark groaned silently, they'd find no safe harbour there. Georgie caught his gaze and shrugged at the thoughts blatantly obvious on his face.

'So we keep on going, what does it matter? If the wind continues being kind to us, we'll make it to Shellharbour in another hour or so. I know a small marina there where we can anchor safely.'

'Ok, it's not like we have a choice anyway,' grumbled Mark as he turned away from the destruction to look out at sea. 'Can't say I've become used to sailing at night though.'

Georgie snorted a short laugh. 'What, you can manage a couple of tours of duty, but you're scared of the dark? Give me a break.'

'Yeah, well it's different when you've got solid ground under your feet. Out here it's just wind, water and pitch black. When I can barely see my hand in front of my face, I keep feeling like we're about to smash into something.'

'Fair enough I suppose, I found it pretty unnerving the first time I did it as well. But give me the water any day rather than being stuck with a bunch of Carriers around us.'

'No argument there, babe.'

Georgie started to bring the boat into the wind to head away from shore again. 'Ready to tack, Mark?'

* * *

Georgie brought the bow into the wind to stall the yacht's progress, causing the sail to flap ineffectively. After leaving Wollongong, the wind had dropped to barely a whisper, making the passage to Shellharbour much longer than expected. The night sky had cleared, leaving behind a crescent moon and a smattering of stars to light the bay. Georgie expertly furled the mainsail back into the mast, securing the lines tightly. With a coughing rumble, the boat's engine stuttered to life for the last few hundred metres.

A small headland sheltered the marina, assisted by two rock walls that sprouted from either shoreline, leaving only a fifty-metre gap between them for access to open water. The interior was tiny, little more than a hundred metres from side to side. Two boats lay partially submerged at their moorings, the only occupants of the marina. Both craft were abandoned and silent, water gently lapping over canted decking.

Georgie guided their yacht within a few metres of one wreck. In the half-light, Mark noted a series of bullet holes down the hull, and dark smears against the pale woodwork of the cabin. He felt certain that the morning light would reveal those same dark smears as dried blood. On the northern shore lay an occupied boat ramp. The roof of a sunken Toyota Hilux Ute poked above the water line with the driver's door open, the likely victim of a rushed boat launch. Streetlights spaced at regular intervals around the deserted shoreline were dead, standing like overgrown black toothpicks against the sky.

Georgie cut the motor, letting the boat glide the next twenty metres towards the centre of the marina before dropping the anchor. As it gripped, the boat slowly came around to face into the light breeze, leaving the chain extending from the bow at an angle as it plunged into the water. They had clear space for at least forty metres to each side.

Mark stretched his arms overhead, easing stiff muscles at each shoulder as his legs naturally braced against the light movement of the deck. Georgie disappeared into the cabin for a few minutes. Mark listened to her light movements while studying the shoreline until he heard her approach behind him. He turned to find her with an old bottle of scotch in one hand, two bashed up metal cups in the other.

'I need a drink. You want to join me?'

Mark nodded with a half-smile on his face, 'You're a life saver. Where'd you find that?'

'My dad's a scotch drinker, I figured there'd be one stashed on board somewhere, and sure enough, he didn't disappoint.'

Georgie passed one of the metal cups to Mark before pouring a sizeable dram into each.

Mark touched the edge of his cup against hers. 'To the end of the world, eh?'

'Not funny.'

'Yeah well, I'm sure it'll only be a temporary state of anarchy. Is Penny still sleeping?'

'She was lying on the bunk facing the wall, if she's not asleep – she obviously wasn't in the mood to talk, so I left her to it,' Georgie said.

'Fair enough, it's pretty fucked up what happened to her family. She's got a right to be a basket case for a day or two I reckon.'

Georgie took a sip from her cup, grimacing at the taste. She hooked her head to the side, indicating for Mark to follow her, then climbed up to sit against the mast on the cabin roof. Mark joined her, their shoulders touching as they sat in companionable silence for a few minutes. Aside from the water lapping at the boat's side, it was quiet. The power was off in the small town, and the streets were empty of movement.

Mark studied her from the corner of his eye. It had only been a couple of days since she dumped him, a few days that had seen their shared world implode. It had allowed him to push aside his questions and hurt to deal with the greater dangers at hand, but he still needed to know why. He took a steadying breath.

'Hey Georgie, the other night when I got back to Sydney, you broke things off between us.' He felt her stiffen next to him at the change in topic. Mark silently cursed himself, but he'd started now. 'What happened to change the way you felt about me?'

Georgie didn't say anything for a moment, taking a slow sip from her cup instead. 'Come on, Mark. Do you really want to do this now?' her voice was tense. Mark didn't answer, waiting for her to continue.

'Fine. Have it your way,' she sighed. 'It's the bloody army, Mark. I never wanted to be a soldier's girlfriend. If I'd known you were a sapper – you wouldn't have got my number that first night.'

'Is it just an issue with me getting deployed, or something more?'

'That's a big part of it, but it's more than that. I know you don't tell me everything that happens to you while you're away. You have hideous nightmares, and then pretend nothing's wrong when I wake you up, even though you lie awake for hours after each one. That's not normal. I wanted to be your girlfriend, not a bloody counsellor.'

'There's not much that happens over there that you don't know about...'

'But?'

'There's some things that I just don't want occupying my mind when I'm home. I can't control what I dream, but I do have a say over what I talk about. Also, it's stuff that once said I can't unsay. Mental pictures that I don't want you associating with me.' He shrugged. 'Anyway, it's not all roses for me when I'm away. How do you think it is when I'm stuck on a base in the middle of nowhere, unable to contact you, and you're going out to the pub with mates, hanging out with a bunch of blokes that have a lot more to offer than I do?'

Georgie's eyes narrowed in anger. 'Nice one, Mark. Play the self-pity and jealousy cards, why don't you. You think I'm out fucking every bloke on campus while you're away, is that it?' She was pissed off. 'Fuck you, Mark. It just shows what you really think of me.'

'It's not what I meant,' stammered Mark.

'Yes it is, and you bloody know it! With everything else that's going on now, thanks for making it just that much worse.'

She drained the last of her cup, flicking the remaining drops overboard. 'I'm going to bed. I'll take the one in the bow, there's another bunk opposite Penny – you can have that one. Just don't climb in behind me.' Without waiting for an answer, she left, letting the door to the cabin bang behind her.

Mark cursed himself. What a fuck up. He considered following her inside to try and fix it, but found that he didn't have the energy. Nor the right words to say. He feared that things had slipped past the point of correction for them.

Mark glanced around the shoreline once more; it was still reassuringly devoid of movement. For all he knew, they were the only people alive in the area. He swallowed the last of his scotch from the tin cup. They had forty metres of clear water around them as a barrier – they were as safe here as anywhere. He was exhausted, but the thought of going below deck after that argument didn't appeal.

Mark picked up the bottle that Georgie had left behind in her haste to escape him, unscrewed the cap and poured a second larger measure of scotch into his cup. He pulled the thick outer coat zipper up high to his chin, and settled back against the mast. He'd let the grog keep him warm, and watch the sun rise from the deck. It wasn't like they'd be in any danger on the water away from shore. The second cup disappeared quickly, followed by a third before the alcohol deadened his thoughts sufficiently to let him slip from consciousness, the cup dropping free of his fingers to roll slowly over the edge and into the water.

Mark's eyes jolted open. It took a few moments for him to work out where he was again while his vision adjusted to the dark. His mind was immediately awake, all remnants of sleep banished in the instantaneous shift from deep sleep to alertness with a burst of adrenaline. The beginnings of a hangover ached in his temples and sat like a sour weight in his gut. He strained his ears for whatever had awoken him, but there was nothing aside from the rhythmic lap of the water against the hull.

He took a deep breath, held it for a count of five then let it go. The following ten breaths he counted slowly, forcing himself to let go of the tension he'd awakened to with a relaxation strategy he used to dissipate anxiety on an all too regular basis. Breath puffed in a white cloud as his exposed skin puckered into goose bumps at the bitter cold of the air.

The anchor chain at the bow gave a metallic creak as the boat moved slightly underfoot. Mark froze for a second, had that been the same sound that had pulled him from sleep? The anchor must be pulling through the sand, trying to find a more solid purchase point to hook onto as the wind picked up. Mark eased himself to standing, his back and neck protesting against his choice of sleeping arrangements. He grabbed hold of the mast next to him as his balance swayed, affected by the excess of scotch he consumed earlier. He mustn't have been asleep for as long as he thought.

Standing on the deck, Mark didn't find the change in weather he'd expected to account for the anchor movement. The water was calm, with only the barest movement of air against his cheek. The tide had receded sharply, and the newly exposed rocks on the shoreline added a tang of salt and seaweed to the air. It was still dark, although dawn wasn't far away. The chain creaked once more, shifting the bow to port by a hand's width. Mark made his way back to a small cupboard next to the cabin door, found the torch he sought, a heavy duty 6V Dolphin lantern and turned it on. A wide arc of harsh light shone from the torch, cutting through the gloom to the shore's edge. Mark swung the beam slowly along the edge to find the marina still empty. The chain drew his attention again. The creaking of the metal links attached to the anchor was now repetitive. Mark climbed onto the cabin roof, and carefully padded along the edge until he came to the bow.

The chain extended from the hull, jutting into the water at a shallow angle. The taught links shuddered every few seconds, sending circular ripples away in the water. Mark brought the harsh beam of the torch to bear on the anchor chain, following it down until it was lost in the hazy green depths.

Breath caught in his throat, and the hairs on the back of his neck rose in alarm. Something was climbing the chain. A hand came into view at the limit of the water's visibility, grasping the chain, followed quickly by a second that was missing the middle and ring finger – each bitten off at the first joint. The chain jerked as the creature hauled its body upwards, bringing a face and shoulders into the beam of light through the swirling water.

Two metres beneath the surface, an Infected was climbing the chain. With body supported on the shallow angle of the anchor chain at low tide, hand over hand, the ghoul pulled toward the surface. Its face was white and bloated from extended submersion, the lips and one cheek gnawed back by hungry fish. Slate grey hair moved about its head in a plume at the whim of the current, except over the right temple, where a fist sized clump had been ripped out, taking the scalp with it. His chest was bare of clothes, an iron coloured mesh of hair stretching from neck to navel, below which a leather belt held up a pair of baggy trousers. A ragged bullet hole was punched front to back through his left shoulder. At a guess, the man had been in his fifties before dying.

Mark eased the sword blade free of the scabbard at his waist, then let it hang loose in his right hand while he waited. He kept the beam of the torch fixed on the Carrier as he consciously slowed his breathing and firmed his stance in preparation for the coming fight. As it drew closer, its eyes fixed on Mark above. Immediately its movements became more frenzied, the arms wrenching forward at greater pace, cracked teeth bared in anticipation. The Carrier's hand punched through the surface of the water to grip the edge of the boat, scrabbling for purchase. Two nails ripped free of their bases, standing obscenely at right angles to the fingertip. Mark chopped his heavy blade down onto the back of one wrist, biting clean through both long bones of the forearm. Still affected by the scotch, he misjudged the amount of force required for the blow, and the sword continued on through the tissue to lodge deep in the timber below. The hand dropped free onto the deck, limp once again while Mark tried in vain to lever his sword free of the wood. The head of the Carrier breached the surface less than an arm's length away from his own. A gout of water poured from its mouth, emptying a stomach full of brine and flesh from a prior meal. A horrid bubbling noise escaped its throat as the water cleared from its airways. It lunged for him.

Mark flinched backwards, the teeth missing his leg by less than an inch. His left foot stepped onto the dismembered hand causing his ankle to twist and give way. He let the torch drop free in an unsuccessful attempt to keep his balance, the lantern bouncing twice before falling over the edge into the water, light tumbling in a slow arc as it fell to the sand deep below. Mark tried to scramble backwards even as he hit the deck. The Carrier now had its torso over the edge of the boat, and with a lightning grab, clamped an iron bracelet of fingers about his right ankle. Mark was on his back and kicked outwards with his left foot, stamping the heel into the pallid, swollen face. Skin and tissue tore free with every strike, but the creature was oblivious to pain. A low cry of terror escaped Mark's lips as his ankle was drawn towards the broken teeth.

A viciously pointed steak knife lunged over his shoulder to bury deep into the eye-socket of the ghoul. Georgie released her grip of the handle as the creature wrenched its head backwards out of reach. Mark thrust his foot forward once more, his heel stamping onto the base of the knife handle, punching the blade deep into the brain until the point burst free of the skull's rear. The corpse flopped onto the deck like a deboned fish, before the greater weight of its legs pulled the limp body back into the water.

Mark drew his feet underneath, then pushed himself to standing. He turned and found Georgie behind him, her face white in the half-light, hands shaking. He enclosed her in his arms, drawing her into a tight hug.

'I thought I was a dead man. If you hadn't… shit, I don't even want to think about it. How long were you there for?'

'I woke up to the noise of it coming up the chain, then I realised you weren't in the cabin, so came out.' Georgie stopped, and pushed back out of his arms until she could look Mark in the eye. Now that the initial surge of adrenaline was ebbing, she was beginning to look angry. 'Don't try to do it alone again, Mark. If you die trying to be a bloody hero, I'm fucked as well,' she said.

'Give me a break, Georgie. I wasn't trying to be a hero,' Mark said. 'I fell asleep up here, so happened to be in the right spot to stop it coming on board. It should have been straight forward, chop the hands off, and it would have fallen back in. How was I to know the blade would get stuck in the wood.' Mark glanced down at the dead hand, still lying like a macabre joke on the deck. 'And that fucking hand…' Mark stabbed a foot at it, kicking it overboard to skip twice on the water's surface before sinking out of sight.

'That's what I'm trying to get at, Mark. You couldn't have planned for that shit, so even more reason that we back each other up when it hits the fan.'

Mark sighed and leant down to remove the sword blade from the edge of the boat. With both hands, he worked it free, wrenching the handle up and down until the wood released the blade with an angry squeal.

'All right,' he said, suddenly sounding very tired.

Georgie let the topic drop with his agreement and now stood with her arms crossed tightly about her, looking across at the two partially submerged yachts that shared the marina with a concerned expression. She was wearing only the t-shirt she'd gone to bed in above a pair of jeans and bare feet. The skin on her arms was puckered, each hair raised in protest at the bitter cold.

'Do you reckon there's any more of those bastards moving around down there?' she asked through lightly chattering teeth.

'Maybe,' Mark replied. 'You should go inside and warm up again though, you look bloody freezing. I'll hang out up here and keep watch.'

Georgie glanced towards him, her eyebrows furrowed with concern.

'Don't worry, I'll call if anything happens. I swear.'

Georgie accepted, and climbed across the frigid roof of the boat and back into the cabin.

Mark was alone once again, and he found his own gaze now drawn back to the anchor line, waiting for it to start creaking under the weight of a second ascending corpse. He suppressed an involuntary shiver at the thought, pulled his coat more tightly about his shoulders and forced himself to watch the eastern horizon for dawn's coming instead.

CHAPTER TWENTY-EIGHT

Harry and Steph were sitting on the edge of the veranda, legs dangling above a new six-foot drop they'd created by removing the steps. Steph cradled a mug of steaming tea between her hands, blowing gently at the surface to cool it. Harry was slowly looking about the perimeter of the paddock in front of them, surveying their efforts of the last two days. They'd worked through every hour of daylight, an intensity of labour driven by witnessing the SCG slaughter on television. And yet, Harry still felt deflated at their slow progress.

He'd sought to prioritise their efforts, targeting easy wins that immediately made the house safer. The first item he ticked off his list was removing the steps to the veranda circling the old farmhouse. The building was perched on high footings, creating a sheltered area for storage that was now just empty space. By ripping out the steps, he created an instant obstacle that any brain-dead Carrier would find difficult to mount. Steph tore out any bushes and items against the side of the house, removing any handhold or structure that could be used to climb up to the veranda. She then attached a ladder to where the stairs had been with thick cable ties. In the event of an emergency, they could sever the ties and pull up the ladder, preventing easy access to the house by anything on the ground.

Next, the two set to reinforcing the fence surrounding the property. Harry and Steph dug out any rotten or broken fence posts, replacing them with star pickets. Once the base structure of the fence was strong again, Harry looked to make it a more difficult barrier to cross. The two of them strung a line of barbed wire along the top of the perimeter posts, hoping to snag any Carrier that tried to mount the fence.

Harry slowly stretched his hands above his head and felt his back creak in protest. He felt like he'd been chewed up and spat out again. Every muscle ached. His hands were a multitude of blisters that wept yellow serous fluid where they had torn open. Despite wearing leather gardening gloves during installation of the wire, needle sharp barbs had punctured his skin more times than he cared to remember.

The next stage of fortification required him to start moving the shipping containers into position around the house, and if Harry was honest with himself, he was starting to question his ability to drive the heavy machinery required. He'd forced open the office door after dawn to get to the truck keys, hoping to make an early start. It wasn't until he was sitting in the driver's seat of the semi-trailer used to move the containers, that he realised he might be out of his league. He had backtracked to the office, looking for a user manual to study. He couldn't afford to do something stupid and break the winches or anything that would prevent them from completing the defences. Better a few days late than a total failure.

He wearily got to his feet and leant against a post at the edge of the veranda. Maybe a change in activity would let his subconscious tackle some of his problems and find an answer.

'How about we ditch this place for a few hours and gather some more supplies before the supermarkets are stripped bare?' he suggested to Steph, who eyed him suspiciously above her mug of tea.

'You've been working like a madman these last two days. Why break now when you wanted to get those containers done? What's happened?'

'Nothing major, I'm just going to have to study some manuals before I can load the trucks – and I can do that at night. I figured I should use the daylight for something a little more useful than just reading,' he said.

'All right. Maybe we should head further away, try Ulladulla before the infection takes hold of the two towns? Might as well save the easier trips for when it gets more difficult to move around. What do you reckon?' Steph said.

'Deal. Are you ready if we head off soon?'

Steph nodded, took a last sip from her mug of tea and threw the rest on the dirt below. 'Let's go.'

* * *

Georgie had successfully sailed them down the New South Wales south coast to reach the harbour of Ulladulla. Two curtain walls jutted from the south and north margins of the harbour entrance, protecting the small marina within from the worst that the ocean could throw at the town. The yacht bumped up against the rubber tyres protecting the pier as they closed the final distance to berth. Penny stumbled, and threw an arm out sideways to steady herself and regain her balance. She had forced herself to get up and move the day before. Grief hung like a haze over every interaction and sight, giving everything a hideous dreamlike quality. The knowledge that her family was dead, was a raw wound on her heart that bled continuously, unseen.

Penny had always pitied those who chose suicide, and was determined to honour her son and husband by fighting until she could stand no longer. She had to keep moving, knowing that if she allowed herself to curl into a foetal position in the darkness once more, the seductive voice of despair would prevent her from emerging a second time. She already carried an additional weight of guilt after sleeping through the attack at Shellharbour, and had no plans to increase that debt by failing her new friends again.

Mark swung himself up onto the pier and secured a mooring line from both the bow and stern to the wooden pylons. He then jumped back down, disappearing into the cabin for a few moments, only to reappear with his loaded rifle in hand. Penny said nothing at the sight. Only weeks before, a heavily armed man carrying a military rifle in an Australian town would have set her heart racing. However, this wasn't the same country anymore. The country that had been their home was lost. Anything the government eventually won back would be a shadow of former glory, the surviving population altered and scarred by their lived history.

She ran through a basic check of her pistol before holstering it once again at her waist. She switched her hand hold to the ladder hanging from the edge of the pier and climbed up. Penny could smell herself as she climbed; she'd lost count of the days that she'd been wearing the same blue uniform. Then again, the trio all smelt the same. Deodorant hadn't been high on the list of priorities when they ran.

Georgie was the last to ascend after she had shut down the yacht's engine and locked the cabin. She accepted a hand up from Mark as she gained her footing on the rough wooden planks of the pier. A sheathed fishing knife from the yacht's supplies now hung from her right hip. In her hands was the Sako 0.22. The day before, the wind had dropped away for two hours, leaving them becalmed. Georgie had taken the opportunity to learn the basics of handling Mark's rifle. Her accuracy proved excellent as she fired at a number of floats Mark had strung out behind the boat. He'd been impressed at the speed at which she'd taken up the skill of managing the firearm, but when he'd commented on her hidden talent, she had frostily ignored the praise, stating that she'd always been good at different sports.

The three of them walked quietly to shore and headed for the car park to find transport. They split up, each checking door handles, praying for an abandoned set of keys and a full tank. Interestingly, most cars had unlocked doors, left carelessly as their owners fled to their boats in the marina.

Mark let out a small whoop of excitement as he found a Subaru Outback station wagon with keys in the ignition, a tank full of petrol and a luggage cage pinned to the roof racks. The engine turned over without hesitation, grumbling into life. Mark drove the car out to the start of the pier to load the few things they'd been able to take from Sydney. Penny and Georgie followed. As they passed the boot of a new Mercedes Sedan, a guttural noise started in the boot, quickly followed by thumps against the metal work that rocked the car on its suspension. Georgie caught Penny's gaze,

'How did a Carrier get itself locked in there?'

'Probably a bitten family member that had to be left behind once the disease took hold. Can't say I'm keen to open it up and confirm my guess,' replied Penny. Both women increased their pace, keen to leave the car behind. Penny helped Mark load the case of ammunition for the Austeyr and 0.22 into the rear of the Outback while Georgie kept watch.

'How far away is your parents' place?' he asked Georgie.

'A thirty minute drive. We'll need food though; I don't think there's much stocked at the house.'

Behind the marina ran the main road of Uladulla, lined with various shops and cafes. Penny pointed over Mark's shoulder, drawing their attention.

'There's a sign for a Coles. Might as well see if they've got food left on the shelves?' Penny suggested. The three of them climbed into the car, and Mark drove out of the marina, following the signs towards the supermarket.

* * *

Steph was glad for the size of the four-wheel drive. It made her feel a little safer being farther off the ground than the usual car. As they drove out of the property, rain had poured from the sky in a torrent before abruptly stopping like a tap had been turned off. The sun had then pushed aside the grey clouds to flood the green paddocks on either side with light. On entering the town, it was clear the infection had started to take hold here as well, continuing its irrepressible march from Sydney.

The beautiful village of Milton that straddled the crest of the ridge to either side of the Princes Highway had changed. Better days would have seen tourists drinking coffee at sidewalk tables, or sifting through the menagerie of homeware and antique shops Not any more. Business windows were smashed; a few buildings had been gutted by fire. She counted five stumbling figures of the Infected as they drove through. One tried to intercept them, forcing Harry to mount the curb to pass.

Steph tried to get the radio to work, but was met with static as she rolled the tuner through the FM and AM bandwidths. Contact with the outside world was shutting down, the TV had ceased picking up any signal that morning as well. Electricity would probably be the next to go. Harry's eyes skittered about the road ahead, looking for obstacles to their passage. Now was as good a time as ever to broach the topic – they needed help.

'Harry, I think we need more people on the property. Looking at this town – we could be attacked any day, and our defences aren't anywhere near complete. Is there anyone at the hospital that might want to join us?' Steph asked.

Harry sighed, scratching at the stubble on his chin while he thought. 'You're right, but I only just got to this place myself last week. I don't know anyone here. We could try and make contact with some of the other farms around us I guess as a starter?'

'Didn't you say that you and that other doctor left phone numbers and addresses on the front door of the ED? We could get in contact with him, see if he can suggest anyone that wants to make an alliance,' Steph said.

'Shit, I'd completely forgotten about that. The hospital's just up ahead,' he replied.

Four of the Infected were slowly walking around at the front of the Emergency Department, probably dumped by family members prior to succumbing to the disease. As Harry pulled in, their attention locked upon the car. He tried to swallow, but his throat had dried of spit.

'Make sure your door's locked. They won't break in if we're quick.'

Steph didn't need any encouragement. She locked her door, then unclipped herself and twisted around to check both back doors were locked and windows firmly up.

'There's a pen in the glove box I think, grab it out for the details can you?' Harry said.

Steph found it as Harry pulled into the ambulance bay, leaving only a foot's width between the passenger window and the entrance. Steph quickly scribbled the details provided on the window onto the back of her arm. Two of the Infected were closing on Harry's window as he watched with concern.

'Have you got it down yet?' he asked.

'Yeah, let's get out of here.'

Harry spun the wheel and accelerated out of the ambulance bay, back onto the main street to leave their attackers behind. After they had put a block between them and the hospital, Harry started to breath a bit easier again.

'Are you still up for getting food? After seeing how this town's already gone to shit, and as much as I would love to give it a miss now, this might be one of our last chances to stock up.'

Steph found herself grasping the handle of the small axe she'd chosen to bring as a weapon in a white knuckled grip. She loosened her fingers, noting the colour return to the skin. Forcing a steadying breath, she answered, 'Let's just get it done and go home.'

* * *

Mark found the Coles a block behind the main street, hidden at the back of a U-shaped complex of shops with a car park in the middle. The place was deserted, allowing him to drive up to the entrance.

The tempered glass of the automatic sliding doors lay in a scattered heap of tiny pebble-like pieces over the tiles both inside and out of the store. Someone had been kind enough to do the dirty work of break and enter for them. Their shoes crunched on the glass as they stepped over the base of the door and entered. Georgie noted a couple of house bricks in amongst the smashed glass that were likely responsible for the destruction.

Mark left the two women at the front as he did a quick walk past the aisles to check if the place was empty. He wasn't just looking for Carriers, but also other people like themselves. After seeing the ruthless way in which some survivors had fought for their own gain on Botany Bay, the group had agreed to treat other people they met with some reserve. Lawlessness was the new world order. It was up to them to ensure their own safety.

The aisles were clear of any movement, although the supermarket had been heavily picked over already. The shelves were half emptied, and the fresh food and deli meats section swarmed with flies over the rotting produce. The lights were off, however, the windows at the store's front provided a weak light source. Most of the aisles were in a state of twilight, with just enough light present to read labels. Mark returned to the others, his rifle now slung at ease over his shoulder. Penny had pulled out three trolleys to fill, and seeing Mark return, she rolled one towards him.

Georgie grabbed a trolley. 'So what are we targeting? Canned vegetables and meat I suppose. Anything else in particular either of you want?'

'Toiletries,' answered Penny. Mark cocked an eyebrow at her in question. Penny sighed with irritation. 'We need more than just food, Mark. I'll get toilet paper, tampons and other bathroom stuff along with some washing powder for clothes, because mine are about to rot off me.'

Mark failed to take offence at her tone. Instead, inspired by her line of thought, he took a whiff from his own armpit and grimaced. 'Ah, can you chuck in a couple of cans of deodorant for me as well?'

Penny's glare softened somewhat.

'I'll go for water and see if I can find anything of use in the electrical and gardening section. If anyone else turns up, we all clear to the far aisle away from the door until we know what's going on, ok?'

The girls nodded in reply, each going their separate ways.

Mark headed to the drinks aisle first, heaving three crates of bottled water into the trolley. He placed his weight up on the handle, scooting the trolley towards the electrical section. Mark had just picked up a torch when he heard a low rumble of a car's engine pulling up to the supermarket. Leaving the trolley where it was, he jogged back to their agreed meeting point, rifle now in hand. The women had beaten him there.

'How do you want to play this?' Mark asked quietly.

Penny answered immediately. 'Start from a position of strength, then ease it down as appropriate. Whoever it is, we want them on the back foot.' She turned to Georgie. 'Are you ok with that?'

'I guess so.' She didn't look too convinced. 'I'm still kind of hoping that we only really need to be afraid of the Infected, rather than every person we meet.'

'Don't worry, I won't do anything stupid. I'll just have a quick conversation and make sure they're not dodgy, then we can finish getting the food,' said Mark, trying to sound reassuring.

Both the women stood back from the edge of the aisle, leaving him at the corner. Penny unclipped her holster, and waited.

*   *   *

Harry pulled up next to the Outback and cut the engine. 'Looks like we're not the only ones stocking the pantry,' he said, tilting his head towards the other car.

'Well, as long as they're not dead, I'm happy to have a conversation with them,' Steph answered as she unlocked her door and stepped outside, unconscious of the fact she still gripped her hatchet at the ready.

Harry looked down at the machete hanging from his own waist. *We may be willing to talk – but are they going to want to speak to us when we walk in armed like this?*

The two cousins paced warily through the broken frame of the entrance, feet crunching loudly in the silence. Harry peered forward into the gloom, trying to take in as much as he could.

'Anyone here? We're just coming in to get some supplies,' he called out, startling Steph with the volume of his voice.

There was no reply. A can skittered in the farther-most aisle, drawing Harry's attention. *Crap. Better not be another of those dead fuckers.* He gently withdrew the machete from the sheath at his waist and held it, point forwards. He turned to Steph. 'Wait here a sec, yeah? I'm just going to check out that sound,' he whispered.

Harry walked slowly, trying to keep the sound of his footfall to a minimum. Glancing down each aisle as he passed, he found nothing but empty linoleum floors and depleted shelves. Coming to the last aisle, he turned the corner, and stopped abruptly. The end of a military rifle was mere inches from his face, the black hole of the barrel giving a wordless promise of death as it loomed directly ahead.

'Stop right there, mate,' ordered the man. 'And drop that blade.'

There was no hope of discussion on the matter. Harry slowly squatted, placing the machete on the ground. As he stood once more, he noted two women standing a few metres behind, both holding firearms. A half smile kinked the side of Harry's mouth.

'Is something funny?' the man ground out tonelessly, his rifle still trained on Harry's face.

'No, sorry,' said Harry, holding both hands palm outwards in capitulation. 'I was just thinking how I'd been worried that we might look too intimidating with our weapons if we bumped into normal people. But hey, we've got nothing on your firepower,' he added, with a short laugh.

The rifleman just looked at him, his face expressionless.

Harry lost his smile quickly and changed tack. 'Look, you've nothing to worry from us, my cousin and I are just stocking up on some food before it's all gone. I'm one of the doctors from the local hospital; we're no threat to you. We'll leave you to it, if that's all right?'

The man slowly dropped the barrel. 'Ok. We don't want any trouble either. Sorry, we've just seen some dodgy stuff of late.'

Steph inched her head around the corner, 'Is everything ok?' she asked quietly.

'Yeah, it's fine,' Harry replied, his eyes still on the rifleman. 'We're all just getting our own supplies and leaving the other alone.'

The man confirmed Harry's words with a slight nod. Harry glanced down at his machete on the floor. 'Can I pick that up now? Because I'm pretty sure I'll need it again before too long.'

Another nod. 'How about we all just keep our stuff sheathed while we're sharing the place though. I don't want any miscommunications turning nothing into something.'

'No worries,' Harry said, easing the machete back into its sheath. Steph stuck the handle of her small axe through a loop of belt, leaving the blade free at the top. With that, they both backed away.

As they pulled out a trolley each, Steph caught Harry's eye. 'Did you see that rifle? That's got to be military issue,' she whispered. 'He's probably an Australian soldier – maybe that's someone we could use at the property?'

Harry shook his head. 'Are you kidding? That bugger nearly made me shit myself!'

'Come on, Harry, one of the women was in a cop's uniform as well – they can't be that dodgy. We're going to have to take a gamble eventually.'

Harry clenched his jaw. 'All right, let's try and talk with them a bit first. I'm not agreeing yet though.'

Steph and Harry split up, quickly moving along the aisles shoving canned food, flour and other baking ingredients and toiletries into their trolleys. Within ten minutes, they were both finished. They met back at the entrance where the shop window provided a little more light.

Steph pulled a few cans of food from her trolley – tossing one to Harry. 'We'll sit down and eat here, then offer to them to join us when they walk past. Can't get less threatening than that, can we?'

Harry nodded in agreement, and parked his arse on the floor while his cousin pulled a few more items out to eat.

Harry was onto his second can of baked beans when the other group walked towards the exit pushing their trolleys. He stopped eating, the plastic spoon heaped with a congealed mass half way to his mouth as he tried to think of something to say.

Steph broke the tense silence, letting him off the hook. 'Were you guys in Sydney during the evacuations?'

The dark-haired woman stopped at Steph's question and looked across to the rifleman, who just shrugged. Taking this as assent, she cleared her throat. 'Yeah, Mark, Penny and I escaped at the same time it was happening, saw the debacle at Port Botany from a distance. We were lucky though, I had access to a boat, so we avoided having to gamble on the government's bailout plan.'

'We watched the SCG blood bath on TV, turned my blood cold that did. We've been working flat out to fortify our farm since it hap—'

'What did you see happen at the SCG?' interrupted Penny. 'One of my colleagues was evacuating a group of people to that location. Did it get overrun?' Her face was white, both hands clenched tightly on the handle of the trolley she had been pushing.

'We only watched for ten minutes or so,' said Harry. 'But it didn't look good. The Infected had broken past the army cordon and were into the crowd on the oval,' he glanced up at Steph for a moment. 'We did see one police officer in the crowd, I don't know if it was your mate or not though.'

'What did he look like?' asked Penny.

'I think he had a close shaved head, pale skin? I couldn't really be certain – we only saw him for a moment,' said Harry.

Penny turned to her companions. 'Jesus, that could have been him.' She looked back at Harry again. 'Do you know if he made it to the evacuation chopper? Please tell me he did.'

Harry shook his head slowly. 'He didn't make it. But he went down fighting, used his last rounds to save others in the crowd.'

Penny closed her eyes at his words; jaw clenched, looking like she was trying to bring herself under control.

'I've never seen anything like it,' continued Harry. 'He fought to the end, didn't give an inch.'

The dark-haired woman placed a hand on the cop's shoulder in consolation. 'It wouldn't have made any difference us being there, Pen. Sounds like it was a dead end with no way out.'

'Yeah, that's twice now I owe you. If you hadn't got me and Georgie to join you, we would have been in that same crowd,' added Mark.

Harry held up his tin of beans, trying to change the topic. 'You guys want to join us for something to eat? We figured it's one less meal we need to carry home. I'm sure Steph would like to hear some other person's voice aside from mine for a while.'

'Yeah, why not?' Mark sighed. 'I'm bloody starving anyway. You girls all right with that?' he asked, turning towards the two women.

The trio joined Harry and Steph on the floor. After introductions were made, and a slow start to conversation, the two groups gradually thawed to each other, each relaying their background and personal experience of the outbreak to date and the horrors that it had entailed.

Steph turned the conversation towards the future, asking what their plans were from here. Georgie described her parents' farm, north of Milton. The rest of her family had the good fortune of being overseas on holiday, leaving the property empty. Once they arrived there, they would try to make the site defendable in the short term.

Harry described the location of his farmhouse, outlining its strengths, the changes that they'd already achieved, and their plans to make the property impregnable via the construction of the shipping container wall.

'We've got the materials to make it safe until the government gets their shit sorted. As we found out on the drive here today, the infection's already hit Milton and I'm starting to worry that we're running out of time.' Harry paused, looking across at his cousin to check she was still in agreement. She nodded, mouthing, *ask them.*

Harry took a breath, and continued, 'What we need, is the right people to join us. Mark, you said that you're an engineer in the army? I take it you've got a heavy vehicle licence then?'

Mark nodded.

'With your help, we could build the shipping container wall in a couple of days. We'd create our own fortress to keep the Carriers out. No more sleeping with one eye open each night. What do you think? Will the three of you join us?' asked Harry.

Mark looked at Penny and Georgie. Both looked torn. 'Thanks for the offer, Harry. It's tempting, but I think we need to have a private chat first. Give us ten minutes, ok?'

Mark, Penny and Georgie walked away to the rear most aisle for privacy. Mark spoke first. 'What do you reckon? They sound like they've thought it out pretty well. Can your parents' place match theirs for strength of defence?' he asked Georgie. She shook her head.

'I don't think so. It's got a good line of sight to see anyone approaching, but the fences are only waist height, built to keep sheep in, not stop a mob of Carriers,' Georgie said.

'He's a doctor too, with emergency department supplies and medicines on hand. That could be just as important for survival as weapons and fences,' added Penny. 'I think we should take the offer. If it doesn't work out, we just leave.'

'I'm inclined to agree,' Mark said. 'Georgie? What's your call?'

Georgie walked back to the end of the aisle, looking towards Harry and Steph who were now quietly grabbing a last few items into their trolleys. 'Ok. Let's do it. Can we agree that this is only a stepping stone towards something else though?'

'What do you mean?' asked Mark.

'We still need to find out how the infection is spreading across the country, and what the government's doing. If there is somewhere free of Carriers, surely we should be heading there?'

'No argument from me,' Mark said. Penny nodded her agreement.

The trio walked back to the supermarket entrance where Harry and Steph now waited with their trolleys.

'So, what's the decision?'

'You got a deal,' answered Georgie, holding out her hand. Harry and Steph both smiled, shaking each of their new members' hands in turn. Things were looking up. Harry grabbed hold of a trolley handle and made for the cars to start loading the food. The rest followed close behind. Time was moving, and there was still plenty to achieve.

CHAPTER TWENTY-NINE

Mark walked slowly around the farmhouse's veranda, looking out at the surrounding paddocks and land features. Harry's appraisal of the place had been honest, but he lacked the eye of an engineer to identify key problems in his suggested use of shipping containers to build a perimeter barrier. He could do it, there was no question that it was a feasible plan. It was just going to be a little more difficult than carting the containers up and dumping them in a square. The farmhouse sat on a slight incline, meaning that the top of the containers would sit on an angle making their top a dangerous structure to fight upon when the need came, and that day would surely come. It was only a matter of time. He would have to dig out footings for each of the containers, providing a level surface on which to dump them.

The equipment yard held the required digging equipment. Mark came to a halt and shoved his fists deep into his jeans pockets as he stared towards the highway and heavy machinery yard. He'd built similar fortifications in Afghanistan with the Americans as they pushed into Taliban-held territory. Their building blocks had been slightly different, wire cages lined with thick cotton that they filled with rubble and sand, but the concept was the same. The makeshift forts could be built extremely quickly. In this case, he thought he could have it up within a few days. Two days to dig the footings, then one more to cart the containers up. They would just have to hope they were far away enough from town that each Carrier stumbling through Milton didn't get drawn straight to them. It was a gamble they'd have to take.

'What do you think? Still interested in joining us?' asked Harry.

'Yeah, I'll get it done. It'll just take a little longer than expected. All the noise is going to drag any Carrier in hearing distance on to us though,' warned Mark.

'I'd rather take that risk now than when we have a swarm of those bastards move through town.'

'True. Your current fence should make it easier to manage small numbers of the bastards. We'll need to come to an agreement on how we take out any dead fuck that stumbles our way. How about we head in and make a plan of attack?'

Tomorrow would see the real work begin.

* * *

Mark had made good progress gouging a strip of soil from the incline to create a flat base for the shipping containers. Based on speed, he'd chosen a Bobcat skid-steer loader/excavator from the equipment yard. It might not have been ideal for the job, but it moved fast. A level base was now prepared at the front and sides of the property, only the rear platform needed completion. After a quick tutorial, Mark had passed over the bobcat to Harry to complete the job while he started to move the first of the shipping containers into position.

Steph and Penny were creating an inventory of everything at hand on the property, a list of all equipment, tools, materials, food and their location. On completion of the barrier protection about the farmhouse, the next item on the agenda for the team would be scouting for required supplies and materials, but first they needed to have a clear idea of what was already on site.

Steph flinched as a high-pitched whistle sounded from the lookout on the roof. She ran out of the shed towards the house, picking up her new weapon from where it stood propped against the doorframe as she went. It was her turn to dispose of the latest ghoul attacking their property. She looked up to Georgie sitting on the apex of the corrugated iron roof. Georgie held up one finger, indicating number of approaching Carriers, then pointed towards the western fence line. The noise created by the heavy machinery had proved a bigger draw card than they had planned for.

The prevalence of the infection in Milton was only beginning, and yet, they'd had to deal with between five and ten lurching corpses per day. Taking turns, each of the group aside from Mark, had completed shifts upon the farmhouse roof as a sentinel, watching for approaching danger. Mark's value as an earthmover had trumped his need to gain a sore arse sitting on the roof.

Initially, when a Carrier had been sighted, everyone had downed tools and approached the threat as a group. The barbed wire fence had proved an effective barrier, allowing relative safety as long as they stayed out of arms reach. Soon, their strategy changed to allow continuous work on the main barrier. For attacks by lone Carriers, only a pair was sent to meet the walking corpse at the fence line; one to engage the enemy, the other as back-up if anything went wrong. The 0.22 was used on each occasion for a close-range headshot, saving the Austeyr ammunition for a later date. They left the bodies where they fell, delaying disposal until the barrier work was completed.

The previous night, Penny had raised a concern about their small ammunition supply. She wanted bullets to be conserved for situations of higher threat, such as the feared confrontation by a Sydney-style swarm of the Infected. The group had spent the next hour discussing possible alternatives that would provide the greatest degree of safety.

Steph now held the prototype of their collective creativity. The end had been removed from a long-handled pick and a hole drilled into the wood to snuggly fit the width of an M9 bayonet handle, three of which Mark had acquired from the Sydney University Regiment weapons store. A loop of metal at the base of the blade served as a fastening point to the end of the pick handle with a washer and screw. Mark had then wound fencing wire around the outside of the shaft housing the bayonet handle, to prevent it from splitting. They had created a mean, short-handled stabbing spear, strong enough to puncture a skull from short range.

Mark had trialled it earlier in the morning with good effect.

Now it was her turn.

Steph gripped the handle tightly in damp hands, concentrating on slow deep breaths to distract herself from what was about to happen. Penny was her back-up, ready with the loaded 0.22 rifle. Neither said anything to the other as they headed towards the western fence. There wasn't much point in fake assurances, it would either go well, or it wouldn't.

Calf-height grass in the paddock, sodden from rain during the night soaked through Steph's jeans and runners within twenty metres. The sky above was clear and brittle with mid-winter cold. Plumes of steam burst forth from each woman's mouth with every breath and despite the freezing temperature, a trickle of nervous sweat oozed from Steph's armpits. She sought to distract herself from what was about to happen. It wasn't her first killing duty, far from it. The execution had become easier as practice grew; however, the anticipation became harder as personal experience replaced imagination.

Mark was unloading the first container at the front of the house. She'd found her eyes drawn to him often over the past days when she thought no one else was looking. Not exactly ideal timing with what was happening, and also, there seemed to be some sort of history between him and Georgie that she was yet to clarify. Reluctantly, Steph drew her focus back to the task at hand.

A woman carrying the infection had tangled herself upon the fence as her stunted brain drove her towards the sound of the machinery. Wicked spikes of sharpened wire had torn long rents through her t-shirt, and ribbons of dry brown flesh hung free of her neck, breasts and arms. One eye was punctured, a grotesque, dried jelly smeared down her cheek from the deflated globe. Suddenly the Carrier noted their arrival. Her head swung around, the remaining bloodshot eye fixing on Steph as she waded forward through the grass. The ghoul's efforts to cross the wire re-doubled, feet stamping up and down, arms flailing. One foot caught purchase on a loop of wire half way up the fence, propelling the body upwards to rip free and topple into Penny and Steph's side of the paddock. It landed face down, before rising like a drunk to stand.

Instead of being afraid, Steph found her dominant emotion to be anger; anger that this creature sought to invade the safe space they were creating to spread nothing but terror and disease. She strode forward to meet it, weapon raised.

'Screw this, I'll shoot it. Save the spear for the next one,' Penny said from behind her shoulder.

'Let me try first, Pen,' muttered Steph through gritted teeth.

The haft of the makeshift spear felt reassuringly heavy as she took a double-handed grip. The creature started forward, letting out a snarl of rage. Thoughts of her pre-rehearsed strategy of a thrust into the eye or under the chin evaporated. She swung her weapon in a vicious arc, slicing the bayonet blade like a long-handled sword through the middle of the corpse's neck. The point of the knife nicked the vertebrae at the back, before carrying on through in a clean sweep to burst out the other side. The head lolled to the side, hanging backwards over its shoulder, held only in place by the dried sinew between the cervical vertebrae of the spine. Over balanced by the wound and displaced head, the ghoul fell backwards, arms and legs now out of control of the infection-ravaged brain.

Steph moved closer, standing over the Carrier's body to look down at the one part still functioning, the head. The remaining eye stared unblinking at her, lips pulled back in a voiceless snarl as the teeth snapped impotently. Steph slid the bayonet point between its teeth, then leant down hard onto the base of the pick handle, driving the knife down and through the brain stem, into the grass beneath.

The Carrier's features slackened as its brain was destroyed, the mouth closing about the blade as the jaw muscles relaxed. Steph braced her boot against the forehead and pulled the long knife free, causing the lips to pucker upwards with the blade's movement in an obscene kiss.

Stepping back from the corpse, the adrenaline that had coursed through her veins moments prior washed away, leaving her feeling strangely lightheaded, shaky and unbelievably tired. She stabbed the point of her makeshift spear into the turf and squatted before her knees unhinged against her will. Steph felt a reassuring hand grip her shoulder, and looked up to find Penny standing at her side, staring down at her with an expression of awe.

'That was amazing. When it starts hitting the fan for real, I want you by my side... Just saying,' she said, before offering a hand to help Steph back to her feet.

Steph felt an unwitting grin kink one side of her mouth at the praise. She was surviving. It was unnerving just how quickly this new demented version of the world was becoming an accepted reality. Because what else could you do? Rolling over and giving up wasn't an option. She accepted Penny's hand, and stood once more, looking over at Mark's progress as he set down the second container at the front of the property. Another day and at this rate, they would have a secure fortress to sleep within. Steph shifted focus back to the motionless corpse she had created. She had no desire to bury it, but leaving it here on their side of the fence just didn't seem right.

'Shall we push that thing back through the wire?'

Each woman grabbed a leg and pulled the body back to the fence line. Penny held up the bottom rung of wire while Steph rolled the corpse back under to the other side. Standing, she wrenched her spear free of the grass again and searched the perimeter fence for any other threat. While the Carriers attacked in small numbers, Steph knew they would manage. But that wouldn't last forever; eventually they'd be hit hard. She glanced back at the start of the container wall, and not for the first time, prayed it would be enough to hold a swarm at bay.

CHAPTER THIRTY

Mark climbed a wooden ladder, another item extracted from the recesses of the farm shed, each rung smooth with a faint oily sensation from half-a-century's worth of use. The end of the ladder was securely fastened to a container in the front wall that now encircled the farmhouse. They had actually done it, had turned Harry's vision into a reality to keep them safe from the infected madness that had turned the east coast into a place of slaughter and horror.

Stepping off the ladder onto the container roof, he turned in a slow circle, inspecting the curtain-wall of shipping containers. Three long containers made up the majority of the front wall. They had found one container with lockable doors at either end, and wider than usual that could accommodate the passage of the Pathfinder easily. This container had been incorporated into the wall as a double-ended gateway for vehicles to enter and exit. The slight incline of the slope surrounding the house meant Mark had not had much earth to move to achieve a flat base for the sidewalls, consisting of three long containers, each rising two feet higher than the previous as they marched up the slope. The back wall mirrored the front in construction to gain a uniform width. The encircling wall left roughly eight metres of space to each side of the house, while the tool shed's rear wall only just fit within by a hand's breadth.

Mark had to admit, he was quietly proud of what they had achieved in a short timeframe, and while under intermittent attack by Carriers. He was the only professional soldier amongst them, and yet each of the team had approached their respective turns to dispatch the stumbling Carriers on the fence line with a grim acceptance. There had been surprisingly little talk about their respective experiences of guard duty, aside from focused discussion that passed on techniques and tips learnt in killing the ghouls. It was as though an unwritten rule now existed amongst them, to not talk of their fear, as if to voice the terrors that each held locked down, might release them to shred self-control and sanity.

The metal roof was greasy from the light mist that had fallen during the afternoon, making the surface treacherous under foot. Some sort of new surface that boots could grip upon would need to be attached to the roof, otherwise the roof itself would become a liability during a fight. It was only one of numerous issues that needed to be solved over the coming days. Somehow, they had to enable their complex to be defended against low numbers without wasting the small amount of ammunition left.

He decided to park the thought for the moment and allow himself a small moment to just appreciate what had been achieved so far. Mark found a patch of metal that had dried in the late afternoon sun and sat down, letting his legs from the knee down hang over the outer edge of the wall. The farmhouse sat to the east of the highway, facing back into the setting sun. Although light clouds obscured it, a light warmth still reached Mark's face as he sat. He heard a light creaking from the wood of the ladder behind him as someone else climbed upward.

Mark looked back over his shoulder to find Steph's head rise above the roof, teeth biting on a corner of bottom lip in concentration as she climbed over the edge. As her gaze met Mark's, a smile lit up her face that Mark couldn't help but answer. She looked away, turning on the spot to look at the completed barricade.

'You did an awesome job with the wall, Mark. There's no way Harry and I would have got it done in this way, or as fast.'

'Thanks, but don't throw too many compliments my way. It was a team effort. Without you guys keeping the Infected outside the fence line, I couldn't have kept working,' he replied, shrugging off the praise.

'Do you mind having some company? This is the first bit of calm we've had in the weather all day, and it looks like you had a prime spot up here to enjoy it.'

'Nah, make yourself at home.'

Steph joined him on the edge of the container, her thigh brushing past his as she sat down and made herself comfortable. Mark found himself hyper aware of each accidental touch between them, in a way he hadn't been since first dating Georgie. She'd been a welcome distraction from the frosty state of play he'd endured from his ex since their argument on the boat.

They both sat in silence looking out across the green expanse bisected by the highway for a few minutes, comfortable in each other's company.

Steph broke the quiet with a question. 'You guys gave us a bit of history when we met in the supermarket, but I'm still putting the dots together. What happened to Penny? I know she was a cop, but she hasn't mentioned family once since getting here, and there's a sadness in her eyes that doesn't move when she tries to smile.' She paused, and there was weight in it. 'They died, didn't they?'

Mark confirmed with a nod. 'She lost a husband and son, killed at home before we could reach them from the University. She blames herself.'

'That's awful.'

'If it hadn't been for Penny though, Georgie and I would have gone to the evacuation attempt at the SCG, so she's saved our lives a few times. She's up and moving and that's what matters. I reckon she's mentally tougher than she's willing to give herself credit for,' he said.

'What about the other two of you?'

'What do you mean?' Mark said somewhat evasively.

'Are you two a couple?' she asked, looking away to the north and avoiding his gaze.

'You get straight to the point, eh?'

'Sorry' said Steph, wincing slightly. 'I'm just trying to understand everyone's background a little better.'

Mark sighed. 'It's all right. Look, we used to be. She broke it off though, just after I got back from deployment when this whole thing started. So I guess, the answer to your question is no.'

'If you're not a couple, why are you both still together through this?'

'Just because she ended it, doesn't mean I don't care about her and want to ensure she's safe.' He paused before adding, 'She's moved on in her mind though, so that's it I guess.'

A small smile brightened Steph's face before she changed the topic. 'What's your plans from here? We're safe for the moment, but it's not like we can live here forever.'

A shout from behind had them both turn before Mark could answer. Harry was standing on the front porch, waving at them to come down.

'Penny's found a radio frequency that the government's broadcasting on. There's a loop of new information playing if you want to come in to hear,' he yelled up to them.

As the pair climbed down the ladder and walked back to the house, Mark saw Georgie for the first time, leaning against one of the poles on the veranda watching him, her brow creased. Mark ignored her and went inside to hear the report. She had made her position on their relationship clear, and he'd be damned if he was going to pander to every change in mood from here on in.

Penny was hunched over an old radio in the corner of the living room, making fine adjustments to achieve a clearer audio. Satisfied she had the best lock on the station possible, she turned up the volume and moved back to sit on a couch out of the way.

Mark, Georgie and Harry filed in behind Steph, each finding a spot to sit. A light crackle of static was all they could hear over the speaker. Mark raised an eyebrow in silent question to Penny.

'Don't worry it'll start off again in a moment. A speech has been looping every couple of minutes. Just be patient,' she said. Mark sighed and settled himself back into the armchair he'd taken and waited.

An articulate voice suddenly boomed into the room. Penny darted across to the radio, dialling down the volume to a reasonable level.

'If you are listening to this emergency broadcast, I congratulate you. To make it this far, you have already proved that you are a survivor, someone who will be crucial in the upcoming fight to regain our country. I'm General David Black, Chief of the Australian Defence Force. I'm here to assure you, that all is not lost. You have not been abandoned. Pockets of resistance exist in each state, employing successful local strategies to repel Carriers. I do, however, provide sobering news. We have suffered significant setbacks, with infestations in all major cities of Queensland, New South Wales, Victoria, the ACT, and South Australia. The federal government has relocated to Tasmania, from where a strategy will be enacted to reclaim lost territory from the swarms of Infected blighting our land. To date we have been successful in preventing transmission of the virus across Bass Strait to Tasmania.

'As I speak, bases of operation are being set up in each state to where survivors will be able to retreat. I can assure you that we have learnt hard lessons from previous evacuation attempts, and the losses previously experienced in each state capital will not be repeated. Once these evacuation points are ready to accept civilians, notice will be provided. I encourage you to check this radio frequency over the coming days, as news will be updated as changes come to hand. So, until next we speak; stay safe, and if you can't – fight hard.'

The radio returned to static once more. Harry walked across and flicked a switch to silence the speakers. 'I suppose we should take some positives from that,' he said. 'Although I'd have to say I was hoping that more of the country was left standing than just bloody Tasmania.'

'Where do you think they'll set up the evacuation centres?' Penny asked. 'They'd want to have a better plan than last time for me to trust them again.'

'I guess we wait and hear on the next report. But after seeing their attempts at the SCG and Port Botany – I won't be trusting anything near a large population centre, that's for goddamn sure,' Mark said.

There was a rumble of agreement through the room. A large gurgle echoed across the room from Harry's belly, breaking the remaining tension.

'My stomach's obviously hungry. Who else wants to raid the pantry?' said Harry, getting up and heading towards the kitchen, effectively putting on hold any further discussion on the topic.

Chapter Thirty-One

The day brought unexpectedly balmy weather for a mid-winter's day. A dry wind through the night had dried the grass in front of the house and blown the sky free of clouds, allowing the mild winter sun to take the edge off the cool morning. Mark stood on the grass providing a tutorial on hand-to-hand combat to his housemates. The latest lesson had left their weapons behind, focusing squarely upon methods of escape from a Carrier's grip. Mark demonstrated one simple technique of breaking a handgrip upon the wrist, then they each paired off to replicate the move.

During the construction, each member had gained experience killing those infected with the virus. Practice had demonstrated that a thin blade or stiletto was effective through the eye. Wider blades became jammed in the socket creating difficulties in removal from an actively biting head. Medium width blades of reasonable length proved most useful in a thrust upwards from under the chin into the brain, while heavier weapons such as a machete, axe, or mason's hammer, chopped through the weakest section of skull with relative ease at the temporal bone.

Each person through practice had found affinity with a particular weapon. For Mark, the Gladius sword had become an extension of his own arm; Penny felt most in control whilst dealing out punishment with the long-handled mason's hammer; Steph and Harry demonstrated considerable dexterity with their improvised bayonet tipped spear; while Georgie achieved uncanny accuracy with an altered hay fork. Mark had sawn off the two outer prongs of the fork, leaving the centre spike intact and hammered straight. In effect, the long-handled tool had been transformed into a functional medieval pike, capable of dispatching a Carrier while staying out of arm's reach.

Throughout construction of the wall, their evenings had been spent creating a small arsenal of hand-held weapons out of pre-existing items on the farm. Mark had proposed creating the larger store of weapons to have replacements on hand for any breakages, and spares that could be used by people taking refuge within their barricade. A rack to store the weapons now sat along the corridor inside the front door. Light reflected occasionally from the array of steel-headed implements through the open doorway, creating a ripple of light across the housemates as they trained. Mark had also made a crate of Molotov cocktails, however these were stored in a cupboard on top of the wall. Harry had found fifteen old wine bottles under the house, the contents of which had long ago turned to vinegar. Once emptied, Mark filled each with petrol. A cotton wick was held in place by a cork stopper. Beside this crate of improvised fire bombs was a jar of kerosene to dip the wick in before use. In practice, once the wick was lit, the bottle was thrown. On impact, the glass smashed causing the subsequent cloud of petrol droplets and vapour to explode in flame.

At the end of the training session, the group headed inside. Harry flicked on the kettle and began putting teabags in mugs for everyone. The girls had pulled up a seat each at the kitchen table, while Mark was leaning against the doorframe, where he cleared his throat to speak.

'Hey Steph, did you find it slippery up on the container roof last night?'

'The rusted sections on the metal were fine, but yeah, the majority where the metal's painted was pretty greasy underfoot. Why?' she asked.

'Well, if we get attacked, that's the only place that we can fight from at the moment. I'm worried that it wouldn't take much for one of us to slip off the roof. If we land on the other side – we'd be torn to shreds. The other problem is, the only weapon I see being any good from the top of the containers is a gun – and we've only got a very limited stock of ammunition. If you stab down from above at the moment, we're only able to hit the top of the skull, where it's strongest. We might get lucky, but I reckon nine times out of ten, the blade will slip to the side and fail to penetrate. That means we need a spot on the ground where we can still use our hand-held weapons,' Mark said.

'I take it you've thought of a couple of solutions?' Harry said.

'I've got a few, but we'd be better to bounce them off each other before we commit to the work required. One of the best solutions is yours by the way, mate.'

'Which is...?' queried Harry, one eyebrow raised.

'Steph told me about it the other day. Digging traps to catch the Infected before they even get to the wall.'

'Can you fill us in a little more on it, we still haven't heard about it,' interrupted Penny.

'Sorry, you dig a deep hole, say ten-foot-deep that a grown man couldn't climb out of without help, then place a speaker in the bottom to attract the Infected. We've all seen them, when it comes to getting a fresh meal – they'd walk straight over the edge of the pit to investigate the sound, and then they're stuck. Spray a bit of petrol, toss a match, then its job done. We wouldn't even have to get them out. If the pit fills up, we just fill it in and dig another. Pure brilliance, Harry. It'll be a lifesaver in the advent of a swarm hitting us,' Mark said.

Harry looked a little embarrassed at the attention. 'Common sense, I thought. Any option that means I can stay at a distance from those bastards is worth trialling in my opinion. What's your idea to meet them on ground height while keeping us safe?'

'I want to take a heavy-duty angle grinder to the front of the containers,' started Mark.

'And what, weaken the structure that you just spent over a week installing?' interrupted Georgie with a snort.

Mark looked at her with a deadpan gaze and drawled, 'Yes, Georgie. I want to cut a big hole so the Infected can come through more easily.' He let the sarcasm drop. 'No, I want to cut a few strips of metal away at roughly head height on the exterior of the containers. They've all got those small side doors that we can enter via, and lock again when needed. If we take out a hands width of metal, it'll be enough for us to stand in the interior of the container, and stab through the gap into their skulls, but not enough for them to reach through and grab hold of us easily. That way, we can save bullets for a real emergency.'

'That should be easily enough done, I guess,' Penny said with a thoughtful expression on her face. 'And the roof of the containers. We still need to make that space useable. Can we rig some sort of waist high scaffold or something on the front edge?'

'No reason we can't bolt some star pickets at intervals and string fencing wire under tension between them,' suggested Harry. 'There's still a massive pile of them at the back of the shed.'

'That's perfect. If there's any left over, we should sink the rest at angles in the turf out front. Make a series of obstacles that might break them up a bit and hopefully impale a few in the process,' Mark said. 'I don't know about making a grip surface for the top though. I was thinking of attaching hessian sacks or something, but we haven't got any. Any other ideas?'

Steph piped up, 'I saw cans of spray adhesive when Penny and I were doing the inventory. Could that be sprayed on the metal, then swept over with dirt? Once it's dried in place, it should be like sandpaper that our boots could grip on.'

Georgie left the room for a moment, then reappeared with a piece of paper and pencil.

'Let's get a plan written down then on how we're going to get this all done, and in what order. If you're starting again with the heavy machinery, Carriers are going to be attracted here once more. Our guard details and sentry will have to kick off again.' She paused, as if deciding about whether to bring up a new line of conversation, before continuing. 'And while we're at it, we need to sort out a roster about simple shit like cleaning, washing and getting food before it gets out of control. I've already done a couple of loads of washing, but I'll be damned if I'm going to be stuck being a maid. If me and Steph are on the front line with those Infected monsters, you guys can do your fair share of mundane bloody cleaning!' she sighed. 'I know we've got bigger fish to fry, but that's the kind of shit that pisses off people in the long run when they share a house, yeah?'

Harry and Mark were both stifling a smile. Harry spoke up first, 'No worries, Georgie. Happy to do it. Actually, I reckon it would weird me out a little having someone else do my washing after all these years living as a bachelor. I normally get down to my last pair of jocks and shirt before I can be arsed doing it though.'

'Yep, all good. I expected to be doing that stuff as well anyway. Sorry, I guess I've just had my head focused on the building projects. How much food have we got left, Harry?' asked Mark.

Harry got up and opened a few cupboard doors about the kitchen. The numbers of cans had diminished somewhat over the past week. 'Less than I expected, we'll have to start rationing stocks a little better unless we can find a steady food source. We'll need another food run by the time the new construction works are finished.'

'I wouldn't mind heading up to my parents' place soon,' Georgie said. 'I can clear out their pantry and they've got a chest freezer that's usually packed with meat.'

Mark felt his mouth start to water at the thought of a flame-grilled steak after the taste deficient canned food they'd been eating.

'Dad's also got a few rifles that we could take as well. Mark and I can take the Outback over once the work's done here and pack everything of use.'

Mark did a slight double take, hearing that Georgie wanted to spend time in his company. 'We can? Ah ok, sure. No worries. Anyway, first things first – who wants to do what this arvo? We've still got six hours of daylight left.'

CHAPTER THIRTY-TWO

Four days later, Mark and Georgie climbed into the Subaru. Penny swung open the far end of the wide shipping container installed as a gate. Mark turned the key, bringing the motor to life, then drove through the narrow confine, metal creaking below until they re-emerged into the winter sun on the outside of the barricade. He braked on reaching the long driveway to look back on the complex that they had created. It still jarred the mind, seeing their creation within the Australian rural setting. Before, the square of shipping containers had looked merely odd. Now however, their defences couldn't be mistaken for anything other than a fort.

The makeshift fence of bolted star pickets and wire about the top of the containers, transformed the roof into a battlement walkway. Flood lights were attached to each corner of the wall, facing outwards, allowing illumination in case of night attack. Hundreds of star pickets and roughly-hewn stakes were hammered into the preceding three metres of ground to the wall, sharp points facing outwards. And yet, it was the simple holes cut at head height in the outer wall of the containers that gave Mark the creeps. Each window appeared pitch black from the outside, and it took little for the imagination to picture a watching sniper, their rifle tracking his head with every movement.

Mark let his foot off the brake and started down the gravel drive to the highway. At the bottom of the paddock, he passed the series of pits that he had dug with the help of an excavator from the equipment yard. A 3.5 tonne Caterpillar excavator had made light work of the earth-moving exercise, enabling him to drop three pits with sheer edges, twelve feet into the ground in the space of one morning's work. The speakers had proved more difficult to achieve a workable option. In the end, he'd stripped wiring from throughout the equipment yard's office and two of the bedrooms in the house. Spliced together, there had been just enough to link a rudimentary switch to a tape recorder and speaker housed in water-tight containers in each pit. A rope with knots tied at regular spaces for hand holds, hung into each pit as a basic means for entry and exit to maintain the speaker set up.

Georgie and Steph had obliged the boys by making the tapes to be played. When Mark had initially heard the recording, his stomach had turned. Both girls had released a blood chilling series of screams that sounded like a poor soul being torn apart. Unfortunately, each had firsthand experience now, and knew just what that level of agony, terror and despair sounded like.

The highway was empty of movement as Mark pulled out to the left, heading back towards Sydney and away from Milton. Georgie's property was only a twenty-minute drive away, up a single lane road that exited from the Princes Highway further along. Both sat in silence between her directions. Georgie fidgeted in her seat, turning frequently to look behind them for signs of Carriers drawn by the car's noise. As Mark turned off the highway to follow a narrow road to the west, Georgie spoke up.

'You and Steph seem to be hitting it off over the last couple of weeks,' she said, looking away from Mark and out her window.

'Yeah, I'm not quite sure what you're talking about, Georgie.'

'Come on, Mark. You're not blind or stupid. She's a good-looking girl, and she's obviously sweet on you.'

'Well, nothing's happened, if that's what you're asking. And if it had done, you've already made it clear that you'd finished with me, so I kind of fail to see where you're going with this,' he replied, a level or irritation entering his voice.

'Fair enough. As you said, you're a free man and all. I wouldn't be the first person to realise what they wanted after it was lost though,' said Georgie quietly.

'You realised what?' asked Mark, his attention taken away from the road by the last sentence.

'Nothing,' replied Georgie with a sigh. 'Take a right onto that road – we're here.'

Mark had to brake heavily to avoid overshooting the entrance. He pulled to a halt and Georgie jumped out of the passenger door to swing open the gate across the driveway. Mark drove through, then waited for her to close the gate once more and climb back in. He almost launched back into their conversation, but pulled himself up short. He'd blown it the last time he'd tried to force the issue, better to let her take the lead on this round.

Her parents' farm lay on the edge of the MacDonald state forest, consisting of sixty acres of mixed paddock and native bush. Mark followed the gravel road deeper into the property. Paddocks of grass lay to either side of the drive, dotted with heavily-fleeced merino sheep awaiting a spring shearing. Two hundred metres in, they crossed a simple bridge constructed from railway sleepers over a creek. Mark's eyes followed its path to the right, seeing where the creek had been dammed to provide an accessible water source for the sheep. Georgie tracked his gaze to the dam and her features softened at the sight.

'My dad taught me to fish in that dam when I was a kid. He filled it with trout especially for us. I used to love lying back in the grass at the edge, not really caring if I caught anything or not. I bet there's some monster sized rainbow trout in there nowadays for anyone keen.'

'I didn't know you could fish,' said Mark with mild surprise.

'There's a lot you don't know about me, Mark,' she said. 'Too much time away was the problem – not that we have that hassle anymore.'

The road wound up a slope to the left, passing through a band of eucalypts before opening out once more. And then there it was. The house was beautiful; no wonder Georgie had always talked of it so fondly. As one of the earlier homesteads in the area, the exterior walls consisted of sandstone that had weathered over the intervening century, softening angles and corners. The single-level house was roofed with silver corrugated iron that thundered during a downpour, making the whole building come alive with the noise of the rain. A small garden extended from the front of the building, consisting of petite box hedges enclosing a rectangle with an ancient Frangipani tree as a centre feature. The tree extended naked silver branches to the sky, all leaves dropped for the winter months. The gravel driveway terminated at the door of a three-car garage that stood off to the left of the house as a separate building.

Georgie got out and typed a code into an electronic pad, causing the door to roll upwards. Mark parked the car and cut the engine, then Georgie quickly closed the door again behind the vehicle. Along the back wall of the garage were numerous inbuilt cupboards and he spotted a chest freezer at the far-left corner. A door was sited at the right, leading to the back of the house. He exited the car, walked outside and silently did a lap of the house looking for any danger, finishing at the front. Georgie's light footsteps crunched on the gravel behind him and he turned to acknowledge her.

'This place is amazing. Is it heritage listed?'

'Yeah, although my dad reckons that's more of a curse than benefit. It's been in the family for generations.'

'I can see why you love the place,' he said. Something caught his eye down the slope in the distance, a moving figure closing in on an unaware sheep. 'Shall we head inside?' he added, ushering Georgie towards the front door quickly. She turned to see what threat had prompted his sudden haste as a high-pitched animal scream emanated from the lower paddock. They both looked back, seeing a man rise from the grass where the sheep had kicked him. The animal in question bolted away, blood streaming from a neck wound. The Carrier merely stumbled onwards, giving up on its prey to continue aimlessly forward.

Georgie hurriedly lifted a plant pot at the side of the path, uncovering a key to unlock the door. Mark followed her into the front hallway. The house was musty from prolonged closure while her parents were away overseas. Georgie pulled close the blinds in each room, trying to prevent accidental attraction of any further Carriers by their movements in the house. Although the heritage listing had prevented her parents altering the outside facade of the house, the interior was a different matter. Modern fittings and cool white walls lightened the rooms. Georgie gave him a quick tour, past the open-plan kitchen and living areas, four bedrooms and study.

'Did you grow up here?' Mark asked.

'Until I was twelve, then my parents moved to Sydney. We still came here for school holidays, which was fine by me. The surf isn't that far away, I spent most summers down the road at Mollymook beach.'

'Sounds nice. So where's the stuff that we need to pack into the car?'

Georgie led him back to the garage and unlocked one of the rear cupboards to reveal a gun safe. She typed in a code and the door clicked open revealing three 0.22 rifles and ammunition. Mark pulled each out in turn, running through a quick inspection of the firearms.

'They're in pretty good condition. Did your dad use them much?'

'Only to knock off a few rabbits here and there,' she replied.

Mark rested them back into the rack for the moment and walked towards the chest freezer. 'Would your parents have left this on?' he asked.

'Worth a try. Mum usually pays one of the local butchers to slaughter and prepare a lamb once or twice a year.'

She joined him as he opened the lid, revealing a whole frozen side of lamb butchered into various cuts. Mark felt his mouth start to salivate at the thought of it cooked. Georgie pointed out a large esky perched on a high shelf.

'We can pack that full of meat to take back with us. I don't think anyone would complain at a change from canned ham and beans.'

Mark grinned as he reached up to retrieve it. 'Anything else in here worth taking back?'

Georgie showed him where a stash of tools and camping equipment were stored, then left him to start loading the car with what he thought was useful. She headed inside to look through the pantry for food worth taking and her bedroom for extra clothes.

After thirty minutes, Mark had the Outback packed. The camping gear had provided a bounty of survival equipment that would prove invaluable if they were forced to leave the farm. Just when he thought he was done, he'd stumbled across a compact diesel generator with two Jerry cans of fuel. The electricity was bound to fail, and having a backup power supply would be a welcome crutch. Mark heaved the unit into the luggage cage on the car's roof along with the Jerry cans.

The car now packed, he did another quick check around the outside of the house for any Carriers, then headed back inside to look for Georgie, entering the backdoor to the kitchen. Two milk crates of food stuffs were packed and waiting on an island bench. The house was warmer, a low background hum indicating that she had turned on the ducted heating. A shower was running in the bathroom. Mark leant forward and sniffed at his armpit, recoiling at the smell. He could really do with a wash himself and a clean change of clothes. The water turned off and five minutes later Georgie came into the room, with a large towel wrapped around her.

'Do you want a shower while we're here? The hot water's awesome! I didn't realise how bad I smelt until I picked up my clothes a second ago on getting out,' she said, her nose wrinkled in disgust at herself.

Mark accepted the offer. Georgie showed him to the bathroom, handed him a bath towel and left him to it. He shut the door and for ten minutes he managed to forget the possible threat of Carriers moving through the property, as hot water pounded the stress out of his shoulders. It took two washes of his scalp to remove the dirt in his hair, and his skin noticeably changed colour to a lighter tone by the time he was finished scrubbing. Stepping out the water, he felt somewhat lighter, like the water had succeeded in washing away a part of the heaviness he'd held in his chest for the past few weeks, along with the grime. Mark dried off, then leant to retrieve his jeans and shirt from the ground. They stunk. Bad. There was no way he could put them back on now after just getting clean. He rolled the clothes up in a ball, and propped them on the edge of the bath for the moment. Hopefully Georgie's dad or brother would have some clothes in their bedrooms that he could borrow for the meantime. Mark wrapped the towel around his waist and left the bathroom.

He walked out to the living room looking for her. The temperature had risen further, with barely a chill left in the air to raise any goosebumps on his arms. A single floorboard creaked behind him, giving away Georgie's approach. He turned, and found her leaning against the doorway into the kitchen, watching him.

She looked how Mark remembered her from before his last tour overseas, when she would spend the weekend padding about his Glebe flat procrastinating from study. She was barefoot in a pair of jeans. A Bonds singlet top hugged her torso and chest, accentuating her slender build. Her hair was pulled up behind her head in a simple bun, leaving her neck exposed. A light blush of colour pinked her cheeks as she stood biting one corner of her bottom lip, her left hand hidden behind her back as she unashamedly looked Mark up and down. She took her hand out from behind her back, displaying two opened bottles of beer.

'I thought maybe you might want to join me for a drink?' she said.

Mark, a little curious, moved forward to accept the bottle, only to have it pulled out of reach.

'It'll cost you, though,' Georgie said, a slight shake to her voice.

'And the price?' a smile started to tug at the corner of Mark's mouth, at the cheesy opening she had often joked with before demanding a kiss when they were together.

'Use your imagination, Mark.'

Mark stepped closer, placing a hand on her hip to gently draw her toward him as he leant down to kiss her. Georgie pressed herself against him in response, answering his kiss firmly. Mark's right hand lifted upwards to cup her breast, the nipple hardening under his palm as he kissed her neck, a light sigh escaping her lips as he reached her ear. Georgie pulled backwards, depositing the two bottles on the sideboard, and grabbed Mark's hand, tugging him toward her bedroom. The beers could wait.

Mark and Georgie were lying in bed, her head resting on his shoulder and hand on his chest where she had drifted off to sleep afterwards. Mark ran one finger lightly over her skin, from shoulder to waist down the side of her body, tracing the soft contours as he tried to burn the memory into his brain. He had no idea if this was a one off, if it was a sign she wanted him back, or if it was just stimulated by jealousy at her thought of Steph being interested. Either way, it had been lovely to have her back again, even just for a short afternoon, with the travesty of the outside world expelled temporarily.

He glanced at his watch, the afternoon was racing away. If they stayed much longer, the others would worry that something had gone wrong. He squeezed his arm lightly about her in a hug at his side. She blinked her eyes open.

'Crap, did I drift off? What's the time?' she said stifling a yawn.

'You've only been dozing for thirty or so minutes. We better head back though.'

'Do we have to?' Georgie said, snuggling further into his embrace.

'As much as I don't want to leave this bed – we've got to get going. I don't want to have to negotiate a bunch of Carriers on the way in the dark.'

'Yeah, well I don't want to meet any, full stop.'

They both wearily sat up, legs hanging over the edge of the bed. Georgie fished her jeans off the ground with one toe, then started to pull her clothes back on. Mark only had the towel still.

'Are there some bloke's clothes here that I could borrow?' he asked. 'As much as I don't want to dress up as your father, I reckon mine could walk off on their own, they stink so bad.'

'There's no chance of you getting back in my bed dressed as my dad, I'd vomit all over you,' Georgie laughed. 'Not that it's any better, but I'll see if my brother's left anything you could use in his cupboard.'

She returned with some jeans, t-shirts and jackets. 'Try these, something should probably fit.' Mark gratefully pulled on a pair of jeans, happily free balling for the moment. The shirts were a little big, but an old-school biker style leather jacket made up for it. Georgie had also grabbed a few items for Penny, taking a guess at her size.

They each grabbed a crate of the food Georgie had packed earlier on the way through the kitchen. Georgie did a last check around the house, switching off lights and heating, then locked the door behind herself, sad to be leaving again. Within five minutes, they were on their way back to Harry's farm.

CHAPTER THIRTY-THREE

Harry pulled into the driveway of the last house on their list. While Mark and Georgie had taken a trip to her parents' place for supplies, he and Penny had begun to make contact with the remaining neighbours in the surrounding few kilometres of land. Progress had been relatively quick initially, with most of the houses empty on arrival. On Penny's insistence, the group had agreed to offer sanctuary to any people nearby in the advent of a swarm moving through their area. The police officer in her still felt an innate need to fulfil a role in community protection, and Harry had been easily swayed. Mark had taken longer to come to the party. He had concerns regarding inviting an unknown variable into a situation that would prove taxing and dangerous enough on its own, however, he had eventually been convinced that added hands to fight would outweigh anything else in the circumstance of an all-out attack by the Infected, as long as any person bitten by a Carrier was refused entrance.

A front curtain twitched as they climbed out of the Pathfinder. Someone was home at the very least. The house was a brick veneer with a black-tiled roof. A large Cyprus pine reared up into the sky to the left of the building, dominating the scene as its canopy spread to a width almost as great as the house itself. They walked up a set of wooden steps to the front door. Penny took the lead in her police uniform, or what was left of it that could be laundered and mended. She raised her fist and rapped on the door sharply three times. Within moments, the door opened a crack, held in place by a short security chain. The face of a man in his early forties peered through the gap at his visitors.

'What do you want?' Although the man was trying to sound rough, his nervousness was evident as his voice cracked at the sentence's end.

'We're neighbours, living in the rental behind the machinery yard. I'm a new doctor at the Emergency Department,' Harry said.

'My name's Penny, I'm a police officer from Sydney, now living with him,' she said, indicating her companion, 'and two others. We thought it would be good to touch base with those around us to see if we could possibly help each other. Could we come inside?'

The door shut for a minute. A muffled discussion could be heard through the closed entrance, then the tinkling noise of the security chain being removed. The door swung wide and the man ushered the two of them quickly inside before locking up once more.

'There was none of those dead bastards out there with you?' he asked, while looking out from the edge of the curtain once more.

'No, just us. Two properties to the north is a different matter. That family's infected, although luckily they somehow locked themselves inside, so they shouldn't be any danger to you,' Harry said.

The man spun back around, looking at his wife whose face had gone deathly pale.

'Dammit. That's the Colemans. We talked to Danny, the father of that family not two days ago. He was heading into Milton to try and scavenge from the supermarket or other abandoned houses if need be. I told him he was stupid, that it was too risky. And I was right, wasn't I?' he said turning back to his wife, a strange look of triumph on his face. 'And then the idiot goes and infects his whole family. I always told you he was a fucking douche bag, Jan.'

'Maybe if you hadn't refused to join him, they'd all still be alive,' said the wife, a look of contempt on her face. 'He offered to find food for all of us, and you couldn't even face helping him. Now the whole family's dead. You're the idiot in this story, Rodger.'

'Fuck you, Jan. You're more worried about your bloody boyfriend down the road than me! How about "thank god you didn't go, you were right, it was too dangerous, Rodger." Maybe you'd be happier without me, eh? Well I'm still here and I'm not fucking going anywhere,' he said, moving towards his wife with his fist clenched.

Harry and Penny caught each other's eye as unbidden spectators to the dangerously escalating argument. A small girl, no older than nine years of age, timidly peeked out from behind her mother's waist, wide eyed at her parents' fight. Harry coughed into his hand, drawing attention back to them in an attempt to stall the fight. Both husband and wife stopped and visibly collected themselves. The wife forced a weak smile.

'Sorry about that, it's just that the Colemans are… were, close friends. Things seem to be only getting worse as time goes on.'

She paused, rubbing the palms of her hands down the sides of her t-shirt to straighten the fabric, or more likely dry sweating palms. Her husband, Rodger, had slumped into an armchair looking despondently into nothing. 'Would you both like a cup of tea?' Jan asked, trying to project an aura of normality over the stilted meeting.

'Thanks, but no,' answered Penny. 'We've only stopped by briefly to offer assistance to you if things become unsafe here.' She nudged Harry to get him to carry forward the conversation.

'We've managed to create a fortified position that should be able to repel any attack by large numbers of the Infected,' Harry said.

'Yeah, we saw,' replied Rodger sullenly. 'All that use of heavy machinery drew Carriers out of the woodwork. We had more than usual walk through our property heading your way, kept us locked inside for days.'

'Sorry about that,' answered Harry, somewhat annoyed. He was starting to regret seeking out this particular couple. 'But it was necessary to create a wall. And now we're offering you the chance to benefit from that work.'

Jan moved forward a little, her eyes widening a little in hope. 'Can our family move in behind the walls with you?' she asked hopefully.

'Unfortunately, we haven't got room to permanently take in a whole family. With regard to danger from the infection at present, I don't think it's necessary for you all to live there yet. However, if you see a large group of the Infected coming down the highway or through your property – make your way to us. We'll let you through the gates. The offer's conditional though.' He paused, looking at Rodger to try and assess how much of a liability he would be. He had no time for insecure bastards that preyed on their own family. 'If you come in, we expect your help in defending the walls. Also, if you've been bitten, you won't be given access.'

'That sounds fair, I guess,' answered Jan.

Harry made ready to leave, 'Thanks for offering the cup of tea earlier, but we better head off.' Harry started for the door, then stopped and turned back. 'One last thing; the Emergency Department's closed, but I've taken a limited stock of equipment to our farm. If you have any trauma or illness that isn't of the walking dead variety, come to me as well and I'll do what I can.' The last sentence he said directly to Jan, holding her gaze. 'If you start to feel unsafe, bring yourself and the girl to our place.'

'Ah, I'm not quite sure what you mean by that, but thanks,' answered Jan hesitantly. Harry turned back to the doorway and headed for his car. Penny followed, allowing Jan to walk her to the door. Rodger stayed behind in the living room, pointedly ignoring her as he continued to sulk after the altercation with his wife and then Harry. Penny took Jan gently by the elbow, getting her to step outside with her for a minute, closing the door gently behind.

'Is everything ok between the two of you?' Penny asked quietly. 'I've assisted in quite a few domestic violence cases as a police officer, and although I know these times would stress the strongest of relationships – something didn't quite seem right before. Are you and your daughter safe?'

Jan froze for a moment, glancing back over her shoulder to the living room as if searching for her husband's proximity to their conversation, 'He's all talk, mostly. Don't worry.'

'Well if that changes, come and see me,' said Penny, giving her hand a brief squeeze to reassure her. 'There's two more women at our house, and the men are solid characters that I'll vouch for. Your girl shouldn't have to see her mum be intimidated like that earlier scene.'

'I have to go,' said Jan, withdrawing her hand from Penny's grasp. She disappeared back through the entrance, shutting the door firmly behind. As Penny turned to walk back to the car, she felt eyes boring into her. Looking up, she saw Rodger glaring at her through a gap in the curtain. They had well and truly outstayed their welcome. Penny only hoped she hadn't made it even worse for the woman and child in the short term.

As the passenger door clicked shut, Harry slowly drove down the driveway, not waiting for Penny to fasten her seat belt. 'That guy was a real knob. I kind of hope that family doesn't have their own gun – they'd probably be safer without one.'

Penny nodded her agreement as she looked over her shoulder at the receding property.

Harry and Penny had been home for at least half an hour by the time Mark and Georgie drove up the long driveway. Penny jumped down from the veranda and unlocked the container door, allowing the Subaru through. Mark parked the car next to the house for ease of unloading, cut the engine and jumped out.

'We come bearing gifts!' said Mark with a fake British accent and theatrical flourish.

'I hope they're of the high calibre kind,' answered Harry dryly. Someone was clearly in a better mood than when they'd left.

'What I've got is better than rifles, although there are a few of those as well. We've got a whole side of lamb, butchered with precision.'

Harry was suddenly serious, 'Don't bullshit me, Mark. Have you really got some?'

'Take a look for yourself, mate,' answered Mark with a smile as he hoisted the esky up to the veranda decking. Harry opened the lid and let out a sigh of contentment. 'We might have to wait until tomorrow for a joint to thaw, but lunch is going to be awesome.' Harry picked up the esky and disappeared indoors, carting it to the kitchen and freezer. He returned moments later to help unpack the station wagon.

Georgie was at the back of the car, lifting out some of the smaller camping items to carry to the shed. Mark rested a hand unconsciously in a caress on her hip as she leant into the back, and Harry noted she returned the gesture at different points through the unpacking. The ice that had been in the air between the two had clearly melted.

Steph had come to help move some of the gear inside the house. After both Mark and Georgie walked off to the shed, Harry casually made comment to his cousin.

'I think you may have missed the boat on that one.'

'What do you mean?'

'Just that our estranged lovers seem to have made up again. You were a bit sweet on him, weren't you?'

'You're a doctor, not a bleedin' matchmaker. Stick to what you know, you twat,' she said, laughing off his comment. Harry let it drop.

The group congregated in the kitchen once the car had been unloaded. A lamb shoulder sat in the sink to defrost overnight, the rest having been loaded by Penny into the freezer. Georgie had brought back the dozen beers she'd found at her parents', and passed one into each person's eager hand. In unwitting tribute to a decades' worth of Victoria Bitter adverts, everyone silently enjoyed their first sip, savouring the flavour.

'Did you guys come across any Carriers when you were out?' asked Harry.

'Only one,' said Georgie. 'It was crossing the paddocks at my parents' place. We saw it attack one of the sheep, so looks like we might not be the only species on the menu.'

'Did you see what happened to the animal later? Did it catch the infection as well?' asked Steph.

'No, we went inside to keep out of sight. I didn't even really think of that as a possibility to tell the truth. It's bad enough having mobs of undead humans, I could do without animals turning on us as well,' said Georgie, looking disturbed at the thought.

'We didn't see any on the road, but one of the local farms has a house filled with Carriers. Their neighbours think the father returned home after being attacked, then slaughtered his own family once he died and reanimated,' said Harry. 'It's made me think – what are we going to do, if one of us is bitten?'

The group remained silent, nobody wanting to state the obvious. The only cure so far was a bullet to the brain.

Mark eventually spoke up. 'If I'm bitten, the last thing I want is to be responsible for the death of my friends. If I'm capable, I'll shoot myself. However, if not, I'd request that someone put a bullet in my brain.' Nobody answered him, each looking away. 'Think of it as euthanasia,' he suggested.

'I closed up the Emergency Department because the state was asking me to do the same thing. I'm not going to kill you, Mark. It's still early days; what if we find out that some people have a natural immunity, or that the wound wasn't severe enough to transfer the infection? I don't want your blood on my hands or in my nightmares, mate,' said Harry.

'If we leave it until the person's converted, it'll place the rest of the group in danger,' Mark said.

'Then confine them until we know for sure. We could use one of the containers, set up a bed and restraint point, then lock the person inside. If they become a Carrier, then we finish it humanely and with respect. Clean shot to the head and burial,' suggested Penny, gaining agreement by all present to the idea.

'What were you saying about wound severity and infection transfer, Harry?' asked Steph.

'I've just been tossing around some ideas in my head these last few days. One of the reports on TV stated the test subjects observed had experienced slower conversion if the bite wound was minor and not involving major vessels. When an artery or vein is pierced, the virus reaches the brain within minutes. If it hasn't damaged these larger vessels, the virus has to travel via the lymphatics system and nerves which is a slower route. My first patient with the disease had a bite like that on her forearm, and she made it all the way from Cairns to Sydney before dying. I can't help but wonder if amputation of the affected limb has been trialled to stop the infection reaching the brain,' theorised Harry.

'Just make sure I'm unconscious before you go sawing off my arm, ok?' joked Mark. 'But seriously, do you think that would work?'

'Probably not. If the bite was bad, I reckon it would be a waste of time. Here's hoping we don't have to find out, eh?' said Harry, wincing at the thought of removing a limb outside an operating theatre.

CHAPTER THIRTY-FOUR

Mark sat bolt upright in bed, his heart thudding in the pitch black of his bedroom. His sentry duty had finished an hour prior, when Penny had arrived for her four-hour shift through the small hours of the morning. He'd passed out within moments of hitting the pillow to a dreamless sleep. There it was again – a hammering on metal, coming from outside one of the shipping containers. Mark swung his legs out of bed, groped for his jacket and boots that he pulled on in a hurry.

He wasn't the only one awoken by the noise. The other bedroom doors were opening, with house members emerging in various stages of undress and exhaustion. Mark took a few quick steps to the front door, grabbed his sword and scabbard off the weapons rack before joining Penny on the veranda.

She was standing alert, rifle in hand. She looked back over her shoulder at Mark.

'What bloody took you so long? Someone's at the front gate. Here, take this,' she said, passing him the rifle and a torch. 'Can you get up top of the wall, take a look and find out what's happening? I'll be at the gate ready to let them in if all's ok.'

Mark nodded his agreement. After buckling his scabbard around his waist, he vaulted to the ground off the veranda and ran for the ladder up the side of the container. Taking two rungs at a time, he reached the top within seconds.

He now heard voices, urgently whispering back and forth, and the sound of a girl whimpering in pain. He crawled forward, keeping a low profile to prevent his body making a silhouette against the sky. Mark popped his head over the edge to find a twin-cab Triton Ute parked at the gate. In the half-light cast by a crescent moon, he made out a teenage boy leaning over a girl in the Ute's tray. A man and woman were standing at the shipping container gate. Mark turned on the torch, shining the beam into the faces of the man and woman below.

'Have any of you been bitten?' he asked.

The man answered in a hushed voice, 'No, I've got a girl with a gunshot wound to her leg. She needs help by the doctor here. Can we bring her inside?'

Mark hurried to the other side of the container, looking down at Penny.

'Open the gate Pen. Some kid's been hurt. I'll get Harry if you let them in.'

As Penny opened the gate, Mark slid down the ladder and jogged back to the house.

'Harry!' he yelled into the house. The doctor appeared within moments at the front door. 'We need your help, mate. A kid's been shot. Where do you want her?' he asked. Mark's face was tense, his breathing tight.

Harry took a deep breath. 'Is she infected?'

Mark shook his head, 'They denied a bite. I think it was an accident, but haven't got any details.'

'Bring her into the living room then. I'll start setting up.' Harry disappeared back inside without another word.

Mark ran across to the dark cavern where Penny had thrown open the container doors to the outside. Within moments he was at the Ute. Penny was speaking to the adults, trying to get a story. A teenage boy was crouched at the girl's side, and the kid looked up as Mark approached.

'She needs a doctor. Can we get inside now, please?' he asked urgently.

Mark climbed up onto the tray and squatted over the girl who was crying with distress. 'Where's the wound?' asked Mark. The boy pointed at her outer thigh where a dark patch of denim lay. 'Is that the only injury?'

As the boy nodded, Mark breathed a sigh of relief. At least there should be only soft tissue in the area of concern. He'd seen a US marine bleed out within minutes from a femoral artery bullet wound to the inner thigh in Afghanistan.

'Let's get you inside. I'm going to carry you in, do you think you can hold on to my shoulders if I lift you up?' he said to the girl, keeping his voice calm.

She nodded, biting her lip to try and remain quiet. He slid the girl forward to the edge of the tray and helped her to sit up. She placed an arm around his shoulder as Mark picked her up. He walked back quickly through the container to the house.

Harry was back out at the front, waiting. He jumped to the ground to help Mark lift her up to the veranda where Georgie and Steph pulled her onto the deck. Harry and Mark carried her to the living room, to where the girls had pulled the dining table as a treatment surface. A clean white sheet had been thrown over the top, giving an appearance of cleanliness.

The light in the living room seemed blinding in comparison to the night, causing the girl to squint and shield her eyes from the globe above. Georgie placed a pillow under the girl's head, trying to make her more comfortable. 'My name's Harry, I'm an emergency doctor. Is it all right if I check out your leg and see what needs to be done to fix it?'

The girl nodded in response. Harry started to cut up the seam of the jeans with a pair of trauma scissors. As he worked to expose the wound, he got the girl talking, finding out that she was a twelve year old named Erin. The boy accompanying her was her brother, Jai, sixteen, who remained at her side, a reassuring hand on her shoulder.

The thigh now exposed, Harry was able to examine the trauma. An entry wound was visible on the outer aspect of the mid-thigh. Approximately ten centimetres to the side was a small, hard lump – likely the bullet. On face value, it appeared that she had been extremely lucky, with the bullet tunnelling through the subcutaneous tissue before stopping. The blood and nerve supply to the leg appeared intact, as did her femur bone.

Harry decided to trial a simple operation to remove the bullet under local anaesthetic. He drew up a dose of midazolam, a sedative that he injected into her left thigh to make the girl more relaxed. Erin's features softened as her muscles released their stored tension and her eyelids drifted shut. Harry held her wrist, finger over her radial pulse as her breathing slowed to a comfortable rhythm in response to the drug's action as she slept.

The living room door opened a crack as Penny slipped inside, closing it quietly behind herself. She padded up to the table for a closer look at their newest charge.

'Is she ok?' Penny asked, concern evident in her voice.

'She's been pretty lucky. The bullet hasn't touched any important structures from what I can see so far,' Harry replied over his shoulder as he began to assemble the equipment needed for the procedure, opening packets of suture material, scalpel and saline water onto a sterile field. 'Wasn't that the couple we met yesterday? How did it happen?'

Penny nodded. 'Turns out he did have a rifle after all. Reckons it was an accident, that he shot the girl thinking she was a Carrier that had broken into his house. They've already left, didn't want to be out at night.'

'That's complete bullshit!' Jai said from the head of the table, where he remained next to his sister. 'He should have known we weren't infected.'

Harry looked at the teenager, who held his gaze defiantly. After meeting the man on the previous day, he was interested in hearing another side to the story. 'What happened then?' he asked.

'We were looking for food and thought the house was deserted like most places at the moment. I knocked on the back door and when there was no response, I smashed out a section of glass next to the lock and released the catch. We were in the kitchen going through the cupboards when the crazy bastard started screaming at us from the kitchen doorway to get out, waving a rifle at us. Before we could say anything, he pulled the trigger. The bullet hit the oven first, sparking against the metal before ricocheting into Erin's leg.'

'What happened then? Did he stop and try to help?' probed Harry.

'When Erin hit the deck screaming, he stopped and just stood there dumbly. Then his wife turned on the kitchen light. Blood was oozing out of Erin's thigh, she gave me a tea towel that I bunched up and pressed onto the wound to stop the bleeding. Eventually they decided to take us to you guys,' said Jai, his hands trembling slightly from a repeat surge of adrenaline as he relived the scene.

'It still sounds like it may have been a mistake, Jai. If he wanted to kill your sister, he could have shot again,' Penny said.

'If we were infected,' countered Jai, 'we wouldn't have been carefully searching the cupboards. He shot Erin because we were taking his food. The guy's a fucking idiot, if he'd answered the door when we knocked, it wouldn't have got to this,' said Jai.

'All right kid, I met the bloke yesterday and I agree with you that he's an idiot. But that doesn't change the fact I've still got to get the bullet out before your sister wakes up. Shall we crack on?'

The teenager nodded and sat back in the chair next to his sister.

Harry injected local anaesthetic at the bullet entry wound and into the skin over the top of the bullet. He sliced the skin with the scalpel, then cut down through the fat tissue until the bullet was exposed. Harry grasped the bullet, a small 0.22 round, with a pair of forceps and pulled it free. Steph shined a torch from above as he worked, helping him to view the wound. The bullet appeared to be intact, meaning there shouldn't be any other fragments left in the leg. One surface was flattened from hitting the stove, accounting for the shallow nature of the wound. Even a low calibre weapon such as a 0.22 rifle would usually inflict much greater damage at close range.

Harry pushed a small tweezer like pair of surgical forceps through the length of the bullet tract, searching for any piece of material that may have been pushed into the wound from her jeans. With a small snort of satisfaction, Harry found a tiny piece of crimson stained cotton deep within the wound. He flushed the bullet tract with a bag of saline in an attempt to wash away bacteria before loosely suturing the two wounds closed and wrapping the thigh in an absorbent dressing. If he had missed any foreign matter in the wound tract, there was still a chance it could become infected. Harry mixed up a prophylactic antibiotic dose, injecting the solution directly into a large vein in her arm as a bolus.

Once the operation and treatment were complete, the four adults each took a corner of the sheet, and carefully carried Erin into one of the bedrooms to sleep off the sedative. Jai stood at her side as she slept, now more comfortably rolled onto her good side.

Harry placed a hand reassuringly on his shoulder. 'She's going to be fine, mate. The wound wasn't too bad, all things considered. Why don't you come and get a cup of tea and something to eat, then you can crash as well. One of us will sit up with her in case she wakes during the night.'

Jai looked up at Harry, seemingly weighing his words and deciding whether Harry could be trusted. The kid glanced at Georgie in an armchair in the room's corner, then nodded and followed Harry toward the kitchen.

Jai slumped back on the kitchen chair, a soft sigh of satisfaction escaping his lips as he folded his hands over a swollen stomach. The teenager had virtually inhaled two cans of chunky meat casserole that Penny had heated on the stove for him. Seeing that his bowl was empty, she placed a large mug of steaming milo within his reach, then joined Mark and Harry at the table.

Harry took a sip from his own mug of black tea, watching Penny from the corner of his eye. His interactions with the police officer had to this date been humourless discussions regarding needed tasks. Aside from work duties, Penny had kept her thoughts to herself. The two kids, however, had brought a different side to light. A mothering streak had emerged, as she sought to feed and console the boy at their table. He knew of her loss, and if she gained some comfort from caring for another's child, then who was he to argue?

While Jai had eaten, Mark had given the teenager a rundown of their groups' collective background, what they had done about the farm to improve safety, and how chores and responsibilities were shared. Now that the boy had finished eating, he asked about his background.

Jai wrapped his hands around the mug and took a tentative sip as he thought where to start. He and his sister had grown up on a farm not five kilometres distant. His mum had died of breast cancer when he was little, leaving his father as the sole carer, a challenge he completed while running a mid-sized cattle farm. When the infection had hit New South Wales, his father had elected to stay put and wait out the disaster in isolation. Nestled at the end of a lengthy dirt road, his father had hypothesised that they would be insulated from the worst. For a number of weeks, the plan had worked. They had closed their gates and withdrawn from interaction with their neighbours and wider community.

The farm held reasonable stocks of food, as a sizeable vegetable garden alongside a small orchard that his dad had cultivated for additional income, ensured fresh vegetables and fruit were available. They'd only been troubled by a handful of the Infected, stumbling corpses that had crossed their property, mostly coming from the direction of Milton.

All this had changed four days earlier. Jai had been outside, preparing food for a pair of ferrets that he kept for rabbiting, when he'd seen two men walking up the dirt road towards their farm. Both men were tall, wearing jeans with dirty Hi-Vis jackets; probably workers from construction of a new section of highway further north. The shorter of the two had grey, unkempt stubble covering his jaw. The other wore a large beard stretching from high on his cheeks to finish over a stained t-shirt at mid-chest, a trucker cap perched on the top of his head. Jai had dropped what he was doing and ran to find his dad who was working in a maintenance shed behind the house.

His dad was underneath the hood of their Ute, a single cab Toyota Hi-lux with a flat tray. Jai caught his attention as he dropped the hood of the engine. On hearing his son's news, he had calmly wiped oil off his hands onto his work overalls, and told Jai to find his sister and stay out of sight in the house.

Jai had run to do his father's bidding and found his sister on her bed reading a book. After passing on his father's instructions he'd found a window from which he could observe the interaction between the unknown men and his father. A soft movement behind his shoulder informed him of his sister's arrival. Jai gently opened the window slightly so he could hear the men speak. His father was waiting calmly in front of the maintenance shed, a heavy wrench hanging from his right hand as the two men walked up to meet him.

'Can I help you?' said his father, his face remaining blank.

The stubble-faced man's face broke into a wide grin, a shark's smile that didn't involve his eyes. 'How you going, mate?' he said, holding out his hand to shake. Jai's father let him hang, ignoring the offered hand that eventually fell back to the man's side. A flicker of irritation caused the man's eyes to briefly narrow while the smile remained fixed. 'My name's Davo, this hulk is Tony,' he said pointing to his silent mate. 'We're on our way south to get away from that crazy shit in Sydney, and was wondering if you could help us out with a few things... like that Ute behind you.' The man's fake smile dropped as his father remained impassive to the demand.

'The Ute's not for sale. I need it for the farm,' answered Jai's dad.

'Oh, I'm not offering to buy it, we're taking it. Tony, check the ignition for the keys, will you?'

The big man nodded, and moved around Jai's father to the driver's door. For the first time, Jai's dad started to look angry.

'I said you can't have the car,' he repeated, his voice starting to escalate. 'You need to leave this property, now!'

'Or what?' replied Davo with a sneer in his voice. 'Are you going to call the cops on me?' He looked across at his accomplice, 'Well, are the keys there or not?' The bearded man just smiled, holding up a small bunch of keys that he'd retrieved from the ignition. Jai's father started to move around the Ute to get his keys back, growling in fury at the theft.

Davo spoke up once more. 'Looks like our meeting has come to an end,' he said, the shark's smile returning as a hammer dropped down his sleeve into view. He swung the heavy tool in a vicious arc, connecting with the back of the farmer's skull in a sickening, wet thud.

His father fell to the gravel; joints unhinged with loss of consciousness. Jai covered his sister's mouth to stifle her scream, forcing her into a tight hug. His own eyes welled with silent tears at the horror of seeing his dad felled.

The two men grabbed a leg each and dragged the farmer away from the Ute. A slow ooze of blood seeped into the gravel from behind his head where he came to lie. Without another thought for their victim, they climbed into the Ute and drove back out of the property.

Jai ran outside to his father. His dad's eyes stared blankly at the sky, irregular rasping breaths escaping his mouth. Jai placed two fingers under the jaw line, feeling for a pulse like he'd seen on television, only to feel a faint one diminish to nothing beneath his touch. He had tried CPR for a few minutes but gave up, not really knowing what to do. He knew his dad was dead. Jai had clubbed enough rabbits himself while ferreting to know the head injury had been lethal.

Jai was unsure how long he and his sister sat next to their father in the cold, his mind empty of anything but numbing pain at their loss. Eventually he had risen and set to work in burying his dad. Erin and Jai had dug a grave in the farmstead's small garden before dragging their father's body into the hole. A bedspread they'd wrapped around his body saved them from witnessing his face as Jai started to shovel soil.

The siblings had left the next morning, unable to countenance remaining on the farm where their father had been murdered. Each had only taken what they could carry. Jai had brought the family's 0.22 rifle for defence and hunting, alongside a set of outlawed rabbit traps. They had mostly camped in abandoned houses so far, still undecided as to which direction to head, with the presence of infection reported in Sydney as well as Melbourne. And now here they were.

The adults sat silent in their chairs, rendered speechless by the lad's tale. Jai's eyes were dry, his voice low as he relayed the story. He may have been sixteen, but his demeanour was that of someone far older. Harry eventually found his voice.

'I'm sorry to hear what happened to your dad. That would have been bloody awful to see.'

Jai clenched his jaw. Avoiding eye contact, he looked down at his cup and traced a crack in the ceramic with a fingertip. 'Yeah, it's fucked. But that's life now – other people have been through the same or worse,' he said with a rough voice. 'But I'm done crying about it. I just have to keep my sister safe and survive. Whatever needs to be done to achieve that, I'll do it. There is no other option.'

Harry glanced at the others briefly. 'I think I speak for the rest, Jai; you and your sister are welcome here for as long as you want, mate.' Penny and Mark nodded their agreement.

Jai accepted the offer with a brief smile, then excused himself to go and sleep, claiming exhaustion. Before leaving, he shook Harry's hand, thanking him once more for treating his sister.

Harry leant back in his chair and sighed as he watched Jai walk away, knowing his experience wasn't unique. Youths all over Australia had lost any chance of a normal childhood.

CHAPTER THIRTY-FIVE

The next day Erin was up and out of bed, gingerly taking weight on her injured leg as she made her way to the kitchen. In the daylight she still appeared exhausted, the trauma of the experience clearly taking a toll. Steph had helped her dress in a pair of loose track pants with a black hoodie on top. Erin was whip thin but healthy, with wiry muscle evident on each limb. Work on the farm and a more recent restriction of diet, had burnt away any softness of youth. She had a short bob of mouse-brown hair that she intermittently tucked behind her ears as strands of hair broke free and fell over her forehead. A speckling of freckles covered each cheek and the bridge of her nose.

There was a clear familial resemblance between Erin and Jai. Both siblings had sharply-defined noses and prominent cheekbones, and a minimalist approach to communication. Neither were given to rambling conversation, keeping their words succinct and to the point. Jai's hair was a darker brown, a buzz cut clipping the hair within millimetres of his scalp. Jai had already completed most of his growing, standing at roughly five-foot-ten, however was yet to bulk out his frame.

Prior to coming into the kitchen, brother and sister had talked quietly in the bedroom, Jai relayed the happenings of her operation, his discussion with the adults and their offer to stay. To the relief of Harry and Penny, the pair elected to remain, but were keen to earn their keep.

A stubborn streak within Jai was quickly evident, desiring to be given the same responsibilities as any of the adults present in relation to encounters with the Infected. The boy had managed to keep his sister safe to this stage, so Mark found no reason to refuse his request, and besides, boys his age had been fighting as men for millennia past. In the destruction of society, any norms of the last century were clearly removed.

Over the coming days, Erin continued to improve. Her limp lessened as the wound began to heal in an absence of infection. Jai provided a brace of rabbits caught in his traps at the back of the property on the second day. After that however, everyone was restricted from leaving the shipping container defences. Greater numbers of the Infected began moving along the highway and, to a lesser extent, the fields to each side in a southerly direction.

All noise was kept to a minimum, lights left off at night in a concerted effort to avoid drawing the attention of the passing Carriers. A four-hourly shift rotation kept watch from the porch through the nights, the guard listening for any signs of an attack on the wall. The low moaning growl of the passing Infected outside, carried in fluctuating volume on the breeze, was enough to keep each sentry firmly awake during their shifts.

Each afternoon, the radio was turned on to the emergency broadcast channel to check for any change in announcement. For the past two weeks there had been no alteration, the same speech by General Black repeating every ten minutes. However, today was different.

Steph flicked on the radio, the volume down low while she sat and listened. She felt a flutter of nerves in her gut as she realised that a different voice was speaking. Steph caught the last sentence, something about the town of Jindabyne. As the voice was replaced by static, Steph gathered the other members of the house to listen. Penny brought a blank piece of paper and pencil to jot down the outline of the speech and any key information.

Jai helped his sister, supporting her left elbow as she limped in to the living room to sit on the couch, her brother perching on the armrest next to her. The other members quickly took seats or sat on the floor. Everyone was quiet, a palpable sense of anticipation present as each waited for the new information. Steph carefully dialled up the volume so each person would be able to hear, and was rewarded by the sound of a woman clearing her throat.

'Good afternoon and congratulations to you, the survivors of southeast New South Wales. My name is Major Williams, and I bring you news regarding local evacuation and resistance efforts. Since the last national address provided by General Black, the army has been working around the clock to establish retreat points across the nation. Your closest point, is based in the alpine town of Jindabyne. Recent research upon Carriers has demonstrated that they freeze in sub-zero temperatures, becoming completely incapacitated. This makes the snow-line the safest place in the state. If you are able to retreat in safety, you are encouraged to make for Jindabyne with speed to join the national resistance effort. The remnants of this winter must be used in preparation for a summer offensive. We look forward to your arrival. So until next time, stay safe. And if you can't – fight hard!'

Static replaced the woman's voice. Steph leaned forward and turned off the radio again, then rocked back on her heels. 'Wow. Looks like the country is finally starting to do something,' she said.

'If that information is right about Carriers freezing solid, then they're right – we should make for the snow line. Once we get there, we won't have to worry about an attack until the spring thaw,' said Harry.

Mark wasn't so convinced. '*Once we get there*, Harry – that's still the problem. We would have to risk a trip of over three hundred kilometres in the open to reach that safety. The numbers of those bastards are only getting thicker out there – what if we run into a swarm on the road? We'd be dead. I'd rather stay and fight from our own small fortress and live.'

'You're right,' said Penny. 'The numbers of Infected around us *are* increasing. But what if we miss a window to escape? If they get any thicker out there, we won't have any choice but to remain.' She firmed her voice, 'I think we should vote on whether to stay or go.'

Georgie appealed to Mark. 'This place was only ever meant to be a temporary base until we knew what was happening across the state and country. We have that information now – surely that means we should move on?'

Mark refused to be swayed. 'We could hold this place against hundreds of them – what a fucking waste of effort just to leave it behind.' He stopped, rubbing his eyes in frustration. 'Can we at least sleep on it before any vote takes place? The logistics of such a journey would have to be considered prior to making a firm decision anyway.'

'So you'd come if you're out-voted?' asked Harry.

Mark glared at him. 'That's a fucking stupid question, Harry. Of course I'll bloody well come. I just think you're all going to get us killed by leaving,' he snapped in reply, walking to the front door. 'I'll take the first shift of the evening.' Without waiting for a reply from anyone, he shut the door, bringing the conversation to an end.

Steph let out a long breath as she watched Mark exit. 'If we leave, we'd be going against the advice of the only professional soldier amongst us.'

'Yeah, one soldier's advice that contradicts the instruction of the army's leadership,' countered Harry.

Georgie stuck up for Mark. 'You're missing his point, Harry. Mark's primary concern is our safety during the trip needed to get there. Everything he's done around this place to date, is to increase our chances of survival. By leaving here, we need to be mindful that we may be jumping, for want of a better description, from the saucepan into the fire. And the burn might be enough to kill us all.'

'If it gives me the chance to get my sister to permanent safety, and then join the main fight against the Infected – then I'm ok with that risk,' said Jai, entering the debate for the first time.

Penny nodded, agreeing with the boy. 'We'd want to make the journey within a single day. I, for one, don't want to be stuck in the open overnight. Let's nut this out then, work out what we'd need for the trip if we're to attempt it,' suggested Penny, moving some chairs over to the dining table. The others joined her and settled in to mind-map a plan.

CHAPTER THIRTY-SIX

An hour later saw the light begin to fade as the sun dipped below the western ridgeline. Mark pulled his jacket more tightly around him as a light breeze picked up, needling any exposed skin with icy teeth. The sound of Carriers had been increasing through the afternoon. A brief peek over the edge of their defences had shown at least eighty ghouls on the highway within sight. Luckily, the barbed wire fence had been enough so far to dissuade any attempt to breach the immediate grounds about their house.

The sound of an engine in the distance, rapidly increasing in volume caught his attention. Mark climbed the ladder to the edge of the front wall to see if the vehicle would turn in their direction, or keep going. With the increased numbers of Infected moving through, he'd expected the approach of at least a few of the families that Harry and Penny had met the previous week. A Ute was accelerating down the highway from the north, swerving around Carriers on the road, knocking others down or bouncing them to the side off the edge of the fender.

In the fading light, Mark could just make out damage to the Ute. The front right wheel arch was badly crumpled and rubbing on the tyre causing it to smoke heavily. The Ute barely slowed as it suddenly made a sharp right into their driveway, gravel spewing out behind spinning tyres as the vehicle hit the new surface. Instead of stopping to open the gate, the Ute careered onward, smashing the wide gate off its hinges, rendering their first line of defence useless. Now any of the infected on the highway could enter the paddock surrounding the shipping containers without impediment.

The collision had been the last straw for the front wheel. The tyre exploded with the noise of a shotgun blast, rubber shredding away in large pieces. The driver lost control, the Ute slewing to the right, off the driveway and into the base of the paddock toward the deep pits. Some luck was with the occupants, as the Ute dug into the soft earth and ground to a halt next to the second hole. Three people emerged from the cab and started to run towards the battlement of shipping containers. Mark's gaze flicked back to the highway and broken gate, now lying bent and useless on the ground. Carriers were starting to file through the space, following in the wake of the family.

Mark swore violently under his breath. The bastards had brought a true storm onto them. He dropped from the side of the container, running for the house to raise the alarm. Mark yelled as he ran, there was no point maintaining noise precautions now. Climbing the ladder onto the porch by every third rung at speed, the other occupants were spilling out of the front door as he reached the top.

'Some bastard's broken down the front gate drawing the Carriers from the highway onto us,' said Mark, pausing to draw in a lungful of air. 'We could be facing hundreds within minutes.'

Each person listening was deathly pale, faces drawn as the significance of his words drove home.

'Shit. We need to enact our major defence plan then,' said Penny, the first to break out of inertia. 'Mark, will you run the show? You're going to be the best one to lead us through this.'

Mark nodded without pause, he would have claimed control within moments if it hadn't been offered anyway. There was no time available to waste on niceties.

Now that the attack had finally become reality, he felt himself begin to slow and think more clearly. He'd always found the waiting to be hardest. Once the fight started, he tried to imagine himself as already dead, freeing himself to act rationally and prevent making decisions based on fear. He could then fall back on training and routine. He saw expectant faces before him awaiting instruction, expressions starting to steady and firm in reflection of their leader's evident resolve.

'I want a ladder over the front to allow the people in, we can't afford to open any of the container doors at this late stage.' He pinned Harry with eye contact. 'Can I leave that to you, Harry?'

He nodded in assent.

'Make sure none of them are bitten, if they are, cull the infected member once the family is out of sight. I'll be there to help you in a minute.'

Harry swallowed gluey spit in a throat suddenly dry. He swiftly descended the porch ladder and was away.

'Georgie and Steph, load hand weapons into each of the front containers ready for use. Penny and Jai, take rifles and ammunition to the top of the wall and complete a weapon check of each rifle – we need them ready for action. We'll all rendezvous on the top of the front wall on completion to assess our next move. I'll make a decision once I see how many of the bastards are attacking the walls and where.' Mark pulled his sword and scabbard from the rack, buckling it about his waist as he talked. 'Right, get moving!' he shouted, pushing each into action.

Mark followed in Harry's wake. He still held a cold fury at whoever it was that had so effectively damaged their first line of defence without need. There had been a good forty-metre gap around the vehicle clear of Carriers, surely they could have opened and closed the gate in time? He also had a nagging feeling that he recognised the Ute from earlier in the week when Erin had been delivered into their care.

Mark's fingers gripped onto the top edge of the container wall at the apex of the ladder, a rough sandpaper texture providing purchase thanks to Steph's idea. Harry was starting to lower a ladder over the front wall, an old timber number that had been left there for such an occasion. Mark joined him, taking a side to lower it downwards.

'Hurry up! They're coming, you've got to let us in!' screamed a man below.

Mark could barely make out his face. Night had now fallen, the half-light of dusk already ebbed to nothing. Multiple snarls came from the darkness surrounding. He'd have to wait until they were on the wall to search for bites – there wasn't going to be time.

After the ladder hit the ground, he pulled a torch from his jacket pocket, shining it onto the group to help them find footing on the ladder. First pushed onto the rungs was a girl of eight or nine who scaled the ladder like a rat, hiding behind Harry to wait for her parents. Next came a woman, her husband pushing at her from behind to urge her upward, but only making it more difficult for her to climb. Tears ran down the lady's face in terror, her mouth open and panting. A set of reaching arms and face lunged into the circle of light provided by the torch, latching onto the man's lower leg as he climbed awkwardly with a rifle gripped in his left hand. He screamed, violently shaking the limb to dislodge his attacker, who ripped free and dropped to the ground, a clump of material in its teeth. The man climbed the remaining rungs and heaved himself over the edge to lie on his back. Without surprise, Mark and Harry identified the man as Rodger, the useless coward that had shot Erin. Harry and Mark quickly pulled up the ladder once more, unwilling to test the abilities of the ghouls below to climb such a structure. The noise of the milling Infected had reached fever pitch, the volume of their animalistic snarling forced Mark to shout above the din to be heard.

'Did that bite reach through to your skin?' he yelled. Rodger scooted backward away from Mark when he stretched down a hand to examine his leg.

'No, no – nothing. We're all fine. Those bastards didn't get a piece of me,' he said in a tumble of words. Mark didn't trust him, the man avoided eye contact like a liar.

'Let me see the leg where you got bitten, you might not have felt the teeth break the skin in the fight.' Rodger refused, shaking his head. Mark was losing patience fast, he placed a hand menacingly on the grip of his sword. 'No one gets in here that's infected – it places everyone at risk. Either raise the leg of your pants and let me see, or I'll throw you straight back over the edge to the mob below. If you're bitten, we'll give you a painless death, better than turning into one of them,' he said, waving at the Carriers on the ground.

Rodger eyed Mark's sword, then winced as he slowly raised the left leg of his jeans. A long pair of gumboots was under the denim, covering the bottom two thirds of his calf. They appeared to have protected his skin from the Carrier's teeth, Mark was unable to see any wound above them.

'Right that wasn't so hard was it? We haven't got time for fucking around here. If you're going to stay, you do as I say, when I say it. Everybody except the kids, fights for their keep. You got it?' said Mark, his tone brooking no discussion.

Rodger and his wife nodded, their faces white with fear.

Steph, Georgie, Penny and Jai had joined them on the container, catching the end of his discussion with the newcomers. Mark acknowledged their presence.

'How did everything go? Weapons all ok above and below?' he asked, mentally ticking off the required tasks for preparation. He received affirmative replies from each of his team.

'Right. They know we're here, so we might as well know what we're dealing with. Shall we light up the place and give ourselves something to fight by?' yelled Mark above the hellish noise.

Penny jogged over to the far-right corner where the switch for the light system had been housed. The floodlights blinked on, bathing a ring of pasture around the wall in harsh white light, illuminating the front paddock down to the pits in the front corner.

A bowel-loosening vision greeted their eyes.

The closest half of the paddock to the container was filled with the Infected, lurching forward to the wall. The walking corpses were in various states of trauma. Clothes stained with dry gore, vomit and filth clung to dead flesh. Some were naked, their injuries in plain sight. Hideous wounds adorned most, brown dry meat hung in tatters at the edges of amputated limbs, torn throats and gnawed torsos. More than one walked while completely disembowelled, intestines ripped clear, leaving nothing but an empty cavity beneath the rib cage. Open eyes were white against the light, a side effect of lids that no longer closed, leading to countless scratches over the eye surface until the cornea was opaque.

The Carriers below were focused on the front wall, hammering in rage at the containers, clawing at the steel in vain attempts to reach them above. They only managed to rip off finger nails and spread gruesome brown trails of abraded flesh, like meat crayons on the painted metal.

Mark forced himself to swallow the bile that had risen to the back of his throat and get back to work. *Compartmentalise the fear, keep the rational thought in command – the monsters below are only dangerous if they get inside. This should be a simple enemy for God's sake. It's not like they can shoot back. I just have to prevent their numbers accumulating to the point that they climb over each other to the top of the wall.*

'For the moment they all seem to be attacking the front, that should hopefully make it easier for us to keep them in check with our small numbers. Therefore, we place most of our resources along the top of the wall and within the base,' said Mark, justifying his plan out loud to the team. He turned to the newest recruits, the family responsible for the whole bloody mess. Mark didn't want them anywhere near an area of need, better out of the way where they would less likely cause another episode of 'friendly fire'.

'Rodger and Jan – you're taking the top of the back wall. I want you to keep an eye out for any of the Infected that start to converge on either the side or back walls that will require us to change our defence pattern. If you can avoid it, I don't want you firing a rifle back there as yet – I'd prefer the Infected to stay congregated where they are for the moment for us to kill in one location. If you fire that weapon, you'll be drawing more of the Carriers towards you – just run and tell us if anything changes.' Rodger nodded, the clear relief on his features at staying out of the action made Mark feel like punching it off his face. It was the wife that questioned what was to happen with their daughter.

'Steph, can you take her to Erin? Tell her she's in charge of the girl, and that they are both to remain inside the house no matter what. Then get back here. You and Penny will take the first shift on the wall. Start picking off the bastards with the rifles. Nothing more than twenty metres away. Slow, even headshots. Make each one count.'

Penny gave a grimace that Mark guessed was supposed to pass as a smile. She grabbed one of the Austeyrs, jogged twenty metres away from the group where she took a kneeling stance, her elbow resting on one knee to steady her aim, and began firing.

'I need three of you with me in the Containers to start culling them through the murder slits we carved in the front wall.' He pointed at different members as he talked. 'Georgie, Harry, Jai. You're with me. We'll take shifts and rotate off the top of the wall. I'm going to set off the speakers in the front pits, then I'll be with you.' Mark ignored how they involuntarily winced with each firing of Penny's weapon. They nodded nervously and quickly headed downstairs.

The battle had begun.

CHAPTER THIRTY-SEVEN

Steph gripped the little girl's hand tightly as she drew her quickly towards the house. The poor girl was whimpering in terror, but she didn't have time to console her. Every few seconds, another rifle shot cracked from behind them as Penny systematically targeted Carriers outside.

Erin was standing on the porch waiting as she approached. 'Steph, what's going on? Where's Jai?'

'Your brother's with Mark – he'll be safe with him while we get them under control,' answered Steph, trying to sound confident. 'I've got a job for you though.' She drew the girl in front and squatted to speak to her. 'See that older girl up there? Her name's Erin, and she's going to look after you while your mum and dad help us to get rid of the monsters outside. I want you to do everything she says. Erin's in charge. Do you understand?'

The girl nodded, snot dribbling down over her top lip as she cried. Steph picked her up under her armpits then hoisted her up to sit on the edge of the porch. For the first time, Steph noted that Erin had armed herself. She constantly forgot that she and her brother had survived on their own for days in the Carrier-infested land without any other help. Erin gripped one of the improvised hay forks – the murderous long-handled pike. She leaned on the shaft slightly, using the weapon as a crutch to support her injured leg.

'Don't worry, Steph. She'll be safe with me. Let the others know I'll bring out containers of water to the porch for easy reach – you'll each need to keep drinking through the fight or you'll pass out. That, and I'm setting up a medic post in the living room again – just like Harry had for me when I came in.' Erin seemed surprisingly in control for a child her age.

'Good stuff. I'll let Mark and Harry know.' Steph gave her another smile, then slipped backwards to the wall once more, leaving Erin to lead her small charge inside.

* * *

Rodger and his wife walked around the top of the wall to the back of the property. Once they were away from the direct gaze of the others, Rodger allowed himself to limp, the pain in his calf was like a red-hot poker. His right boot squelched with each step as it filled with blood from the bite wound. The Carrier had bitten down to the muscle before he shook it free. The gumboot had been half dislodged from his foot in his hurry to get up the ladder, exposing his calf. When Mark had demanded to inspect the area, he'd stamped his foot down into it properly, the rubber top rising to conceal the wound from his view.

Rodger had no desire to let Mark know of his injury, he knew he'd follow through on his threat to kill him. Why tell anyone? For all he knew he might be an anomaly, someone that could survive the infection unscathed. Yeah, that was what was going to happen, he just knew it.

Jan noticed him limping, and looked at him with concern, 'Are you ok, babe? What's wrong with your leg?'

'Nothing, Jan. I just pulled a muscle or something coming up the ladder, I'm fine,' he answered, looking straight ahead. He'd always been a crap liar and knew his wife would read him like a book. 'How about we each take a corner at the back? That way we should be able to observe the rear of the property as well as the sides?'

Jan nodded, walking onwards to the other suggested post while he crouched at the first corner. He couldn't have given two shits about watching for Carriers. How could they possibly hurt them up on the wall? Rodger just wanted his wife gone so he could suffer in peace.

* * *

Mark knelt at a power board on top of the wall and picked up the plug marked with red tape for the speakers in the front pit traps. Shoving the prongs home into the electricity source, he waited for the tape of screaming to reach him from the base of the paddock.

Nothing.

It had been tested before, and he knew it should be easily heard over the murderous din created by the Infected below. He began trouble shooting the rig by ensuring the power board was connected, then running his hand along the cable from the power board to where it exited the wall; that left damage somewhere between the containers and the pits themselves as the problem. He peered over the edge, following the line down through grass until he saw Rodger's car. The bastard had run over the cable when he burst the front tyre and crashed into the field, pulling it free from the tape and speaker set up in the pit bases. Yet another key defence measure had been ruined by the man.

'That fucking bastard, I'll kill him myself if we live through this bloody night!' he cursed, thumping the metal wall in frustration. They were left with a finite amount of ammunition and their hand weapons to see them through. Mark hocked a mouth of gluey spit in anger, then ran for the ladder. He had to join the fight below.

CHAPTER THIRTY-EIGHT

Harry raised the lever with a metallic squeal to open a doorway into the front containers. Shafts of light cut through the darkness of the interior from the narrow slits cut horizontally at head height in the front wall. Carriers' faces could be seen at these gaps, hands wrenching uselessly at the sharp edges, or sticking whole arms through. The agitation of the Infected outside escalated with their presence. The volume of noise within the enclosed space was awful. Guttural snarls and moans bounced back and forth off the metal walls, so that in the darkness it gave an illusion of being surrounded by the beasts.

Harry gripped the bayonet tipped spear tightly in his right hand, and with a force of will, stepped forward into the killing room. He hung a camp lantern from a hook in the middle of the ceiling. The light swung slightly, creating an eddy of light against the walls.

Georgie and Jai entered, heads down as if the wall of demonic noise was a physical barrier to be overcome. Jai held another bayonet-tipped spear like Harry's, Georgie gripped an altered hayfork, the remaining middle prong sharpened to a wicked point. The three spread apart along the front wall. The joining walls between the three containers that comprised the front line of defence had been cut to allow a small doorway for access to allow free movement by the defenders through the whole front wall to reach areas of need.

The Carriers outside fixated upon each of them, following them as they moved, hands reaching through the holes, desperately trying to grab hold of a limb to pull back into a hungry mouth.

Without a word, Jai was the first to act. He lunged forward, his blade piercing through an open mouth. The Carrier clenched its teeth together about the knife, upper incisors snapping free. Jai shoved forward again, driving the blade upward to puncture the brain stem. The ghoul went limp, hanging as a lead weight on the knife blade, almost ripping the shaft from his fingers. Jai braced a foot on the front wall and wrenched the handle back, salvaging the knife for his next target.

Harry and Georgie followed suit, trying to block out the cacophony of screams. Mark stepped through the doorway in time to see Georgie drive her narrow pike into the right eye of a Carrier, causing jelly from the ruptured globe to spurt onto her chest as she rammed the weapon deep into its brain. She gave a small yelp of disgust, before ripping free the metal to find another target.

Mark waded in, spurred on by the view of his mates attacking the enemy. He drew his sword from the scabbard in a fluid motion and stepped almost within reach of a set of hands grasping ineffectually through the metal slit. Mark chopped viciously into the two arms to clear space. The severed hands flopped into the container to lie about his feet. Grasping fingers removed, he was now able to stab ahead. The strength and weight of the blade allowed him to be less picky in his targets, as he punched through skull at the temple, stabbed into open mouths, or merely incapacitated via slicing through the spinal cord of an exposed neck.

They settled into a gruesome pattern of work. Pick a target, stab, repeat. Steam billowed from their mouths as chests heaved with exertion. Sweat poured from their bodies despite the midwinter's night, making weapon grips treacherous and slippery.

Georgie rubbed the back of one wrist across her forehead, trying to move loose pieces of fringe stuck in place by sweat. She glanced down at her watch, noticing for the first time the layer of gore spattering her shirt.

Harry cursed as yet another blister tore open on his palm, straw colour fluid dribbling down to his fingers from the wound. Both hands were macerated from the rough wooden handle of his bayonet spear. He clenched his teeth against the discomfort and continued.

It had only been thirty minutes, but it felt like an eternity.

CHAPTER THIRTY-NINE

Jan shivered. The night grew colder as time crept forward. The Infected continued to target the front wall, ignoring the sides and rear for which she and her husband were responsible. Jan's guilt at bringing this influx of Carriers into their current location was a sour weight in her gut. She glanced across at her husband, a black silhouette on the far corner of the wall. He hadn't moved since taking up his post, just sat there with knees drawn up to his chest, shivering. As she watched, he fell to the side, the dull thud of his head against the metal drowned out by the battle which had so far forgotten them. Jan swore under her breath, something was wrong with him. She knew he had been lying earlier; the man wore every thought on his face like a banner.

She glanced desperately around for anyone else she could call to for help. No one was near. She abandoned her post, jogging across the back wall to her husband. He was lying on his side, eyes staring blankly ahead, motionless. She grabbed him by the shoulder and shook him roughly, yelling into his ear to wake up without effect. Tears started to well in her eyes as realisation hit – he was dead. She rolled him onto his back. Beads of sweat clung to his forehead like a swarm of fat bed bugs that scattered, running down the sides of his cheeks and temples with the change in position. A fine spider web of dilated blood vessels spread upward across his cheeks. A look of surprise was frozen on his features, as if he couldn't believe that death had finally caught him.

Jan still couldn't believe he might be really gone. She leaned forward over his face, feeling for air movement against her cheek as a sign he might still be breathing. Her heart skipped a beat and she found herself conflicted. Part of her quailed in fear of losing a husband, and another silently exalted that she might be free of him at last. She pressed two fingers into the side of his throat, feeling for a pulse under waxen skin that made her recoil inside at the sensation. Nothing.

Out of her periphery, she noted his fingers tremble by his side, then form a fist. She jerked backward from her husband's body. His eyes suddenly opened, locking onto the form of his wife at his side. Lips pulled back into a grimace, teeth exposed.

Slowly, as if the nervous system was navigating control of a foreign body for the first time, the corpse drove itself to a sitting position. Jan was speechless in terror; her mouth silently formed the word 'No' again and again as she scooted backward on her bottom to stay out of reach.

Warm piss soaked her jeans as her bladder released. She drew closer and closer to the inside edge of the container wall. Her husband's corpse lunged forward, hands reaching hungrily for her throat. She leaned backward, and suddenly there was nothing behind her except air. Jan fell headfirst, a short scream extinguished by a wet crunch on impact with the concrete path below. Dark blood crept away in a spreading halo from the back of her skull, crushed like an egg by the fall. Throughout the years of verbal and physical violence that marked their relationship, Rodger had always promised to kill her, but it had taken his death to make it a reality.

On top of the wall, the corpse rose to standing, then stepped into the void in mindless pursuit. It hit the ground feet first, both ankles shattering on impact. The tibia of the right lower leg burst through the shin as a bloody spike of bone. The Carrier attempted to rise once more, however, the two ankles now lacked the structural integrity required to stand. The ghoul fell ungainly to its side, sprawled into the garden. Limbs thrashed in the air until eventually it managed to turn onto its stomach. Its first victim now forgotten, the Carrier dragged itself toward the house in search of warm prey.

CHAPTER FORTY

Penny fought to retain control of her thoughts against a mounting panic that threatened to reduce her to an incoherent mess. A carpet of dead extended thirty metres ahead, gaining depth the closer it came to the wall.

And still they came; stumbling over the meat underfoot or crawling forward to the containers. The defenders below had been effective in cutting down those that reached the wall, maybe too effective. Wickedly sharp metal flashed out of the narrow holes cut in the front wall, killing any Carrier within reach. The carcasses themselves now created a problem for Penny and Steph as death upon death made a fleshy ramp. The Carriers were almost within hand reach of the top, fingers scrabbling at the metal in a frenzy driven by the defenders' proximity. Exhaustion decimated Penny's accuracy with the rifle. She was missing up to half of her headshots as her arms trembled beneath the weight of the rifle that had previously seemed so light.

She fired once more, the shot going low and wide, blasting flesh from the right shoulder of a Carrier below. Penny swore bitterly to herself as she pulled back from the edge to reload. They desperately needed support or a short break. Steph's magazine ran dry and she stepped back to join Penny in reloading a handful of magazines with ammunition.

'Where's Mark? We need help here or they're going to reach the top,' spat Steph. Rather than scared, she looked furious. Rage driven by her perceived failure to keep the Infected at bay.

'They'll join us soon I reckon, the Infected will be too far above their holes now to reach effectively.' Penny looked over Steph's shoulder to the containers at the rear of the house, searching for Jan and Rodger. 'What happened to the people Mark sent to the back wall? We need those useless bastards here.'

Steph scanned the skirting wall herself, incredulous that they could have left their post unattended. 'The fuckers are gone,' she breathed unbelieving. 'They didn't even have to do anything back there…'

A scream echoed from the container beneath their feet, cutting over the horrendous noise of the attacking ghouls outside the wall. Both Penny and Steph froze, then looked at each other, neither wanting to admit what the noise heralded.

'You go see what happened, Steph. Try and bring them up here if you can. If we don't get help, we're all dead anyway.'

Steph nodded, then scrambled for the ladder to the ground. Penny rammed a magazine into the military rifle, clamped down on her fear and returned to work.

* * *

Erin bit her lip in frustration. She felt useless stuck inside while the fight continued at the front wall. After preparing the living room as a medical clinic and putting the water on the front porch – which had remained untouched – Erin had floundered for an activity to occupy her mind. She'd given up trying to talk with the smaller child. The girl had refused to speak, growing ever more distressed away from her parents. Erin found a viewpoint from within the house so the little girl could watch her mother through a back window. The girl sat on a kitchen chair, knees drawn to her chest and thumb in mouth, her behaviour regressing to that of a toddler during the night's terror.

Erin spent the next hours restlessly pacing between checking on the girl, to listening at the front door for any change in activity, desperately trying to determine what was happening. From the back room, she heard the girl yelp with anxiety and then a rapid patter of footsteps into the adjacent room. Erin quickly walked to the rear of the house to find out what was happening. She found the girl with her hands up against the glass, staring up at the wall.

'Is everything ok?' Erin asked.

'Mummy just ran to Daddy for something, I just wanted...' the girl suddenly emitted a terrified shriek as she saw her mother fall.

Before Erin could react, the girl was past her, running for the front door. Erin screamed at her to stop and wait, but the girl scrambled down the ladder, off the porch and out of sight.

Erin bolted after her. The gap between the containers and the house appeared pitch black in comparison to the blinding floodlights at the top of the wall. She grabbed a hand torch from next to the front door then stepped outside. Ignoring the ladder, Erin dropped her long-handled pike off the porch then jumped the six feet to the grass below. As she hit the ground, the force of impact tore her stitches, laying her thigh wound open. She stifled a scream at the burning pain, biting on her lip until the metallic taste of blood filled her mouth. Erin grabbed the pike off the ground, used it as a crutch to force herself to standing, then limped in the direction the young girl had run. She was determined not to fail Steph in the one task given to her while the others did the real fighting.

Within moments, she had rounded the corner of the house to find the girl crouched above a motionless figure. Erin shone her torch, providing a halo of light about daughter and mother. Dark blood lay in a rapidly-congealing pool under the woman's skull. The girl was hysterical. She screamed at her mother to wake up, thumping her chest with tiny, balled fists in desperation. Tears welled in Erin's own eyes as she stood next to the girl feeling useless, unsure what to do in the situation.

A snarl emanated from ahead. Erin froze. The sound was close, from inside the compound. The younger girl was oblivious, now hugging her mother's body as she cried. Erin moved the torch's beam ahead, pointing toward the noise's origin. Out from the shadows emerged the infected corpse of the girl's father, hands used to drag itself forward on the ground, eyes fixed upon his child.

CHAPTER FORTY-ONE

Inside the container wall, Harry had given up on using his spear. He'd discarded it after the blade snapped off in an eye socket. Now he held a long-handled axe as the implement to transform his fear and anger into trauma upon the Infected outside. He swung wildly in a horizontal arc through the narrow window, and buried the metal wedge deeply into any flesh he could reach.

The four had been forced to come closer to the windows, angling their weapons upward to reach the heads of the Infected that now stood higher, atop a pile of corpses mounted against the wall. Fewer hands came through the windows as the attention of the Carriers was taken by Penny and Steph above.

Georgie had steadily grown bolder, periodically reaching her arm outside of the window to stab upwards. Seeing a target within reach, she did this once more, burying the tip of the pike deep into an exposed neck. A hand darted in from the left, snapping a ringlet of unforgiving fingers about her wrist and yanked her hand downwards with savage strength. Georgie shrieked in agony as her elbow dislocated on the window's edge. Mark and Harry rushed to her side to help. Harry wrapped both arms about her torso, pulling her backwards, however, the creature outside the wall refused to relinquish its hold. Georgie screamed again, her arm jerking wildly in the steel opening as the hand was savaged out of sight. Mark brought his own face to the edge of the window, within reach of the milling Infected directly outside, and found his target. He stabbed the point of his sword hard into the face of the Carrier terrorising Georgie, forcing it to momentarily let go. It was enough, allowing Harry to pull her to the ground. He knocked the hanging lamp, causing the light to swing wildly up and down the edges of the interior.

Small arterial jets of blood spurted in rapid staccato of her heartbeat from three severed fingers, now just stubs of flesh beyond her knuckles. A mouth-sized chunk of tissue had been ripped clean away from the side of her palm, bone and tendon clearly visible. She whimpered in pain and shock at the injury. Mark grabbed a jumper off the ground that had been discarded earlier and wrapped it tightly about the fingers in an effort to slow the bleeding. He looked up at Harry, his eyes pleading.

'Harry, you've got to help her. Please mate, I can't lose her again.' Mark's voice was hoarse.

Harry's face was pale as he grunted assent. 'We haven't got much time.' He removed the jumper to examine the hand. 'The teeth have bitten through arteries and veins – the infection could be at her brain within minutes.'

Georgie stared at Harry with wide eyes, lips trembling as he used a belt to tourniquet her arm at the bicep.

'Lie her down, I need that arm on a flat surface.' Harry's voice was hard, leaving no room for negotiation. 'Mark, hold the hand. I need it out straight.'

Georgie whimpered on the floor, looking up at Harry who now gripped his axe. 'What are you going to–'

Harry brought the axe down in a savage blow, sparks glinting off the steel floor as the blade severed her wrist. Georgie screamed, tendons standing proud from her neck, her face a rictus of agony. Harry ignored her cries as he roughly hoisted Georgie off the ground in his arms, blood weeping from the amputation despite the tourniquet.

Mark stared at Georgie's stump, mouth moving wordlessly and eyes wide with horror.

'How else did you think it would happen?' muttered Harry, already moving for the door. 'The hand had to go to buy us some time. I'm going to take her inside and finish the job properly.' Harry stepped out of the container towards the house, staggering slightly beneath his patient's weight.

Mark went to follow, but a hand gripped his shoulder from behind, forcing him to turn. It was Steph.

'Let Harry sort her out. We need your help on the wall.'

Mark looked away from her back to Harry and Georgie for a moment, tracking their movement up onto the porch.

'Now, Mark! They're almost at the top of the wall. If we don't do something, it won't just be her that dies.'

Mark took a deep breath and forced himself to disengage from what had just happened. He nodded his acceptance to Steph and tapped Jai on the shoulder for him to follow. Steph led the way back up onto the wall, her rifle bouncing from a sling across her back as she climbed the ladder swiftly.

* * *

Erin shone the torch at the creature. The facial expression upon the ghoul had none of the love a father should show towards his daughter, only rage fuelled by a relentless hunger. It was less than a metre away from the girl and her mother. One last dragging movement brought the creature within arm's reach. It lifted one hand and wrapped a grip about the girl's ankle.

Finally, the girl awoke to her danger. Looking up, she screamed as her father's corpse drew her leg to his mouth. Erin drove the needle point of her pike deep through its right eye, transfixing the skull on the modified farm implement like a fly on a pin. With a second heave, she followed through on her lunge, driving the Carrier's body backward onto the garden soil. She let go of the fork's handle and clutched her thigh, ramming a fist against the wound to slow the seepage of blood.

The long handle stood vertical, the point buried deep into the earth behind the corpse's head. Erin pulled the eight-year-old to her feet, holding the girl's head to her chest to stop her from looking at her father's body. With a trembling arm, she shone her torch in a circle, looking for any other danger.

Nothing.

Erin mumbled soothing noises to her charge as she firmly led her back along the darkened path to the front entrance of the house. With her own adrenaline surge gone, Erin felt like her muscles were made of water. With all her heart, all she wanted to do was sit down inside, away from the sounds of the Infected where she could have a good cry and pretend for five minutes that this was all a hideous nightmare.

CHAPTER FORTY-TWO

Half way across the living room, Georgie fainted from the pain, becoming a dead weight in Harry's arms. He finished the last few steps to the dining table, easing her onto the surface.

He gave a silent thank you to Erin for trying to get the room ready ahead of time. Before she had a chance to regain consciousness, Harry drew up and administered a dose of Ketamine as an injection into her thigh muscle, straight through the denim of her jeans. The sedative would act as a painkiller while also preventing her from waking up.

The axe blow through the wrist had been critical to try and stop the movement of virus into her body. But despite his quick action, he didn't like Georgie's chances, there had just been too much large vessel damage done by the bite in the first place. Harry shrugged aside his concerns. All he could do now was give her the best overall chance of survival, and that included a clean surgical wound that decreased the odds of sepsis killing her instead. He needed to amputate again, this time higher up at the elbow.

Ideally, he required a bone saw to rapidly remove the limb, but he already knew that this item was not part of his supplies. Harry quickly emptied different items of suture material, dressings and scalpel onto a sterile field. In absence of a saw, he'd be forced to complete an amputation through the joint.

Harry splashed some Betadeine over the elbow, tightened a tourniquet about the bicep, then smoothly made a series of deep cuts around the joint. Skin, muscle, tendon and ligament parted like butter beneath the razor-sharp scalpel. Within moments the joint was displayed, the cartilage end of the humerus bone shiny in the living room light. Harry let the forearm drop to the carpet, forgotten for the moment as he tied off the major vessels, then roughly sewed skin together over the stump. He stuck a wad of gauze over the suture line and secured this in place with a bandage.

Gunfire escalated in frequency atop the wall, causing the glass panes to shudder lightly in their frames. Harry was unhappy with his job, but it was the best he could manage in the circumstances. He desperately needed to get back onto the wall to help defend the farm.

Harry eased Georgie to a sitting position, then picked her up. Although she was slightly built, he still found himself straining in effort as they crossed the threshold like a macabre bride and groom in reverse. He awkwardly lowered her to the ground from the edge of the porch, cursing himself for removing the steps. Georgie stared blankly into space throughout the transport, completely dissociated from any discomfort inflicted on her body thanks to the Ketamine.

Moments later he reached the container that they'd set up for this very purpose mere days before. A mattress covered with a fitted sheet lay on the floor next to the opposite wall. Harry eased Georgie to the makeshift bed, laying her in the recovery position on her side. He checked the bandage around the stump to ensure she hadn't started to haemorrhage from the operation site. The stump was dry, her breathing was slow and even, and a strong pulse gave evidence of adequate blood pressure. There was little more he could do to help her beat the infection.

Harry tied a rope about her ankle, then fastened the other end to a steel ring in the wall above her. If she became a Carrier, it would prevent her from attacking them in the morning. Lastly, he hung a battery-powered lantern on the opposite wall to provide light in the windowless compartment, then exited, padlocking the door from the outside.

The noise from the front wall was deafening. Suddenly an explosion of flame reached towards the clouds, buffeting his face with hot air even this far back from the wall. *What the hell is happening!* Harry sprinted to join his mates again, leaving Georgie to fight her battle against the infection on her own.

* * *

Hand over hand, Mark climbed a ladder to the top of the wall. As his head came over the edge of the container, the sight before him made his jaw drop. From below, the small windows had prevented any clear view of the ongoing scale of attack. He'd allowed himself to become distracted by the fight, failing to monitor how Penny and Steph were coping above. Immobile corpses lay in an ever-increasing depth toward the front wall. Above the carpet of infected flesh, stumbled and crawled more Carriers. A brief glance across the paddock brought Mark to a rough estimate of two hundred active Infected. The steady stream of Carriers flowing in from the highway seemed to have finally dried up.

Penny stepped back from her firing position to join Mark. 'We're running low on ammo. I don't know if there will be enough to kill the rest of these bastards,' she panted. Her face was drawn, exhaustion plain to see. Behind her, the floodlights dipped, then died, plunging them into darkness once again as the generator ran out of fuel.

'That's just perfect,' he muttered under his breath before speaking up. 'We'll just have to do what we can. Once the bullets run out, it's back to hand weapons,' he replied, trying to convey some sense of confidence.

'Why don't we turn on the speakers in the pits? Surely that would remove most of them from the wall?' asked Jai.

'The line got torn when the Ute crashed. I tried to turn them on without success hours ago.'

'So the tape and speaker set up in the pits themselves should still be working though, you think it's just the connection to us that got damaged?'

'Yeah, but that's beside the point. There's a couple of hundred Carriers between us and the pits. Even if you got down there, as soon as you turned the speakers on, you'd draw them all directly to you. It'd be suicide,' advised Mark.

'I can do it,' said Jai. 'I'll skirt around the main group. Those buggers only shuffle anyway, I'll just outrun any of the creeps that come near me.'

Mark just shook his head, 'Don't get any ideas kid. You're not going.'

Jai clenched his jaw in frustration, 'If we don't get them working we're screwed and you know it.'

Mark's gaze rose to take in the horde of undead still attacking the front wall. As much as he wanted to deny the fact, Jai was more than likely right in his bleak assessment. Mark's right eyelid began to twitch, an unwitting symptom of his stress. 'If you're right, then it will be me taking that risk, not you.'

'No, we can't afford to lose you. My sister can't afford for you to not come back,' the kid said, grim determination in his eyes and voice. 'You're the leader, and that means getting stuck with the shit decisions, like deciding which person's most likely to get the job done and return – and you know that's me.' He stepped towards Mark. 'You know I'm the fastest here, I can outrun any of those bastards and be back again in ten minutes.' Jai was adamant, the self-confidence of youth outweighing any doubt of his own ability.

Mark's gut clenched, bile rose at the back of his throat at what he was about to agree to. How did his previous commanders live with their decisions, when in the end, every single one eventually resulted in risking someone's life? He was left with a numbers game, risk Jai's life in the hope it saved the rest of the people under his care.

Mark unbuckled the sword and tied it about Jai's waist. Watching the lad's face smile in triumph only shoved the blade of guilt deeper.

Mark's voice was pure gravel as he began to give instructions. 'Go wide immediately. Jump the barbed-wire fence and don't re-enter until you're level with the pits. We'll try to put on a show up here to keep their attention firmly on us until the speakers start. I'll have a ladder at the back ready for you on return. And make sure you get back – you said you could do this, now bloody well prove yourself right.'

'Mark, no!' Penny was aghast at the scene unfolding. Jai ignored her as he took his own rifle and jogged off to the right. 'You're not killing my boy again. This is wrong!' Tears of frustration rolled down her face.

Mark clenched his fist in anger. As if he hadn't already cursed himself for the decision. 'Penny, he's not your son,' he growled, 'and secondly, he sure as hell isn't a boy anymore. Not in this new age. He's fought all night alongside us, taking every risk that we have. I think that gives him the right to decide what he is and isn't capable of.' Mark tried to spit the sour taste from his mouth, but his saliva had dried to the consistency of glue. 'If you want to help him, let's give him some space by taking out as many of these bastard things as we can.'

Penny turned to watch Steph help Jai lower an emergency ladder over the far wall, and abruptly, the boy was gone. She turned back, her face white with rage. 'If that boy dies, Mark, I hope the guilt fucking rots you from the inside out.'

Mark raised his hand to grip her shoulder, finally lost for words, only to have it slapped away in disgust. Penny ran towards Steph, stopping her from pulling the ladder up again. She clambered over the edge in pursuit of Jai, Glock at her waist and rifle slung across her back.

Suddenly it was only Mark and Steph left on the wall.

'We need to keep the attention of the Infected on us to give those two a chance,' he yelled at Steph as he ran for the storage cupboard located in the far-right corner of the front wall. 'Increase your rate of fire, I'm going to light them up!'

Steph started to release short bursts of automatic fire at head height into the crowd, punching ghouls from their feet. Mark ripped open the cupboard door, exposing a milk crate filled with Molotov cocktails. Stiff wads of cotton stood proud at the top of each petrol-filled bottle, held in place by the cork. He quickly unscrewed the lid of a jar filled with kerosene then proceeded to dip each wick into the accelerant, making them ready for use.

Standing clear of the crate, he gripped the first one by the bottom third of the bottle while lighting the wick. His cigarette lighter barely sparked in the stiff breeze that had sprung up, but it was enough to set the kerosene-soaked rag alight. Mark's heart rate doubled with a surge of adrenaline at the fear of one of the improvised incendiaries exploding in his own grasp. Before the cork had a chance to burn through, he tossed the bottle far into the heaving press of Infected, the burning wick a tiny meteor of flame as it arced through the air. The aged glass shattered over the scalp of a Carrier sending a spray of petrol vapour and droplets that instantaneously exploded in an inferno of heat.

The flames engulfed ten Carriers, burning clothes and melting flesh away from bone. The senseless monsters continued to walk onwards, oblivious to the hideous trauma as they unwittingly set others alight. Mark heaved more bottles into the crowd, sowing a crop of flame from one side to the other.

Thick acrid black smoke blew back onto the defenders making breathing difficult. Mark wrapped a strip of cloth over his mouth and nose, doing the same for Steph while tears streamed from reddened eyes.

A horrid roast pork smell mixed with the burning petrol had Steph gag at the stench. The dead were now able to reach the top of the wall, fingers searching for purchase to drag themselves over the lip. Five metres to the left, a charred forearm snapped into view followed by a skull, still glowing with lurid blue and yellow flame that danced over the surface of the bone. Mark took two steps, and kicked the corpse flying backwards once more.

Harry climbed onto the wall to find a medieval representation of hell. The burning corpses provided the only source of light between eddies of smoke. His eyes were drawn to those Carriers impaled upon the row of sharpened stakes below. The mindless creatures had skewered themselves on the sharpened points in the press of bodies. Some stakes held as many as three Carriers, transfixed like bugs on a pin, arms reaching to the wall above in vain.

Mark met him as he stood, his eyes searching Harry's face for any sign regarding his girl. 'How's Georgie?'

'I amputated again cleanly at the elbow. She's sleeping off the anaesthetic now – we won't know until morning if it's worked or not.'

Mark gave his shoulder a quick squeeze in thanks.

'Jai and Penny are activating the speakers in the pit, we just have to hold out long enough for them to do their job,' he said, passing an axe to Harry.

Harry grimaced at the weapon, it didn't bode well, 'How much ammo's left?'

'There's a handful of magazines; enough to get the job done.'

Yeah, bullshit, thought Harry fatalistically. He swung the axe head deep into the side of a snarling face that broached the top of the wall next to his feet. Levering it free, he readied to strike at the next one.

They had maybe fifteen minutes before the Carriers breached the walls in numbers too large to manage.

CHAPTER FORTY-THREE

Jai eased his body between strands of wire in the fence to reach the other side, carefully avoiding the barbed wire at the top. Free once again, he burst into a sprint, rifle in hand and sword slapping painfully against his thigh with each stride. The sodden, calf length grass drenched his jeans and caught at his feet, threatening to trip him as he ran. To his side, an explosion sounded making him flinch away from the fireball that soared skyward. He stayed about twenty metres outside the fence, avoiding a handful of Carriers stuck upon the barbed wire. As he neared the base of the paddock, he veered inward, slipping through the fence once more en route to the pits. The base of the paddock was free of the Infected, all now converged to attack the wall.

The first of the two pits lay ahead, a cavernous black mouth in the grass. At the near corner, a star-picket had been driven deep into the turf. A rope with knots at regular intervals had one end tied to the base of it, the rest lying in neat coils on the grass. Jai flung the rope over the edge and clambered hand over hand down the twelve-foot drop. Ankle deep mud sucked at his shoes, the bottom turned to a glutinous bog by the winter's rain. The base of the hole was ink black, the high edges blocking the weak light of the moon. Jai pulled out a pen torch from his jacket pocket, flicked it on and grasped it in his mouth to free his hands. The light reflected into his eyes off a stainless-steel toolbox in the middle of the floor, causing him to wince.

He lurched toward it through the mire and threw open the lid. The case had served its purpose in protecting the old cassette tape recorder within from the elements. Two outdoor speakers were bolted to a milk crate behind the toolbox, connected to the cassette recorder by a short length of insulated wiring. Jai ensured the volume was at maximum and depressed the play button. Gut wrenching screams blasted from the speakers, buffeting painfully against his eardrums. He flipped the lid closed once more on the box to protect the tape recorder then made for the rope. Escape was harder than entry. The rope was slippery from the mud on his hands, however the adrenaline powering his muscles was enough to propel Jai upwards. He dug his toes into the dirt wall and scaled the last few feet with scant regard for the skin ripped from his palms by the coarse weave of rope.

He could now make out darkened outlines moving his way against the fire lit backdrop of the slope. Pushing them out of his mind, Jai ran for the next hole and repeated the drill; down the rope, volume to max and tape on. With the second set of speakers working, his job was done.

All he had to do was go back the way he'd come. Jai grabbed hold of the rope, gritted his teeth and began to climb once more.

On the third handhold, the rope slipped. Jai's heart rate bolted. He shot his other hand forward for the next grip but it was too late. The knot gave way around the star-picket, unravelling under his weight. Arms windmilling to right himself, he fell backwards into the mud landing with his rifle behind his back. Winded badly, he gasped for air like a fish on dry land. The rope lay on his chest in a treasonous pile. He cast it to the side and got to his knees. Mud clung in a thick layer over most of his body making him feel like he was carrying double his body weight.

The speakers screamed beside him, echoing the panic inside that threatened to unhinge his knees. He had to get out! Ice-cold mud suddenly splattered against his face. Something had fallen into the hole near him. Jai fumbled the torch out of his pocket, directing its small beam of light over the floor of the pit. Two metres away, a Carrier dragged itself to standing, eyes reflecting white against the beam of light as they centred on him. Jai grasped the sling of his rifle, bringing it roughly over his head. He swore violently. The weapon was useless, damaged past repair by his fall. The barrel was filled with mud and bent. In anger, he flung the rifle at the Carrier; the stock smashing teeth free as it connected. Jai backed away. Something tugged at his waist, stopping him from going any further back. He glanced down and felt his first glimmer of hope. The end of Mark's sword had dug into the wall behind him, pulling at the scabbard's attachment.

Jai ripped the blade free and attacked, burying the edge of the sword deep into the ghoul's neck. He felt the metal grate against vertebrae as he wrenched it free. The Carrier's head now hung unnaturally to the side, the neck wound opening in a sick smile. Jai chopped into the same wound twice more, finally severing the head to plop into the mud at his feet.

Three more splashes. The speakers were working. Jai's heart dropped as he recognised failure. He'd succeeded in his task and his reward would be nothing less than drowning in a writhing mass of the undead. Jai waited for the three creatures to come to him, torch in one hand, sword in the other. He panted with fear, his legs and arms felt leaden.

Gunshots. One, two, three muzzle flashes from above and the Carriers were down. Jai's heart leapt as he looked up and saw Penny gesturing frantically at him, her voice drowned out by the speakers beside him. Jai splashed over to the pile of rope on the mud and threw a handful of coils up to the surface.

Penny caught hold of the rope. There wasn't time for any fancy knot, a glance behind informing her they were about to be engulfed in a crowd of Infected. She wrapped the rope around the star-picket four times, then held the end, taking on the job as anchor; one foot braced in front against the post, while she knelt. The rope went rigid, quivering with strain as she felt Jai begin his climb. She silently urged him onward, biting down on her terror at the encroaching monsters.

A ring of burning pain suddenly consumed her mind, causing a momentary loosening of her grip on the rope before she clamped her fingers tight again. Her eyes bulged in agony as she felt teeth rip another chunk of tendon and muscle free of her lower leg. A Carrier lay in the turf at her feet, having pulled itself through the deep grass unnoticed. The ghoul lay on its torso as it fed, nothing existing below the rib cage. Penny was powerless to fight back. She didn't have the strength to hold Jai's weight with one hand. If she let go, her lone chance to save him would be gone. Penny made her choice and held on tight to the rope, screaming her tortured agony in sync with the speakers below.

With a grunt, Jai pulled himself over the edge and rolled onto the grass to face uphill. Only thirty metres separated them from the advancing crowd of undead, backlit by the fires on the slope above.

Penny's screams finally registered in his mind. Jai scrambled to his feet and unsheathed the sword. He kicked the creature off her legs, stabbing the hardened steel point deep into the Carrier's skull.

He squatted, trying to grab Penny under her armpits to stand, but she batted his embrace away.

'You need to go; you won't make it if you're carrying me.'

'I'm not leaving you here, get up Penny!' yelled Jai, desperation making his voice crack.

'I'm bitten. I'm dead anyway,' she said, her face crumpling in pain.

'You don't know that for sure,' he said uncertainly. Jai began to back away, if she wouldn't let him help her now, he'd be out of time.

Penny pulled her Glock free of its holster. 'Get out of here, now!' she screamed.

Jai's nerve broke. He sprinted for the fence, running parallel to the advancing front of the Infected. At the fence he skidded to a halt and turned back. In the silver light of the moon above, he saw the first of the Infected approach Penny. She raised the gun, took aim and fired three separate shots, dropping a Carrier with each one. Then she reversed the barrel placing it between her teeth.

A sob ripped out of Jai's throat as he saw her head jerk backwards and her body slump to the ground. He couldn't watch any longer. With vision blurred by hot tears, he slipped through the fence and ran for home.

CHAPTER FORTY-FOUR

Hideous screams cut the air, drowning out the rage of the Infected assaulting the wall. Mark felt an empty click as he pulled the trigger. His last magazine had just run empty. Reversing the weapon, he rammed the stock down into the snarling face of a corpse mounting the wall at his feet. The frontal bone caved in, splattering his feet with gobs of brain. He looked for his next target, and came up empty. The wall was finally free of attackers.

Mark looked down the slope in wonder, seeing only the backs of the Infected as they stumbled towards the pits, attracted like vultures to carrion by the tortured screams of the recording.

A hand clasped his shoulder, spinning him around. Both Harry and Steph were at his side, their faces quietly stunned.

'They bloody did it!' said Harry in awe.

Steph's face cracked into a grin as she hugged her cousin in celebration with one arm, holding the other out to Mark to join in. He allowed himself to be pulled into the embrace for a moment before gently stepping back.

He couldn't celebrate. Not until he knew. Mark left the pair to watch for Penny and Jai, and climbed down from the wall, heading towards the container Harry had locked Georgie in. Each step felt heavy, requiring a force of will to continue.

Then he found himself standing at the doorway, padlock at his feet. The handle protested against being opened, emitting a high squeal of ungreased metal as he lifted the lever and eased the door open. Georgie stood quietly, facing away from him. Her manacled foot prevented her from leaving her bedside. Mark noted the bandaged stump, his mind reeling at the trauma he'd requested Harry to inflict upon her.

'It's over, Georgie,' he said. 'The wall's finally clear, I think we're going to be ok now.'

Nothing.

'Are you ok? I'm so sorry about...' he trailed off to silence, noticing how pale the exposed skin of her other arm was for the first time. She started to slowly turn, shuffling in small steps to face the doorway. She was staring at the ground, then slowly raised her face to his.

Lips curled back to expose teeth, her face transformed to pure rage. She launched forward at him, fingers of her remaining hand clawing out towards his eyes before the restraint at her foot stopped her momentum, causing her to fall to the floor.

Mark stared, hair rising on the back of his neck. His mouth moved wordlessly, unable to match his memories of Georgie to the writhing beast on the ground. *She's a Carrier.* Grief welled in his chest; a physical pain like someone twisted a knife sadistically in his heart. The room felt empty of oxygen, he couldn't breath. And he couldn't bear looking at her any longer. Mark backed out of the doorway, his gait unsteady, until he bumped up against the outside wall of the house.

Harry found him there ten minutes later.

'The kid's back,' he said, the pause between his next words heavy with intent. 'But Penny didn't make it.' Any joy of their victory had already turned to ash.

Mark barely acknowledged his presence.

'How's Georgie? Did it work?'

As Mark slowly shook his head, Harry's shoulders slumped. He forced himself to stand a little straighter, Mark had carried the weight of command through the night, and it was his turn to ease some of the load.

'We said we'd do it quick if this happened, give the person dignity. Do you want me to?' Harry asked, his knuckles showing white against the grip of the rifle in his hand.

Mark turned, his eyes red and hopeless. 'I can't do it. I just can't.'

Harry nodded. Without another word, he stepped through the doorway, lifting the rifle to his shoulder. A single shot echoed off the walls of the container. Outside, Mark sunk to the ground with the wall at his back, his head lowered to his knees as he sobbed.

CHAPTER FORTY-FIVE

The battery packs powering the speakers finally gave out an hour later. The ensuing silence seemed unnatural after the previous night. Harry emerged from the house to find Steph sitting on the porch, her back against the wall. He could see clearly now, dawn bringing a soft light that displayed everything in countless tones of grey. He eased himself down next to her, groaning softly as his muscles protested the movement, and placed a towel-wrapped item to the side.

They were both exhausted, their clothes were filthy and torn, covered with an abattoir's assortment of flesh and gore. Harry examined the torn palm of one hand, the medic part of his brain dully curious to the mix of blood borne diseases he had acquired as tissue and body fluids of those he had killed contaminated the wound.

'We can't stay here, Harry,' Steph said.

He nodded his agreement, there was too much death here now. The price for their survival made Harry feel ill. His eyes were dry though. He'd left something of himself behind during the night. He felt hollowed out, like some spark particular to him was squashed.

'I've given the little girl a sedative to make her sleep – poor kid's going to be fucked up for life. Jai and his sister are passed out on the couches.' Harry pulled a list from his back pocket, passing it to Steph. 'That's the list of stuff Penny came up with for the trip to Jindabyne. I agree – we need to get out of here today, if another swarm like that comes down the highway, they'll walk straight over the walls.'

Steph got to her feet with a groan. 'I'll start getting it together,' she said, then pointed at the towel wrapped object. A pale finger had slipped outside the covering. 'Is that Georgie's...?'

Harry nodded, frowning. Steph put a hand to her mouth, turned and leant against a post, emptying her guts off the edge of the porch. Harry stood and helped pull her hair out of the way. Once her shoulders stopped heaving, he left her to recover. His grisly package in hand once more, he climbed down the side of the veranda and left to find a spade. The mass of infected outside the front wall could rot in the sun for all he cared, but their friends deserved better.

* * *

Within the square battlement, to the left of the house stood an old apple tree. The winter had robbed its greenery, naked silver branches now reaching to the clouds. Steph felt its stark appearance fitting for how she felt internally; stripped bare and raw. Behind the tree they had buried the husband and wife together, supporting the young girl while she said goodbye to her parents. She'd now withdrawn once more, mute to any attempted interaction.

To the other side of the tree, Harry and Mark had dug two shallow graves side by side. Georgie's amputated arm was with her body, as whole again in death as they could achieve.

Penny's remains sadly filled little of her trench.

Harry, Mark, Jai and Erin stood with Steph before the graves, each silent with their own thoughts. She felt she should say something, but her mind was blank. Mark knelt beside Georgie and reached out his fingers to gently caress the waxen skin of her cheek one last time, then rose and picked up the spade and began to fill in the two holes. Dirt steadily covered the bodies until their likeness was removed from sight, but not memory.

Mark leant onto his shovel, staring down at the black soil covering his girlfriend. His eyes were dry, as were those of all present. It was if by some unwritten agreement, they had placed grieving on the backburner, setting it aside for a time when the war was won.

'I fucked up last night. I made the wrong decisions, and it got them killed,' he said quietly. Harry and Steph both looked up sharply at the statement.

'That's bullshit, Mark. The only thing responsible for their deaths is the fucking virus,' muttered Steph, shaking her head.

'No, it was the tactics I chose. I lost track of time fighting in the containers. We should have been on top of the wall much earlier. If I'd started by using up the ammunition, killing anything before it came within twenty metres of the wall, the ramp of bodies wouldn't have been created. Then we could have finished off the last of them from below, safe in the knowledge that the wall wouldn't be overcome.'

'Shut up, Mark. Hindsight thinking's bullshit,' said Harry. 'We gave the burden of leadership to you last night, and we didn't question a single decision. If you want to wear blame – we own it together.' Harry looked him straight in the eye. 'This was our first real fight, and the majority of us survived. I reckon that's a good outcome. Next time, we won't make the same mistakes. And that's how I'll choose to honour them – by fighting on, and killing more of the bastards.'

Mark held his eye for a moment, jaw clenched in anger at Harry's challenge. Anger for not even being allowed one moment of self-pity. Slowly, he unclenched the fists bunched at his side and exhaled. Harry was right. He'd turn that rage he'd been readying to direct at himself, and vent it with abandon against those carrying the infection. But he'd not lead again; he was done with that. Let someone else choose who got thrown into the mincer. He'd rather take on the risk himself than ask it of another again.

'We need to get going if we're going to have any hope of making Jindabyne by nightfall.' Harry turned to Steph. 'Did you find the stuff on the list?'

'Yeah. We're ready to go. Jai helped me pack your car,' she replied.

'Ok, there's just one more thing I want to do before we go. Mark, you might want to join me for this. One last moment of payback.'

Mark raised an eyebrow in query, then followed in Harry's wake.

CHAPTER FORTY-SIX

Harry stood at the edge of the pit, staring impassively at the writhing mass of flesh below. One hand grasped the handle of a tank attached to a spray-gun, usually reserved for pesticide or weed killer. This time around, it was filled with petrol. Mark held a Jerry can filled with the same fuel. The Carriers in the pit clawed at the walls of earth, desperate to reach the warm flesh at ground level.

Harry pumped a handle to build up pressure within the tank, then commenced spraying fuel over the manic bodies below, drenching clothes and skin in the accelerant. He repeated the process at the second pit. Mark roughly poured the Jerry can into the pit, walking around the perimeter in the process. He then pulled out a bottle of kerosene and splashed a trail leading backward from each hole for thirty metres.

Off to the right on the driveway was the Pathfinder; Steph and the kids waiting for them to finish the job so they could get on the road. Harry pulled a crumpled packet from his front pocket and carefully straightened a bent cigarette to light. He took a deep drag on the smoke, then offered it to Mark.

'Nah, mate,' he said, waving it away. 'Those things will kill you, and I got enough other things trying to do that already.'

Harry grunted a short laugh. 'I think it'll prove more dangerous to them than me.' He flicked the cigarette to the ground, sparking off the trail of kerosene. A strip of flame ran along the ground, heading toward both pits. As the flame hit the petrol, a fireball roared to the sky above the two holes, incinerating the Infected.

Harry lifted a hand in front of his face, warding off the heat. Even at thirty metres back, the temperature was roasting.

'Time to go, yeah?' said Mark, gesturing toward the car where Steph was beckoning them.

Harry nodded and headed over to the Pathfinder.

EPILOGUE

Six and a half hours later, they drove into the outskirts of Jindabyne as night began to fall. Outside, the air was bitterly cold. A light sifting of snow gently fell from the air, coating the asphalt in a thin layer of white. The car dashboard reported an outside temperature of minus-three-degrees Celsius. Any Carrier outdoors would be incapacitated and frozen solid, or as Erin had so charmingly referred to them, a 'meatsicle.'

They were safe for the moment.

Harry was at the steering wheel, fighting exhaustion of two days without sleep. He followed the signs erected by the army toward the processing centre. He inwardly smirked. The government had spent the last two decades enforcing a morally corrupt border policy that refused entrance of any refugees by sea crossing, and now here they were, citizens of Australia, reduced to seeking protection themselves.

Finally arriving, he pulled up in a car park at the side of the school hall. The large building enclosed a basketball court and stage that had been requisitioned by the army as a processing centre. They joined a file of people at the front door, and slowly worked through the registering process. The little girl was registered as an orphan and removed from their care by a female army nurse with a kindly face. Harry felt somewhat guilty at the relief he felt in handing her safety over to another.

At sixteen and twelve years of age, the siblings were deemed competent to make a choice regarding their own welfare. They decided to remain with the group of adults. Paperwork completed, the group wandered into the hall. At one side lay tables where essentials were allocated, such as blankets and warm clothes. The other side was pure military. Twenty desks were manned by officious-looking clerks in khaki uniform signing up volunteers to the armed forces. Above the clerks hung a massive poster on the wall. The poster depicted an Australian army lieutenant, his finger pointing out of the picture toward the reader. "Your country needs YOU! Join the fight against the ZOMBIE THREAT!"

The group stopped and read the sign. With barely a word of discussion, each filed forward, taking a seat beside a free army clerk.

Their war was just about to start.

End of Book 1

CHECK OUT OTHER GREAT ZOMBIE NOVELS

DEAD PULSE RISING
by K. Michael Gibson

Slavering hordes of the walking dead rule the streets of Baltimore, their decaying forms shambling across the ruined city, voracious and unstoppable. The remaining survivors hide desperately, for all hope seems lost... until an armored fortress on wheels plows through the ghouls, crushing bones and decayed flesh. The vehicle stops and two men emerge from its doors, armed to the teeth and ready to cancel the apocalypse.

TOWER OF THE DEAD
by J.V. Roberts

Markus is a hardworking man that just wants a better life for his family. But when a virus sweeps through the halls of his high-rise apartment complex, those plans are put on hold. Trapped on the sixteenth floor with no hope of rescue, Markus must fight his way down to safety with his wife and young daughter in tow.

Floor by bloody floor they must battle through hordes of the hungry dead on a terrifying mission to survive the TOWER OF THE DEAD.

CHECK OUT OTHER GREAT ZOMBIE NOVELS

DEAD ASCENT
by Jason McPhearson

The dead have risen and they are hungry...

Grizzled war veteran turned game warden, Brayden James and a small group of survivors, fight their way through the rugged wilderness of southern Appalachia to an isolated cabin in the hope of finding sanctuary. Every terrifying step they make they are stalked by a growing mass of staggering corpses, and a raging forest fire, set by the government in hopes of containing the virus.

As all logical routes off the mountain are cut off from them, they seek the higher ground, but they soon realize there is little hope of escape when the dead walk and the world burns.

CHAOS THEORY
by Rich Restucci

The world has fallen to a relentless enemy beyond reason or mercy. With no remorse they rend the planet with tooth and nail.

One man stands against the scourge of death that consumes all.

Teamed with a genius survivalist and a teenage girl, he must flee the teeming dead, the evils of humans left unchecked, and those that would seek to use him. His best weapon to stave off the horrors of this new world? His wit.

facebook.com/severedpress
twitter.com/severedpress

CHECK OUT OTHER GREAT
ZOMBIE NOVELS

Z BURBIA
by Jake Bible

Whispering Pines is a classic, quiet, private American subdivision on the edge of Asheville, NC, set in the pristine Blue Ridge Mountains. Which s good since the zombie apocalypse has come to Western North Carolina and really put suburban living to the test!

Surrounded by a sea of the undead, the residents of Whispering Pines have adapted their bucolic life of block parties to scavenging parties, common area groundskeeping to immediate area warfare, neighborhood beautification to neighborhood fortification.

But, even in the best of times, suburban living has its ups and downs what with rosy neighbors, a strict Home Owners' Association, and a property management company that believes the words "strict interpretation" are holy words when applied to the HOA covenants. Now with the zombie apocalypse upon them even those innocuous, daily irritations quickly become dramatic struggles for personal identity, family security, and straight up survival.

ZOMBIE RULES
by David Achord

Zach Gunderson's life sucked and then the zombie apocalypse began.

Rick, an aging Vietnam veteran, alcoholic, and prepper, convinces Zach that the apocalypse is on the horizon. The two of them take refuge at a remote farm. As the zombie plague rages, they face a terrifying fight for survival.

They soon learn however that the walking dead are not the only monsters.

15204627R00122

Printed in Great Britain
by Amazon